WAYNE STINNETT

RISING THUNDER

A JESSE MCDERMITT NOVEL

Caribbean Adventure Series

Volume 17

2020

Library of Congress cataloging-in-publication Data
    Stinnett, Wayne
    Rising Thunder/Wayne Stinnett
    p. cm. - (A Jesse McDermitt novel)

ISBN-13: 978-1-7339351-6-6
ISBN-10: 1-7339351-6-9

Cover photograph by Rainer von Brandis
Graphics by Wicked Good Book Covers
Edited by The Write Touch
Final Proofreading by Donna Rich
Interior Design by Ampersand Book Designs

This is a work of fiction. Names, characters, and incidents are either the product of the author's imagination or are used fictitiously. Any resemblance to actual persons, living or dead, businesses, companies, events, or locales is entirely coincidental. Many real people are used fictitiously in this work, with their permission. Most of the locations herein are also fictional or are used fictitiously. However, the author takes great pains to depict the location and description of the many well-known islands, locales, beaches, reefs, bars, and restaurants throughout the Florida Keys and the Caribbean to the best of his ability.

In memory of my first boss, Fred Sicilia, Sr., who was recently reunited with his bride of sixty years. I grew up learning what a good work ethic was from my dad.

It was through Mister Fred that I learned a good work ethic was something all dads had in common.

Thanks for the lessons under cars and over sodas.

"One should judge a man mainly from his depravities. Virtues can be faked. Depravities are real."

—Klaus Kinski

If you'd like to receive my newsletter,
please sign up on my website:

WWW.WAYNESTINNETT.COM.

Every two weeks, I'll bring you insights into my private life and writing habits, with updates on what I'm working on, special deals I hear about, and new books by other authors that I'm reading.

The Charity Styles Caribbean Thriller Series

Merciless Charity
Ruthless Charity
Reckless Charity
Enduring Charity
Vigilant Charity

The Jesse McDermitt Caribbean Adventure Series

Fallen Out
Fallen Palm
Fallen Hunter
Fallen Pride
Fallen Mangrove
Fallen King
Fallen Honor
Fallen Tide
Fallen Angel

Fallen Hero
Rising Storm
Rising Fury
Rising Force
Rising Charity
Rising Water
Rising Spirit
Rising Thunder

THE GASPAR'S REVENGE SHIP'S STORE IS OPEN.

There, you can purchase all kinds of swag related to my books. You can find it at

WWW.GASPARS-REVENGE.COM

MAPS

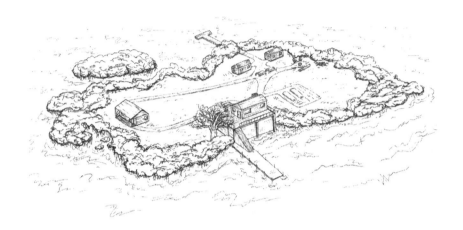

Jesse's Island

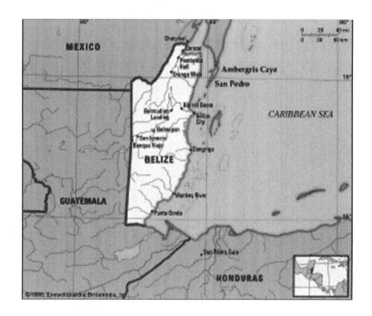

Belize

CHAPTER ONE

I felt the heat of the morning sun on my back. It'd only been an hour since it had risen into the Western Caribbean sky, but mornings were short lived this far south. Feeling invigorated after a deck shower to rinse the night's salt off, I let the warmth of the sun dry my skin. Its rays felt good, but I finally shrugged into a light-weight, long-sleeved shirt. Too much exposure could be painful, especially in the tropics.

Salty Dog held a steady course toward the south-south-west, heeling only a few degrees on a beam reach. A near-constant eighteen knots of true wind speed had powered her through the night at a very consistent seven knots.

In fact, the night had passed easily and not a single change in the sail plan had been needed. The *Dog* had added another eighty miles under her keel since nightfall and slightly more than that the previous day. We'd probably traveled 175 nautical miles since weighing anchor off the coast of Cozumel just over a day ago.

It was hard to believe that less than two weeks had passed since Christmas Eve, when I'd taken my little Grady-White out on the Gulf of Mexico to meet up with Savannah and Florence. It seemed like a lifetime. We fit together better now than we had when we'd first met.

The sun was hot on the left side of my face and I relished the cool feel of the fresh, easterly breeze. The sky was clear, and the air smelled clean, as if scrubbed by the sea.

I checked the wind instruments. We had a true wind angle of 82° and in that direction, I knew there wasn't anything—no land mass of any kind—all the way to the Windward Islands in the Eastern Caribbean, more than 1600 miles away.

Temperatures didn't vary a whole lot between seasons in these little latitudes of the Caribbean. The Tropic of Cancer was a couple hundred miles astern. In early January, when a lot of folks were putting on heavy coats and boots, I preferred putting on a mask and fins. Always have.

South of the Yucatan, temperatures were in the low eighties by noon, and it rarely got below seventy at night. Add five degrees to both for summer and you had a year-round spread of only 15° between the coolest winter night and warmest summer day. With such perfect year-round weather, it was a wonder the beaches went unspoiled.

Just over the horizon to the west I knew there were miles and miles of mostly desolate beaches, punctuated here and there by small fishing villages; *pueblos*, as they were called in the Yucatan.

Exactly where we were didn't matter all that much. I was living in the now and taking pleasure in every moment of it.

The autopilot controlled our direction and the wind governed our speed. Savannah and I took four-hour watches through the night, with me taking the mid-watch from 2200 to 0200. I'd relieved her just before sunrise and both she and Florence would be rising soon.

The course I'd laid in the previous evening took us through the middle of a sixteen-mile wide, two-thousand-foot-deep gap between the mainland and the atoll reef of *Banco Chinchorro*. We'd passed the narrowest part when I'd taken over, and I'd made a very slight course correction to reach our destination sometime later in the evening.

I glanced at my dive watch. Based on our current speed, I knew we were somewhere between Mahahual, Mexico and San Pedro, Belize, and I'd guess twenty-some miles offshore.

Finn came up from the companionway, followed closely by Woden. That meant the girls were up. Finn was my ten-year-old yellow Lab mix and Woden was a comparably aged rottweiler belonging to my daughter and her mom. The two dogs were about the same size—big.

Being on a boat with two large-breed dogs wasn't easy. Fortunately, both of them were mild-mannered, due to their ages, they'd both grown up on boats and were well-trained. Like me, they'd mellowed as their facial hair turned gray. Also like me, they could, I knew, be very dangerous if provoked.

"You had a call," Florence said, as she came up the steps after the dogs. "And Mom wants to know what you want for breakfast."

She held my satellite phone out to me. Not my private one, but the one Jack Armstrong had given me. I was one of many problem solvers for his global corporation, Armstrong Research. I contracted with the company's Mobile Expeditionary Division, otherwise known as ARMED.

"Thanks," I said, taking the phone. "Are there any of last night's lobster tails left?"

"For breakfast?" she asked, as she sat on the starboard bench and looked toward the invisible shoreline.

"Ever had a lobster omelet?" I asked.

Finn and Woden walked around the helm, then sat down on opposite sides of it, both looking forward. Florence stroked Woden's shiny black fur, then turned toward me, her eyes questioning. "I like lobster and I like eggs. Are they good together?"

"I like it," I replied, looking at the recent call list on my phone.

"Then I'll like it, too," Florence said confidently. "Who was it?"

"John Wilson," I replied, attempting to mask the concern in my voice.

Florence's face became grave. "You said he was your handler?"

"I don't think that was the word I used. He sometimes gives me assignments."

"Do you have to take them?"

"No," I replied. "I can say no, any time I want. I'm not an employee."

"There are two-and-a-half tails left," Florence said, rising from the bench and putting an arm around my shoulder for a quick hug. "I'll go tell Mom we're having omelets."

After she left, I hit the redial button to call John back. He answered right away. "Where are you headed?"

"Ambergris Caye," I replied. "What's up?"

"Remember I borrowed *Floridablanca*?"

"Yeah," I said. "That was six weeks ago."

"There's been a development," John said. "Weller's mission didn't go as planned."

Ryan Weller was another contractor, like me, but he worked for Dark Water Research. Though I'd never met the man, I'd heard of him a few times, and knew that the two organizations worked together on occasion.

"Is he okay?"

"He's hooked up with a bat-shit crazy woman," John said. "Weller couldn't make the shot; the target was holding a baby. The woman snatched up his rifle and emptied the magazine. They both got out, and I took them up to DWR's headquarters in Texas City."

"So, what's the problem?"

"He's going back to finish the job."

"What?" I said, surprised. "That's suicide. His target's bound to be ready."

I knew only the basics of what John had been up to these last few weeks, and that was only because I owned *Floridablanca*. I'd bought her from John several years ago, after he'd lost an eye in a submersible accident. John had been providing logistical support for Weller, getting him in and out of Mexico, somewhere about 250 miles south of the Texas border. Dark Water didn't have assets in the area, so they called Armstrong. All I knew was that Weller's target had been a drug cartel boss.

"That's why I'm calling you," John said. "He might need some backup. A person who can reach out and touch somebody from a great distance."

"When?" I asked. "And how long?"

"In two days," he replied. "In and out in a matter of hours."

I didn't want to. I wanted nothing more than to spend as much time as I could with Savannah and Florence. But my sense of duty tugged at my ear.

"Contact Charity," I said. "She's in the Caymans. Have her pick me up at the airport in Chetumal tomorrow morning."

I ended the call just as Florence came back up the steps, carrying a water bottle in one hand and a Thermos in the other. Savannah came up right behind her, carrying a large, covered plate.

"Scootch over," Savannah said, smiling brightly. "Let Flo take the wheel. We already ate."

Doing as I was told, I rose and moved to the port bench. Finn looked up at the dish Savannah was carrying and licked his chops.

"It's on autopilot," I said.

"Is there a change in plans?" Savannah asked, handing me the plate. Our daughter put the water bottle in a cup holder and refilled my mug from the Thermos.

"A slight change," I replied. "I have to leave tomorrow, but I'll be back in two days."

Both Savannah's and Florence's faces fell.

"I know we talked about it," Savannah said. "But I didn't think something would come up so soon."

I removed the cover from the plate and smiled. "I never know when or where," I said, picking up a strip of crispy bacon. "But they don't come often. And this isn't a real job. I just need to go help a friend."

"Someone like yourself?"

"Yeah. But he works for a different agency."

"And what exactly will you have to do?" Savannah asked.

Florence was pretending not to pay attention, but she didn't have much of a poker face.

"Provide support for a team that's going after the leader of a drug cartel."

Savannah looked out over the bow. "Are these men… this team…are they friends of yours? Do you know them?"

A very astute question. I didn't actually know the men I had been asked to assist. I knew a little about them, had heard their names mentioned in quiet conversations with other operators, but that was it. What kind of allegiance did I owe?

"I know *of* them," I said solemnly. "But never met either of them. One's a former SEAL and the other one's a Ranger."

"So how do you know anything about them?" Florence asked.

"Spec Ops is a small community within the military," I replied. "Of the two-and-a-half million people in the U.S. Armed Forces, less than half a percent are Spec Ops. Of those, only a couple hundred would be in leadership roles. Exploits are talked about."

"What exploits do you know these men were involved in?" Savannah asked.

"They're men like I once was—snake-eaters—the pointy tip of the spear. They stand with clear minds and strong arms and say, 'not on my watch.' They are men who understand the true meaning of *molon labe.*"

"That means 'come take them' in Greek," Florence said, looking slightly bewildered. "I saw it on a car's bumper once and looked it up. But I don't get what it's supposed to mean. Come take what?"

I gazed up at my daughter. She was highly intelligent, just like her mom. She'd seen a good bit of the world—more than most seventeen-year-olds, and under Savannah's tutelage, she had a better education than most college grads. But having been boat-schooled, as they called it, she'd led a bit of a sheltered life so far, naïve to the evils out there.

"People who put it on a bumper sticker have no idea of the true meaning. They use it as a protest, thinking the government wants to take their guns away. They strut like peacocks and say, 'come take them.' Most couldn't pour sand out of a boot with the instructions on the heel."

"What's it really mean, Dad?"

Could she understand? Could anyone who'd never had to fight for their life and the lives of others ever understand the kind of commitment it took to stand between the innocent, faceless masses and an enemy bent on destroying them, knowing that the best you could do was slow the inevitable?

"*Molon labe* was the Spartan king's response when Xerxes demanded they lay down their weapons and surrender during the Battle of Thermopylae about twenty-five hundred years ago. Leonidas replied, 'Come take them.'"

I saw her confusion as she frowned at me. "Who won the battle? Xerxes or Leonidas?"

"Who ultimately won the battle is the reason the term is important," I replied, studying her face. I bent and patted Finn on the shoulder as I looked out over the water. "The Spartans were vastly outnumbered," I said, not looking at her. "At least two hundred to one, though some scholars say that number might have been more than a thousand to one. They didn't have any chance of *surviving* the battle, much less winning it. That wasn't what they fought for. The Spartans gave their lives, every single man, defending a pass to slow the Persian invasion and give the Greek army and navy time to fortify. The Spartans all died on that pass, yes. But their stand saved hundreds of thousands of their people. In the end, thanks to the time Leonidas and his Spartans provided, the Persians were turned back."

I could see her eyes moisten a little. "They fought knowing they would *die?*"

"Yes," I replied frankly. "They knew their sacrifice would save others."

"Will that happen to you?" Florence asked.

I leaned over and put my arm around her. "No. Leonidas and his men had warrior hearts, of that we have no doubt, but today's warriors have the advantage of a lot of technology. I'll be back in a couple of days."

She looked into my eyes and nodded. "I believe you. You're kinda scary-looking sometimes."

I laughed and pulled her head to my shoulder. "Scary worked for Blackbeard."

"I know you said these calls were infrequent," Savannah said, sitting next to me, her bare thigh against mine. "I just thought we'd have a bit more time together before you had to go."

"It's likely to be a good while before the next one."

She smiled, but I could still sense the worry. Finally, her eyes seemed to resolve. "You *have* to go," she said flatly. "You're the kind of guy who stands up for two sisters who drank too much. It's one of the things I love most about you."

The memory of my first encounter with Savannah and her late sister, Charlotte, came vividly to my mind. They'd been targeted by human traffickers and were probably just minutes from being abducted when a friend and I waded into the fray. The two of us took on four guys who were bigger and we stacked them up like so much cord wood.

"I just happened to be in the right place at the right time," I said.

I could see the spark of memory in her eyes, too. "Don't worry," she said. "We'll be fine. It's not like Flo and I haven't spent time alone on a boat before."

That was true. Savannah had lived on her fifty-foot Grand Banks trawler, *Sea Biscuit*, since before Florence was born. She knew people in Belize, and it was a safer place than many others in this part of the Caribbean Basin.

"Do you really have to go?" Florence asked.

The night Savannah and Florence had invited me to dinner on *Sea Biscuit* to watch for Santa Claus, I'd explained to them about my work with Armstrong Research. Probably too much. But that hadn't turned Savannah away.

I smiled at Florence. "You know I don't. But someone needs help with a problem he encountered and it's right here in Mexico."

Florence looked at the chart plotter. "Mexico's eastern coastline is over fifteen hundred miles long, Dad. All but about ten nautical miles of that are *behind* us."

"True," I said, taking a bite of the omelet and savoring the flavors of the grilled lobster, eggs, peppers, and spices before swallowing. "But I won't be following the coastline. It will only take me a few hours to get to where John is and figure out what to do. He said it'd only take a couple of hours. So, I'll be back in two days. Think you can plot us a course to Chetumal?"

"Why there?" Florence asked, working the chart plotter.

"Customs," I replied. "No sense for me to clear into Belize, then turn right around and clear back into Mexico. It'll save a lot of time to fly out of Chetumal."

Not that I expected or even planned to come in contact with any Mexican customs agents. Where I'd be going would be more like The Wild West on steroids.

"Will we be waiting there in Chetumal?" Savannah asked.

"No," I said, putting the last forkful in my mouth and washing it down with coffee. "You can handle the *Dog* up to your friend's place without me. Once I finish up, I'll have Charity drop me off in Belize City, clear customs and meet you there."

"Course laid in for the ferry dock," Florence said. "But there's a long peninsula to get past. It goes all the way down into Belize."

"Zoom in on the skinny part," I told her. "Look for Zaragoza Canal. It was dredged to nine feet just a few months ago."

"Got it. It's eighteen nautical miles at a heading of two-four-zero degrees, Captain. We can probably get there at high tide. Spinnaker?"

I smiled at her. Florence was an excellent navigator and becoming an astute sailor. Once we turned, we'd have the wind on our port quarter, not quite a downwind run, but close.

"I'll break it out," I said, gulping down my coffee.

Savannah took my plate and empty mug and headed for the companionway. "Give me a minute to put these away and I'll douse the mizzen."

As Florence furled the genoa from her place at the helm, I went forward, opened the sail locker on the bow, and lifted out the spinnaker bag. *Salty Dog* started turning as I hoisted the spinnaker and Savannah lowered the mizzen sail. Florence eased out the main as she made the turn.

"Take up that starboard spinnaker sheet a little," I instructed Florence when I got back to the cockpit.

She inserted the winch handle and trimmed the sail, bringing the big, asymmetrical spinnaker slightly around on the starboard side.

"Is that good?" Florence asked.

I looked up at the sails. "What do you think?"

She followed my gaze and nodded. "Looks good. We'll reach the canal before the noon high tide."

"We'll have to drop the sails and start the engine to get through the reef and the canal. Then it's another three hours through Chetumal Bay to get to the ferry dock."

"That will put us there before sunset at least. Go get some rest, Dad."

"Yeah," Savannah added. "I'll wake you when we have the markers in sight."

Savannah and I had pulled the night watch after Florence had gone to bed. I'd held her in my arms, lounging in the cockpit, and counting shooting stars for a couple of hours. Then I'd taken a four-hour nap and afterward relieved her so she could get some sleep.

Minutes after my head hit the pillow, I heard the creak of the second companionway step. Then Savannah opened the hatch and came into the cabin.

"Flo's having fun," she said, closing the hatch behind her. "She's fine in daylight. Move over."

CHAPTER TWO

E arly the next morning, we pulled anchor and motored over to the ferry dock. I hugged them both tightly, not yet ready to be separated after not having been a part of their lives for so long.

I waited for a cab to take me to the nearby airport as I watched *Salty Dog* head away from the dock. I had no idea what the future held in store for me, but I wanted Savannah and Florence to be a part of it.

I'd only brought a go-bag with a couple of changes of clothes. Anything else I might need, I'd get from *Floridablanca*.

When I got to the private aviation building at the airport, Charity Styles was waiting. She was standing on a ladder, checking the turbine on her shiny, black Bell UH-1 Iroquois, commonly called a Huey. She wore a matching black flight suit and jungle boots.

"Anything wrong?" I asked.

Charity looked down at me and smiled. "Nothing now. I had a fluid leak some time back and I just like to keep an eye on it."

She closed the panel and climbed down, still smiling. "It's good to see you again, Jesse," Charity said, hugging me tightly. "Rumor has it you have some passengers aboard *Salty Dog* these days."

News traveled fast. Especially in the social circles the two of us moved in. I had no doubt that the information about my sailing off with Savannah and Florence had reached everyone I knew by now. And probably a lot of people I didn't know. My first mate, Jimmy Saunders, had been there at the dock when we left. The two fastest ways to spread the word around the Keys was telephone and tell Jimmy.

Our decision had been spur of the moment. I'd just blurted it out and asked them to go sailing with me. When Florence had asked where to, I'd jokingly told her anywhere she wanted to go. She'd chosen Belize. Savannah and I had just looked from Florence to one another for a moment and smiled.

"We're taking one day at a time," I said. "Any idea what John's into up in Tampico?"

She slid the cargo door open and took my pack before climbing aboard. I followed and she tossed my bag on a seat, then opened the storage area built into the floor. Inside was a bunch of camera equipment—lenses, camera bodies, flash attachments, all kinds of gear— each piece nestled into a fitted foam insert.

After looking around, she quickly pushed a release catch hidden on an equipment rack and I heard a click.

"I figured you might want this," she said, lifting out the tray full of camera gear.

Inside the cavity lay a black tactical rifle case. I opened it and found an M-40A3 rifle. I'd used similar weapons while in the Marine Corps.

"Who does it belong to?" I asked, lifting it slightly and checking the action.

"You, now," she replied. "I was planning to wait until your birthday. I had Sherri rebuild it and zero it to three hundred yards."

I looked up at her. "Sherri Fallon?"

"We stay in touch," Charity replied. "You never know when you'll need a good armorer."

Several years ago, Sherri Fallon had been a part of Deuce Livingston's Homeland Security team. Deuce was now my partner in a security business in Key Largo. Before joining Deuce's team, Sherri had been an armorer for Miami/Dade PD and had returned to that job after the team was broken up. She'd also been an accomplished stage actress and had helped the other team members improve their ability to think on the fly through improvisational skits.

"Or a good improv actor," I added, placing the rifle back in its case in its hiding spot. "Thanks. That's a very thoughtful and timely gift."

"You're easy to shop for," she said with a smile. "Guns, ammo, or tackle."

I smiled back at her. Charity and I had an odd relationship. We'd both been in tough situations, though I couldn't imagine the horror she'd endured at the hands of Taliban captors not long after 9/11. She'd been tortured, raped, and degraded, but in the end, she'd cut the leader's throat with his own knife.

"How soon can we make Tampico?" I asked.

Charity inserted the false bottom and closed the hatch. "Oh, we're not going to Tampico. At least not directly. We're going for a boat ride."

She closed the cargo door and then carried the ladder back to the hangar before the two of us climbed into the cockpit. Charity went through a quick preflight before firing up the big turbine engine. Ninety minutes later, we made visual contact with one of Dark Water's ships, the *Star of Galveston*, a long-range tug. It wasn't easy, and if it had been anyone else at the controls, it would have been scary, but Charity managed to put the bird down on the boat's long work deck at the stern.

She shut down the turbine and started her postflight as I got out. Several deck hands immediately began lashing her helo to the deck.

"Jesse McDermitt?" a man said as he approached.

"Guilty as charged," I replied.

He extended his hand. "Rick Hayes," he said. "I've heard of you."

I shook his hand. "All good, I hope."

"Depends on if the legend of Mogadishu is true," he said, as I opened the cargo door to get our gear out.

I stopped and turned to face him. "I don't count that as a win," I said. "I made the shot, but the kid was killed an hour later."

"But a thousand yards? And a moving target?"

"Guys are shooting a lot farther today with even more precise accuracy. And like I said, my time in the Mog was a failure."

He searched my eyes a moment, then shrugged. "Is that a woman I saw flying that bird?"

"One of my associates, Charity Styles."

"She sure looks fine from what I see. C'mon. I'll show you to the bridge. We'll be meeting up with John Wilson in a couple of hours."

At noon, *Floridablanca* came into sight on the horizon. As she got nearer, I went to the stern with my gear. Hayes accompanied me; a backpack slung over one shoulder.

"If you don't mind," Hayes said, "I'm going to ride along. You'll need a good spotter and Weller's my partner."

His words were a statement of fact, not a question of permission. One glance at his steely resolve and I knew I'd have done the same had it been Deuce.

"Could be a shit storm where we're going," I offered.

Hayes looked over to where Charity was coming down the ladder from the bridge. "It'd be worth a shit storm to hang out with your pilot friend. She single?"

"She is," I replied. "But I wouldn't take that as encouragement."

Floridablanca was soon alongside, fenders out all along her port rail. The tug slowed and *Floridablanca* matched her ten-knot speed. Both boats were heavy steel vessels, though the tug was twice the size. They each bulled through the heavy chop with little effort. Stopping would cause both boats to be less stable.

The tug's open deck was a little lower than *Floridablanca's* cockpit rail. When the fenders made contact, John turned slightly, welding the two hulls together for a moment.

I tossed my gear down into the aft cockpit and grabbed the upper rail over its roof, swinging feet first over the tug's rail and down to *Floridablanca's* deck. Charity landed nimbly beside me, and Hayes came over right behind her, grinning.

I nodded toward the little red light on the camera mounted to the corner of the overhead and *Floridablanca* turned away from the tug.

"Just drop your gear anywhere," I told Hayes, as I opened the hatch for Charity and followed her through the salon. She went down to the cabin area as I mounted the steps to the command bridge.

"Welcome back," John said to Hayes, when we joined him at the helm. The fact that they knew each other wasn't a surprise. They'd probably met during Weller's first failed attempt. "Jesse, if you'll take the wheel, I'll bring the Mercedes engines online, and we can be in Tampico before nightfall."

After John went aft, Hayes said, "I asked John if you guys could keep the helo local until this is over. *Star of Galveston* will remain six miles off the coast."

"That have anything to do with the pilot being a blonde?"

"Didn't know that when I made the request," he replied.

"That's completely up to her," I said. "But since she's here and her bird's lashed down on your boat, I assume she's already agreed."

"We'll meet up with Ryan and Kendra tonight. We have good intel on what's going to go down. Ryan's bringing the bait in after dark and we have a rental that can take us to the spot where you need to be."

After the clandestine meeting with Ryan Weller and Kendra Diaz, we had a rudimentary plan. No plan survived first encounter with an enemy force, so you laid out and coordinated the launch of the operation as best you could, included a couple of possible scenarios for when the shit hit the fan, and outlined the rest to the final objective.

When Hayes took us back to *Floridablanca*, he handed me a set of keys and pointed to a black truck in the corner of the lot. "I checked it out. It's banged up but everything works."

The truck was a Nissan Titan. A big four-door 4x4 with a stubby utility bed. It had oversized all-terrain tires, heavy duty bumpers and a brush guard, or what the locals called a *tumba burro*, which means to literally "knock out the donkey." It was fitted with big driving lights. It'd seen some abuse, judging by the dented fenders and doors on the passenger side—it appeared to have rolled over at some point—but the doors worked, and the fenders were still solidly mounted.

After moving it closer to the boat, Hayes helped us load our gear into the backseat.

"I'll meet you out there at dawn," he said when we'd finished.

"You're not staying?" Charity asked.

"No...I'm, uh, sleeping in the bush," he replied.

I nodded, knowing exactly where he was going. Weller was the one putting himself at risk. He had the most to gain and the most to lose. Hayes was his partner and he was going to go out to the rendezvous point and scout the whole area, making sure there were no surprises.

"In the bush?" Charity asked.

Hayes took a step back and pointed south. "Yeah. Out there. I need to make sure nothing's out there that might keep things from going as planned."

He turned and hurried toward his car.

Charity and I went back to the boat. John was coming down the dock step, carrying a seabag over his shoulder.

"Where are you going?" I asked, recognizing his luggage.

He pointed to the top of a luxury hotel. "Got a penthouse room," he said with a wink.

Or maybe he'd just blinked. With his other eye missing and the socket covered with a patch, you couldn't tell.

"Penthouse?" Charity asked.

"Go big or go home," he said. "I met a lady here two weeks ago. She agreed to meet me for drinks in the hotel bar tonight. I have just enough time for a shower. Besides, you won't need me for two days, so I'm going to make the most of it."

He, too, hurried off, leaving us alone on the dock.

"You can have the master," I said, never sure around Charity.

"No way," she said. "Your boat, your bed. And I kind of like that little forward cabin, anyway. Reminds me of *Wind Dancer* in a way."

We went back aboard, and I got two beers from the fridge, offering her one. She nodded and I removed the tops, then handed hers over.

"What do you think of those guys?" Charity asked.

She'd been flirting with both men, even with Kendra right there. Hayes and Weller hadn't even noticed, but the Latin lady did.

"What do you mean?"

She turned and faced me. "I'm here as your backup. I don't know them, but I know about them. Or at least what each did in the military. So, why are they doing this now? Is there some intangible reward we don't know about?"

Even though she'd flirted with them, she still suspected their motivation. After the things Charity had endured, it was a wonder she wasn't more jaded. But the relationship we had wasn't like ones she had with anyone else. At least not that I knew of. With Deuce and the others, she'd always been slightly aloof. In public, or around people she didn't know, like tonight, she played the part of the fun-loving California girl she might have been, had circumstances not been what they were.

But I knew the real Charity; all her insecurities and weaknesses, her convictions, what drove her, and what kept her going in the face of so much adversity. When it was just the two of us, she wasn't afraid to be herself.

"Let's go up to the bridge," I said, and led the way up the three steps to *Floridablanca's* nerve center.

I sat down at the helm and looked out over the bow toward open water. Charity sat on the low nav station desk, then swiveled around, bringing her feet up on the desk and wrapping her arms around her knees. She looked out over the water, leaning against the glass on the starboard side of the raised pilothouse.

How long had it been?

Ten years? No, it was eleven years ago. Charity and I had gone after a man named Jason Smith. He'd once been the head of Deuce's Homeland Security team, but he'd turned out to be a murderer.

Smith had been responsible for the death of a young Marine named Jared Williams, whom Charity had been involved with.

We'd chased Smith from island to island for weeks, always a step behind. During many of those nights, Charity and I had sat as we were now; me at the helm, and her sitting beside me.

We'd finally caught up to Smith in the Turks and Caicos Islands, southeast of the southern Bahamas. Charity had snapped his neck in an alley in Cockburn Town.

We hadn't returned straight home after that. Call it decompression or coming to grips, but we'd continued our nightly talks. We'd opened up to one another. I'd told her of the dreams I sometimes had, dreams of dead people.

Charity had later told me that our time on the water, just the two of us, was better than all the time she'd spent talking to therapists, psychologists, and even Victor.

"Weller has a vested interest," I said, in answer to her question. "Taking out the cartel means there's no longer a bounty on him."

"And Hayes?"

"Hayes is you."

"What's that supposed to mean?" she asked.

"He and Weller are friends," I said. "Like you and me. With special skills that complement each other. They might have their faults, but ethically?" I thought about it a moment. I was a good judge of people. Or I liked to think so. "I trust them," I said. "They're a couple guys I know I can count on and I know they'll do what's right."

"What about you and Savannah?" she asked, looking through the windshield toward the channel markers in the distance. "Is she finally the one woman who can bring down the legendary Jesse McDermitt?"

I laughed. "Legendary?"

She turned and looked directly at me, her pale blue eyes becoming more serious. "You've been through a few women, Jesse. Some you scared away, some you sent away, and one who—"

"You're keeping tally?" I asked, avoiding the mention of Alex.

"It wouldn't be a legend unless it was epic," she said. "Come on, you really don't know?"

"Know what?"

"The man who disappeared from the legend a few years ago," she said. "Nobody in the cruising community knows where he went or why, but his name has been made into a verb. I hear it mentioned sometimes on one of the nets."

She was talking about one of the many amateur radio cruiser networks, which shared news and information among the cruising community all over the world, though I had no idea how any of that applied to me.

"You really haven't heard?"

"I haven't tuned in on any of the nets in a while," I admitted. "What are you talking about?"

"You weren't the first," she said, suppressing a grin. "And you certainly won't be the last, but among younger cruisers these days, if a guy drags a girl along and then dumps her in a strange port, it's called *pulling a Jesse*. It's even the same if it's the other way around. I've pulled a Jesse myself once or twice."

CHAPTER THREE

Rick Hayes lay beside me, staring through a pair of binos. Though he wasn't a trained spotter, he had the right equipment to give me distance and windage information.

We'd watched Weller and Kendra, along with several of her people, move a stack of bags, each about the size of a brick into the abandoned hospital and stack them carefully on an old pallet.

What we didn't see coming was when Kendra pointed her gun at Weller. Her men quickly seized him and forced him onto his back, on top of the bags of cocaine. I hadn't even opened my rifle case before it was over and Kendra and her men had piled back into their truck and left.

I'd brought the M-40A3 Charity had given me, though John had told me that Hayes had a couple of solid rifles to choose from. I'd used the M-40 in one variation or another throughout my twenty years in the Corps and I'd stayed proficient with it ever since. It was like an extension of my own body. With the butt plate firm against my shoulder and my cheek welded to the stock, we became one thing. One very dangerous thing.

Everyone had a calling in life, something they were meant to do. Some were accountants, some wrote books, and others might be musicians, something I'd been trying to learn to be for quite a while now. But it wasn't my calling, so the learning was slow and tedious.

I was a shooter, and in my last years as a Marine, I'd found that my calling had been identifying those who were like me and making them better; teaching them to detach themselves from the violence they were about to inflict.

I was not an active duty Marine anymore, and the US wasn't at war with Mexico. This was a different situation. These drug cartels, particularly the one Weller had his sights set on bringing down, were run by the worst kind of thugs. They reigned over the populace with impunity, paying the police and military to look the other way as they took whatever they wanted, and killed anyone who got in their way.

My new target was 833 feet from our perch on the roof of a deserted house—not even 300 yards. That was the *intermediate* distance Marine riflemen qualify from with open sights, even the clerks and musicians snapping in every year, starting in boot camp.

The new M-40 came with a very familiar Unertl scope, the same as the one on the rifle I'd left at home, and the same one I'd used from my first day as a scout/

sniper trainee to my last day as a scout/sniper instructor twenty years later.

The trajectory to the target was nearly flat. There was a steady crosswind at about ten knots, and I'd added the windage dope to the Unertl. At this short a range, a wind gust would only make a millimeter's difference to where my round hit, and my mind compensated for it instinctively.

I felt supremely confident that I could make the shot count the first time, even shooting through a cold barrel. Sherri Fallon was that good and I trusted her dope.

Why Kendra Diaz had double-crossed Weller, we didn't know. The "bat-shit crazy woman" had apparently been posing as both his partner and his lover. She knew we were on the rooftop and timed it just right, so we could see it, but not stop it. It was a trap and it looked for sure like this wasn't going to end well. But sometimes it was better to be lucky than good. We hadn't had a chance to stop the abduction, but we could still help.

Weller had his legs tied to the slats of a cargo pallet and one hand cuffed to a water pipe as he lay on his back on top of the millions of dollars' worth of cocaine. The coke was to have been the bait to lure Orozco to this place. For whatever reason, Kendra Diaz had changed her allegiance.

Hayes and I had a clear line of sight. The windows of the old hospital had been broken out years or maybe decades ago. There was nothing to impede the bullet's flight. Had Diaz staked him out as bait anywhere else in the building, we'd have had to move from rooftop to rooftop to find an angle.

Whatever Diaz's motivations were, I had no way of knowing. We'd watched helplessly as they'd boo-by-trapped the pile of coke, using claymore anti-personnel mines before strapping Weller on top of it. It looked like she wanted him *and* the cartel boss dead.

It had all happened so fast, by the time I had my weapon ready, I couldn't engage. After my first shot, the rest would take cover and likely kill Weller.

"You see this?" Hayes whispered.

Peripherally, I could see everything going on. But my right eye was focused on the scope, waiting for the shot. Several vehicles pulled up to the front of the hospital and armed men jumped out. The vehicles were stripped down, lightweight 4x4 pickup trucks. Machine guns were mounted in the beds so the gunner could shoot over the cab, or swivel around and shoot in any direction.

Technicals.

These vehicles were widely used not just by drug cartels, but by many warlords and despots for their speed, maneuverability, and fire power.

The technicals' machine guns were all trained on the hospital.

"The only thing I don't see is Kendra and her people," I mumbled, breathing slowly.

"I'm guessing they're holed up in that defile beyond the tree line."

After securing Ryan to the booby-trapped pallet, the crew had piled into a big Ford F-250 and disappeared down the road.

"Charity, do you have eyes on Kendra's people?" I asked.

Charity's voice came through my headset like she was lying right beside me. "I've got the drone up, but not for much longer with the weather coming in. I see several trucks arriving at the abandoned building to the south."

"Copy that," I said.

Kendra and her people had pulled back but stopped. My guess would be that they'd wait until the right moment to remotely detonate the claymores. That was good and bad. Good because it meant there wasn't a trip wire. The way Weller was thrashing around, he might have set it off. Bad because Kendra could blow Weller to smithereens if she thought her plan was going south, then *didi mau* out of the area.

Hayes had the hots for Charity. Out of the corner of my eye, I could see him grin just hearing her voice. I'd caught him staring after her, slack-jawed, after our meeting and had told him that he wasn't her type. He'd grinned then, too, saying, "They're all *my* type."

He'd probably have to learn the hard way. That is, if Charity ever gave him the chance. Since she'd lost Victor, she'd stayed pretty much to herself and didn't remain long in any one location. He'd been murdered in Nassau several years ago.

Hayes's voice turned serious. "Orozco just got out of an SUV in front of the hospital."

I ignored the urge to readjust the scope. "I need Ryan to move so I can take the shot."

I waited patiently. The shooting solution was dialed in—an easy shot at this range. All he had to do was drop his head for just a second.

"I'm bringing the drone in," Charity said. "The gusts are too strong at the altitude I need to fly to remain unseen."

I didn't answer, but Hayes did. "Copy that. Stay with the Nissan and be ready for a quick exfil."

Charity's drone had given us a good overview of the area, but we no longer needed the big picture. The action was unfolding right in front of us.

Hayes watched through the binoculars, waiting for me to take the shot. It was up to Weller, struggling on top of the pile of coke.

"Is the wind going to bother you? It's holding at ten knots right now."

"Not one bit," I replied.

A gust of wind tossed my hair. It was strong, heralding the coming storm. But with a muzzle velocity of 2350 feet per second, the Hornady SST ammo would have the bullet finding its mark in less than half a second.

I concentrated on my breathing and waited for the shot, the slack already out of the trigger and the crosshairs just inches beyond Weller's nose. His head was still blocking me from making the shot.

Weller seemed to have found something in the stack of cocaine packages with his free hand and was struggling with it. He palmed whatever it was in his free hand, glanced down, and then turned his head to look out the window at the sound of the men outside.

I squeezed the trigger.

"Hot damn," Hayes muttered as Weller's handcuff shattered.

Watching through the scope, I saw Weller lift his arm, examining the broken chain. In his other hand, he held a knife. He quickly sat up and cut through his foot restraints, just as Orozco stepped into the room with several of his men crowding in behind him. Weller glanced out the broken window toward the trucks.

Orozco stepped closer to the pallet. The men behind him had their guns up, leveled at Weller. Suddenly, Weller dove backward, falling into an empty swimming pool.

A deafening explosion caused me to duck below the ridge of the house for a moment. I could hear shrapnel whining and ricocheting throughout the old hospital and the area around the open windows.

When I looked again, I saw a fog of white powder settling on everything. The detonation had come from the four claymore mines we'd watched them hide in the cocaine.

I scanned the area. Orozco and his men had all gone down in broken and bloody heaps. Wherever the powder settled on the dead and dying men, it congealed into a pasty pink mess of coke and blood.

The blast seemed to rock the building to its foundations.

As the powder continued to settle, Weller raised his head above the pool deck. He scrambled out and crawled across the floor toward the hallway.

"Watch your man," I told Hayes. "I'll check Orozco's men for signs of life."

"Weller lived through that?" Charity asked over my comm.

"Boy's got more lives than a cat," Hayes mumbled.

Weller needed better weaponry than a knife, but after the explosion, I doubted he'd find a working gun.

Suddenly, all hell broke loose. Gunfire from AKs, M-4s, and machine guns split the air. My primary concern was Weller, but it seemed as if there were two forces colliding outside and he was between them,

There wasn't any movement from any of Orozco's men inside the hospital. They were all dead. I moved the scope back to where Weller was. He grabbed up an AK-47, examined it, and cast it aside before dragging its owner out of sight.

I raised my head and surveyed the scene. What was left of Orozco's crew, perhaps eight or ten well-armed men, was engaged in a firefight with a larger force. Though they had better weaponry, the cartel soldiers were being picked apart by the new arrivals, who were firing handguns and old hunting rifles in a steady and very coordinated attack.

Weller returned, wearing a bloodied vest and carrying what looked like a Belgian-made FN Five-seveN semi-auto pistol. He moved tactically through the chaos, weapon up and sweeping from side to side. He quickly scoured the mens' bodies lying about the floor, scavenging a couple more magazines. Then he picked up another AK and racked the bolt. Satisfied, he shoved the pistol into his waistband and relieved the dead man of his magazines.

Men shouted down below. Then bullets struck the concrete ceiling above Weller's head, showering him with shards as he retreated toward the hallway.

A technical came charging around the corner from the east, machine gun blazing toward where Weller was hunkered down on the first floor. I acquired the new target.

My M-40 roared again, silencing the machine gun as the gunner spun around, flying from the bed of the truck. I moved the crosshairs to the cab and fired again. The truck veered hard right, bounced over a sand dune, then crashed nose first into the beach below.

Just beyond the hospital, another gun battle raged between a technical and a force hidden behind the rubble piles. Suddenly, Weller appeared in a window and raised his AK, shooting the machine gunner first and then the two men firing over the hood.

I grinned when he put another round into each man's lifeless body for good measure. I once had a friend—my old platoon sergeant and Deuce's dad, Russ Livingston, who used to say, "Ammo's cheap and lives are expensive. Anyone worth shooting is worth shooting twice."

Then, just as suddenly, Weller disappeared.

"Think he knows he has friends out here?" I asked.

"He knows," Hayes replied. "That technical had someone pinned down."

"The enemy of my enemy?"

"Sometimes works that way," Hayes replied.

A bolt of lightning split the sky, followed by a deep, thunderous boom I not only heard, but felt.

Another technical poured rounds into and around an F250 with *Autodefensas* markings. Weller suddenly appeared and fired on the men defending the technical, silencing the machine gun.

The friendlies who had been firing on the cartel vehicle moved cautiously toward the entrance to the building. One of Orozco's men, a big, barrel-chested guy, was holding Diaz, a gun at her head. This was coming to a swift and bloody end.

"Don't move or I'll kill her," Barrel Chest yelled.

Weller appeared again, raising his rifle at the man. Suddenly, the rain began to come down in icy sheets from the low, scudding sky. The sudden heavy downpour completely blotted out my line of sight.

I could make out people running, then one of the vehicles sped away toward the beach. Through the blinding rain, I couldn't tell anyone apart. I felt helpless.

Hayes and I lay still on the rooftop, watching, trying to see through the haze as the rain came down in blinding sheets. I heard a small outboard start and moments later, the sound of Weller's boat's diesel engine. Was it him, making his escape?

"That's Ryan!" Hayes said. "On the beach with one of the *autodefensas* guys."

"Charity," I barked, rising from my position. "Get down there and pick up our friend. He seems to have had his boat stolen."

"Roger that," she replied.

As we made our way off the rooftop, I could hear the engine of Charity's Nissan as she raced toward the beach. A moment later, I could hear her side of a conversation with Weller over my earwig.

"I'm Charity," she replied to a garbled question. "I'm with the sniper team. Rick Hayes sends his regards. Get in."

I could just make out the black Nissan on the beach and over Charity's comm, I could hear Weller's voice but couldn't understand what he said.

"I know," Charity replied. "Get in. I brought your friend KRISS."

She was referring to Weller's weapon of choice. The Vector didn't have much range—it fired the same

9mm round from the same magazine used in a Glock 19 handgun—but it made up for its short range with the versatility of interchangeable mags and its faster target reacquisition after the first shot. With its stock being higher than the barrel, there was less upward recoil.

Charity spoke in Spanish to the man who was with Weller on the beach. *"Deja que los muertos entierren a los muertos."*

I knew the phrase. Let the dead bury the dead.

"Yeah," Charity replied to another garbled question.

Then came the sound of three truck doors slamming and I could hear Weller's voice more clearly. "Who else is here with you?"

"Rick and a friend of mine, Jesse," Charity replied. "He's the one doing the shooting."

With the rain letting up, Hayes and I quickly climbed back through a busted-out window into the filthy, graffiti-covered interior of the house. I heard Weller say something over the comm, but the sound of the Nissan's engine buried his voice.

Glancing back through the window, I saw them stop next to one of the technicals.

"Charity, give Weller one of your earwigs," I said, as I followed Hayes down the stairs to the front of the house.

"Roger that." Then, speaking to Weller, she said, "You get the technical and I'll pick up the sniper team." There was a rummaging sound, then she added, "These will put us all on the same net."

Ryan's voice came over my earwig, speaking in Spanish.

"You on the net, Ryan?" Rick asked, as we got to the front door.

"Yeah," Weller replied.

Hayes and I flanked the doorway, each of us looking outside in opposite directions.

"I got a message from Mango for you," Hayes said, grinning at me. "He said, 'We saved your ass again, bro.'"

"I knew it wasn't you shooting that rifle. You couldn't hit the broadside of a barn with your dick. No offense, Charity."

Charity laughed. "None taken."

I heard Weller chuckle. "Who else is on the net?"

"Just you, me, Charity, and our master sniper, Jesse McDermitt."

"Nice shootin', Gunny," Weller said.

"Glad to be of service," I replied.

I didn't see any movement outside. Hayes's eyes moved back and forth across the terrain he could see, not fixing on anything. It was clear outside. Hayes pulled a GPS device from his pocket and studied it for a moment while we waited to be picked up.

"Ryan," Hayes said, "we overheard your conversation with Charity on the beach. *Kaytlyn's* AIS shows her headed north at ten knots."

"If she's headed to the port," I said, picturing the bay in my mind, "then we have some time. It will take them over an hour to get there."

Weller asked a question in Spanish, calling someone Miguel. I heard another man reply over the comm, also in Spanish. My linguistic skill wasn't anywhere close to that of Charity's or Weller's, especially in the clipped Spanish of the other man, but I could tell Weller had asked a question and Miguel had answered, *"Treinta minutos"*—thirty minutes.

"We'll have time to do some recon," Charity said.

"We'll follow you, Charity," Weller said. "Let's exfil Rick and Jesse and head for the port. Rick, you keep an eye on the GPS tracker in case *Kaytlyn* deviates from our suspected course."

"Copy," Rick and Charity took turns saying.

I could see Charity's truck approaching as the man with Weller started speaking in rapid-fire Spanish. Other voices—off mic—spoke back to him.

"They are with me and want to help," Miguel said in broken English.

Charity slid to a stop in front of the house. Hayes and I wasted no time—we bolted out the door and climbed in before the truck's springs stopped rocking.

Charity rocketed away, following the narrow gravel road past a beach club and then onto a sandy double-track through the dunes paralleling the beach. The technical charged up behind us, several men in the back hanging on for their lives and shouting at the driver to slow down.

"No puedo," the man shouted back. *I can't.*

Minutes later, the road got smoother as we entered a newly built subdivision. Charity turned left onto blacktop and then right onto Luis Donaldo Colosio Urban Corridor. The technical stayed right with us, tires screeching in protest as it made the turn.

The rain let up to just a mist and rays of sunlight could be seen shining on the wet, black pavement ahead.

"I will lead," Miguel said. "No one questions a cartel technical."

Charity waved him around and the truck passed us at better than sixty miles per hour. The men in back were hunkered down below the roofline. A moment later, the technical swerved onto an exit for the port, then onto Boulevard de los Rios.

Eight minutes later, the technical slowed and turned off the blacktop onto a dirt road. Just past the turn was a giant blue sign with business names and arrows pointing to the various port entrances.

"This is the back way in," Miguel announced in Spanish. "We would never get by port security without authorization."

Charity translated for Hayes, who knew less Spanish than me. "We have an M-60 for authorization," he muttered.

Miguel must have understood some of what Rick said, because he replied in Spanish, "*Sí, señor*, you do, but they will only tell the cartel we are coming. I have been this way many times."

Weller repeated his words in English.

"You trust this guy, Ryan?" I asked.

"Yes."

"*Vamos, amigo,*" I said, my voice low and calm.

The technical swayed as it crossed over a railroad track onto a hard-packed sand maintenance road running beside the tracks. The opposite side was overgrown brush and trees. The road crossed the rails again, but instead of following it, the technical bounced the passenger-side tires over the rail and straddled it.

"Don't worry," Miguel said. "Only one truck that I know of has ever been hit by a train."

"That's comforting," Weller replied.

The tall trees around us gave way to low scrub as the technical moved onto a bridge crossing a lagoon, whose flat waters reflected the setting sun. Charity didn't hesitate and followed the other truck. If a train came at us now, regardless of the direction, we were screwed. When we reached the other side, the technical turned off the tracks.

"We don't have to do that again, do we?" Charity asked.

"No, *señorita.*"

We followed the technical onto a road that ran under a canopy of trees. "The lab is about two miles from here. Once we cross Gulf of Mexico Boulevard, we'll be on pavement."

We drove on blacktop for over a mile before the technical again slowed and turned onto a dirt road, this time stopping at a gate in the chain-link fence.

"Where does this road go?" I asked.

"To an old dock," Miguel replied in English, "then around the end of the canal to the container facilities and the cargo cranes you can see in the distance."

Over the treetops, the upraised arms of the massive gantry cranes were visible, the sun glinting off their blue-painted steel.

"Let's get close and use the drone," Charity said.

"It's best if we go to the dock," Miguel replied.

One of the Mexicans hopped out of the truck bed and disappeared into the brush. A moment later, he came back with a key. He unlocked the gate and we drove through it, then he closed and locked the gate behind us before jumping back into the truck. We started moving again toward the deteriorating concrete wharf.

Closer to the port, we parked under the shade of what I thought was a mesquite tree. Hopefully we wouldn't have to go through one of those thorny thickets.

When we were all standing at the back of Charity's Nissan, Weller stuck his hand out to me. We shook hands and nodded. Nothing needed to be said.

Charity unpacked the drone and I held it aloft. With a sudden whine, it rose quickly to the sky and Charity piloted it north along the edge of the canal. The drone quickly rose completely out of sight.

Hayes moved in close to Charity to watch her screen. Weller looked over his shoulder and I looked over hers. Four of the Mexicans had spread out to form a security perimeter while the man I now knew as Miguel stayed close to us. Apparently, he was the leader of this rag-tag militia group.

The drone gave us a view of the muddy shipping channel. It was almost a thousand feet wide in some places. The trees bordering the western edge before the Aztlán Cartel compound came into view. Like the other businesses along the port's canal, the complex had a concrete wharf running along its length.

There was a Fountain 47 Lightning and a center console fishing boat with twin outboards occupying the dock space at an inset boat ramp, their bows pointed out, ready for action. A gantry crane mounted on railroad tracks added more authenticity to the cartel's ruse as a valid port operation instead of a smuggling ring.

An eight-foot chain-link fence topped with razor wire ringed the entire complex, except for the seven hundred feet of waterfront. Just a few feet inside the fence was a two-high stack of cargo containers butted end to end, forming a second layer of protection against intruders—a sixteen-foot steel wall.

Large forklifts and reach-stackers roved the pavement, placing containers on waiting tractor-trailers or moving them from one side of the yard to the other.

From every vantage point, the place looked like a genuine cargo-handling business. Well, except for the extreme security fence and container wall surrounding it. From overhead, we could see another two-high stack of containers forming a rectangle in the center. A quick count showed the rectangle was seven containers by four. If they were standard forty-foot containers, the rectangle was 280 feet long and 160 wide on the outside.

Charity zoomed the drone's high definition camera in for a closer view. Inside the steel rectangle were more containers, placed side by side. They probably had openings cut in the insides, allowing movement from one to the other; sort of a container office building.

"What's inside the fort?" Weller asked Miguel.

"*Los laboratorios de drogas.*"

No one needed a translation.

Charity zoomed in on a three-story building.

"That is the office," Miguel said in English.

The first and second floors were solid concrete block, while the top level was a wall of windows resembling a penthouse. Or a prison guard tower. From there, a person could see the whole property.

"Looks like roving patrols along the fence perimeter," I said. "But no technicals."

"Miguel, where are the technicals?" Charity asked.

"*No se.*" He shrugged. "But they have cameras all over the yard and along the fence."

"What about *Kaytlyn*?" Weller asked Hayes. "Where is she?"

Hayes retrieved the GPS tracker from the truck. He and Ryan watched the blinking dot move along the coast to the east.

I stepped away from the group, rubbing the stubble on my chin as I considered the options.

"What are you thinking?" Hayes asked, following me to the edge of the water. I looked down the length of the channel at the silent cranes hovering over massive cargo ships. Lights were coming on as darkness fell. If we had scuba gear, we could get a lot closer without being seen. One of the dormant gantry cranes on the other side would be a logical nest. They towered higher than even the office building.

"How well do you know this woman?" I asked Hayes.

"Obviously, not as well as I thought I did," Weller said, joining us.

"What if she's part of the cartel and only used you to help change the power structure?"

Weller pursed his lips in thought. "I don't think so. Orozco forced her to become a *sicario* when he discovered she was an undercover *Federale* and then killed her family when she didn't bring me back to Mexico."

Forced to become a contract killer? A hitman?

"Why did she want your help?" I asked.

"We had mutual interests," Weller replied. "She knew I would be the perfect bait. Do I think she planned to stake me out the whole time? I don't know."

I waited silently. There was always more. You just had to give a person time to arrange the words in the right order.

"I appreciate you saving my ass back there," Weller said to me, delaying what I knew he wanted to ask. "But you've got no skin in this game. Me? I have a two-million-dollar bounty on my head still. As long as this cartel is functioning, me and my partner are at risk. This is my fight and I'm not asking you to get involved any more than you already have."

I didn't hesitate. "I'm in."

The fact that Orozco had put a $2,000,000 bounty on the guy's head went a long way in my mind. Weller must have really pissed the guy off. I liked to align myself with such people.

"Thanks," he said, then pointed at the distant gantry crane across the shipping channel, its long boom extending out over the water. "Think you can use that as your office?"

I grinned. "It'll work. Charity is also skilled at long-distance shooting. I'll take her with me, so we have two shooters. We should be able to see a lot of targets from up there."

Hayes looked up from his screen. "Ryan, your boat just stopped about halfway into the port."

CHAPTER FOUR

We'd all studied maps of the area and seen a drone's-eye view through Charity's screen. I knew that Puerto de Altamira was a T-shaped port with one leg running in from the Gulf, a dredged inlet, and two legs running north and south. We were on the landward side of the southern leg. I remembered seeing a marina located just inside the inlet; *Muelle Norte*, which meant North Dock. I didn't recall seeing a south dock in the inlet.

"Charity," Weller said, "does your drone have enough range to fly to where the *Kaytlyn* stopped?"

"Yes." She manipulated the joysticks on the controller.

"Do you know what's over there, Miguel?" Weller asked.

"*Un Puerto Deportivo,*" he replied, "*para barcos de pesca y otras embarcaciones pequeñas.*"

A marina for fishing boats and other small vessels. I understood Spanish better than I could speak it. Sometimes, that was a good thing.

On Charity's screen, we could see the cartel's center console pull away from the dock and speed toward the entrance channel.

"Did that log just move?" Hayes pointed at an area of disturbed water next to where we stood.

"Probably a crocodile," I replied, nonchalantly. I'd seen a few tracks already. "Either an American or a Morelet's."

"Me and Charity are ground pounders," Hayes said. He must have checked her out. Charity had once been a Blackhawk pilot in the Army, and I knew Hayes was former Army. He visibly shuddered at the dark water and what it hid. "You Department of the Navy types can play in the water all you want."

I grinned. "I was in the men's department."

"I didn't know you were a Navy SEAL," Weller retorted with a grin.

I rolled my eyes.

Interservice rivalry was still alive and well. Each branch of the U.S. military had its place, cogs in the American military machine. In some places there was overlap. The Army had boats and choppers, the Navy had planes and ground troops, even the Air Force had Spec Ops people whose only contact with airplanes was when they flew to get from place to place and often that was on a commercial flight. The Marine Corps operated on land, on the sea, and in the air, as well. Many times, it incorporated all three into a single op. I'd worked closely with people of all branches and the jibing was always in jest.

Well, most of the time.

Charity smirked but remained silent as she flew the drone high and behind the center console now cutting a wide wake through the port.

Weller watched the monitor as she followed the boat. "You think the center con is picking up Kendra, Sour Face, and Barrel Chest?"

"I think you need to be more creative with your nicknames," she replied.

I grinned. In her own way, she was flirting with Weller.

"Well, next time I'm in the heat of battle and need to come up with one, I'll call you," Weller said, smiling at her profile.

She glanced at him with a coquettish smile of her own. "Is that a promise?"

"Whoa. Whoa. Whoa." Hayes made a time-out sign. "That's enough. Let's look at the pretty boats on the screen."

I suppressed a laugh. I only knew these guys by reputation. The fact that they had served and survived some of the deadliest places in the world was impressive. Still, they were both out of Charity's league and had no idea who she was or what she'd once been—an assassin. They just saw a pretty face and cool toys.

We watched in silence as the boat rounded the bend into the inlet and angled toward the little marina, where several fishing and crab boats rode at anchor. The center console maneuvered alongside what I assumed was Weller's boat. It looked like the same spot Hayes's GPS was pinpointing. The center console took on three passengers, then sped away, heading back toward the compound.

Charity kept the drone steady as she raced the boat, staying well to the west to keep the sun, which was almost below the horizon, from glinting off the drone's black plastic body. When the center console pulled into its slip, she swung the drone around and focused the camera on the boat's occupants.

Weller pulled Miguel over and had him watch the feed. "Tell me who those men are."

"The tall one is Juan Herrera and the other is Andre Sagaste. Both are Orozco's lieutenants."

"Is one of them *El Matador*?"

Miguel looked puzzled. "Neither of them are bull-fighters."

My eyes were fixed on Kendra Diaz. She climbed from the boat and followed the two men along the dock. That told me a lot. With no gun to her head, she looked a lot more like a willing participant than a kidnap victim.

"What's the objective here?" I asked.

"Shut down the drug labs," Weller said, not looking up from the screen.

"All right," I said. "I think we should send you and Rick in through the wire while Miguel and his *amigos* hit the front gate for a distraction. Charity and I will take our truck and drive around to the crane."

"How long do you need to get into position?" Hayes asked.

"Good question," I replied. "Give us about an hour. We'll give you a shout when we've got eyes on the target. What's our exfil route?"

"Is John hanging around off the coast?" Weller asked, pulling up a map on his phone.

"Yeah, he is," I replied. "He's our ride back to the helicopter."

"Then let's use one of the cartel's boats to meet with John," Weller suggested, moving the map image around on his phone, then pointing to a location on the screen. "There's a small fishing pier on the south jetty where we can pick you and Charity up on the way out of here."

The pier was less than a mile from the gantries. I nodded and Weller turned to Charity. "Got any explosives in those bags?"

"I've got blocks of C-4 and remote detonators."

"Rick and I will set charges in the drug labs."

Charity nodded as she brought the drone in for a smooth landing beside the truck. She packed it into its case while Hayes pulled on his tactical gear.

With darkness came mosquitos and the occasional deep, throaty grumble of a crocodile. Miguel and his vigilantes didn't seem to mind, but the mosquitos were terrorizing the others. Since I lived on an island in the Keys, they didn't seem to like my salty blood.

Hayes retrieved a can of bug repellant from Charity's truck and everyone passed it around, using it liberally.

Weller exchanged his blood-soaked vest for a new one loaded with spare thirty-round mags for the KRISS Vector and the Glock pistol Rick had also brought for him. He slipped the FN pistol he'd liberated from the dead cartel man into his back pocket just in case.

Ryan steered Miguel away from the rest of us and toward the technical. They spoke in Spanish, so I couldn't tell what was being said, but Miguel's voice sounded very sad and Weller seemed concerned.

Charity and I grabbed up our gear and loaded it into the Nissan as Miguel called to one of his men—a kid really, probably no more than seventeen or eighteen. Weller said something to him, and he took off on foot. Weller joined Hayes, who was loading C-4 into a backpack while Miguel talked on the phone. Hayes kept glancing at Charity as they talked. It didn't take a rocket surgeon to tell what they were discussing.

I went around to the driver's side as Charity climbed into the passenger seat.

Weller slung the backpack over his shoulders and turned to Charity. "We're ready to roll."

"What did you say to Miguel?" she asked.

"I told him to call his friends and have them hit the other drug labs and Orozco's house while we do God's work here."

"*Excelente*," Charity said with a smile, as I started the truck.

I backed the Nissan around, headlights stabbing through the darkness to illuminate the rutted dirt road we'd need to follow.

CHAPTER FIVE

The headlights of the Nissan worked both ways. They allowed us to see where we were going, but also gave away our position to anyone looking in our direction. But if we encountered anyone, we'd look even more suspicious driving in the dark, so I left them on.

To the north, the T-shaped port was occupied by a handful of businesses. They were primarily natural gas and oil storage facilities, and other related industries.

Charity pointed to a sign. "Relatives of yours?"

Interestingly, one of the businesses was called McDermott Oil Rig Construction and it took up the bulk of that end of the port. Pap had told me that he'd had distant cousins in the old country who'd spelled their name with an o, but I'd never met them. I was the only child of an only child, and Pap had three sisters, meaning I was the only McDermitt in at least three generations of our branch of the family tree.

I shrugged and drove on. "It's possible, I guess."

The rest of the north side of the port was undeveloped land similar to what we were driving through, surrounded by trees and croaking frogs.

At the southern end of the T-shaped port was the main part of the shipping activity. The land between the canal and the Gulf was covered by large, concrete parking areas, with roads painted on them and railroad tracks traversing the whole area. A sea of containers and new cars awaited shipment, all stacked and parked tightly between the painted roads.

Hayes called on my sat phone to tell us there had been a change in the cartel's hierarchy and Kendra Ortiz was suddenly on the outside. I'd thought that she'd seemed more complacent when her men were strapping Weller down, but I hadn't given it much thought. Killing him hadn't been her idea.

The trip around to the other side was uneventful. Once we got away from the cartel's compound, we were just another *gringo y gringa turista* in another small tourist beach town in Mexico. But the drive around the canal still took more than half an hour.

Where were the technicals? The Aztlán Cartel controlled this area and from all I'd heard, they weren't bashful about making their presence known.

Finally, we found a spot where we could hide the Nissan and get over the fence of the abandoned shipyard undetected.

Weller's voice came over my comm. "You in place yet, Jesse?"

"Another ten minutes or so," I replied, studying the giant framework of the gantry. "We had to do more driving than planned."

"Copy that," Weller said. "We're going in."

Up at the top of the gantry was a large, square structure, which was where the operator controlled the crane's thick cables and blocks to raise and lower cargo into and out of a ship. In the moonlight, I could see that most of the windows were missing.

I touched Charity on the shoulder. When she looked over at me, I switched off my earwig and pointed to hers. She nodded and did the same.

"You okay with this?" I asked, knowing she would understand.

"In your own words," she said, her eyes turning to cold, blue stones, "these people are turd-fondlers. They rape, torture, and murder innocent people indiscriminately for fun. They pay off the corrupt police, who turn a blind eye. They ruin lives and families."

"Then let's do it," I said and nodded toward the easiest point of ingress; a metal emergency ladder enclosed by a round steel cage.

The bottom rung was at least ten feet above the ground. Too high, even for me. I looked around for something to stand on.

"Give me a boost," Charity said.

"You can't haul me up," I replied.

"I won't need to. Just boost me up and trust me."

Interlacing my fingers, I bent and Charity put a booted foot in my hands. With her hands on my shoulders, I easily lifted her to where she could grab the bottom rung. When she reached for it, her shirt rode up and her bare belly pressed against my face.

I pushed her up to the next rung.

The cage around the ladder didn't start until five feet up. Just below that, Charity slid her legs between the first two rungs, sitting on the first one like a child's swing. Then she leaned back and rotated her legs upward, wrapping them around the outside of the ladder above her and hooking her ankles under the fourth rung. When she unfolded herself, hanging upside down, her face appeared just a few inches above my own and her blond hair dangled in front of me like a veil.

"Tie all our gear together," she said. "There's some paracord in the middle pocket of my backpack."

I quickly lashed our packs and rifle cases together, leaving the long end of the tough nylon cord free.

"Hand me the bitter end," Charity said.

When I gave it to her, she did a vertical sit-up and held it for a moment while she tied the end of the paracord to the rung at her knees. When she unfolded again, her shirt once more slipped down, exposing her tanned belly.

"See if you can grab my belt and pull yourself up," she said. "I'll get your feet once you're high enough.

I reached up and could just get my fingertips over her belt, which was threaded through wide straps in her tactical pants. I grabbed it and pulled, testing if the loops, or even if Charity herself, could hold my weight.

"Grab the sides," she instructed. "I don't want a two-hundred-pound wedgy."

"Two-twenty-five," I said, releasing my hold and stepping back from her. "This is ridiculous. I'm nearly twice your size."

Charity's upper body swung freely back and forth. "I know that, Jesse. And I also know my limitations. I can't lift you up here and I seriously doubt I can support you on my shoulders." She gave me a coy smile and put a finger to her chin in mock innocence. "You Jarheads can scale fifteen-foot walls by climbing up one another's bodies. Is it because I'm just a girl?"

The new Charity Styles was taking some getting used to. When we'd worked together before, she'd always been as cool and emotionless as the proverbial cucumber. After all she'd been through, that was understandable. But in the last year or so, she'd undergone a transformation. She'd become more animated and even playful at times; like an hour ago, flirting with Weller and Hayes and playing one against the other.

I wasn't sure which Charity I preferred working with.

"Get over it, Jesse," she said, her eyes suddenly cold. "I got you."

Charity Styles was a warrior woman. She'd always done whatever had needed doing to accomplish a mission. She would have my back, the same as I'd have hers. We both knew that.

I reached up and grabbed her belt at the hips and did a dead arm pull-up, literally climbing her body, until

I felt her grab my right ankle. I lifted that leg slightly and she got both hands around the sole of my boot. I pushed, while releasing one hand and reaching for the first rung of the ladder. From there it was an easy hand-over-hand climb.

Getting above her, I looked down. She did another impossible vertical sit-up and unthreaded herself from the ladder. Then she quickly untied the paracord and handed it up to me.

We pulled our gear up, separated it, and started up the ladder to the gantry operator's position. It was at least a hundred feet above the abandoned dock area. I knew the base of the steel gantry had an elevator, but I also knew there was no chance that it was in service.

When we finally reached the door in the bottom, it was locked. I withdrew my suppressed Sig Sauer 9mm and looked down at Charity.

"Watch yourself," I said. "I gotta blow the lock."

"Hold on," she hissed, turning her head.

I followed her gaze. A technical was driving past, shining a spotlight through the fence. Had we been discovered? It was the first one we'd seen. Why now?

The beam of light passed over the ground, swinging left to right and moving out to the dock edge and back. It never even illuminated the bottom of the ladder, much less our perch ten stories above it. The untrained thought horizontally. They never expected their foe to be anywhere other than on the ground where they were.

I always taught my people to think vertically. Dig in or gain the high ground.

Once the technical had moved on, Charity whispered, "Let me get by you. I'll try to pick the lock. Even suppressed, a ricochet is going to make a lot of noise."

She was right. I stuck the Sig back in its holster as she shrugged out of her pack in the tight confines of the ladder's safety cage.

"Here," Charity said, handing her pack up. "Hold this and I'll squeeze past you."

I braced my feet and leaned back against my own pack, allowing about a foot of room between me and the ladder, then reached down and took her pack while I held the top rung with my other hand.

Charity came up between my legs, flattening her body to the ladder as she wedged herself between it and me. In any other circumstance, I might have enjoyed the proximity of those last few minutes. But the idea of the technical's machine gun ripping us to shreds in that position wasn't appealing.

With Charity sitting on my chest, I moved my lower body closer to the ladder to help support her while she let go of the handholds to get her tools out.

"You know," she whispered, "I've thought about climbing you a time or two."

"What stopped you?" I countered.

"A lot of things," she replied, pausing to look down over her shoulder at my face, crushed between the small of her back and the cage. "Most recently, Savannah."

She went to work. After a moment I heard a click.

"Got it," she said, throwing open the floor hatch and climbing up into the operator's room.

She knelt and reached down. "Gimme my pack, then get your unusually lanky body up here."

"Switch your comm back on," I told her, flicking the tiny switch on my own earwig.

When I climbed up, I noticed that there were two control consoles, each with its own set of levers, switches, and gauges. But more importantly, each had its own seat. Between each seat and console the floor was missing. There had probably once been tempered glass windows there, so the operator could look straight down at what he was lifting as he moved the control room in or out along the crane's boom. But with no air conditioning, I imagined the workers here had removed all the windows. Workplace safety organizations had no control in most of the world.

"You take that one," I said, pointing to the left console. "Just don't look down."

Over my comm, I heard Miguel whispering something in Spanish to someone named Maria. From my limited understanding, it seemed as if he was promising to carry her into battle.

"Miguel, you still with me?" Weller asked.

"Yes, I am here," came the vigilante's response, as if waking from a dream. "We are waiting for your signal."

"You got eyes on us yet, Leatherneck?" Weller asked.

"Two mikes," I replied, opening my case.

"Let us know when you're set. Take targets of opportunity. Miguel, that will be your cue to attack the gate. Come hard, guns blazing. Rick and I will infiltrate the labs and plant explosives."

A chorus of affirmative replies came over my earwig, including one from Charity.

I unfolded my M-40's bipod legs and placed them on the far edge of the control panel so the muzzle extended outside the window. After testing the seat before stepping past it to straddle the hole in the floor, I sat down and positioned myself with my feet braced on a pair of footrests on either side of the console.

Once the lens covers were open, I switched on the optics in front of the Unertl scope. The SPi-manufactured X27 low light imaging scope had been a Christmas gift from Deuce. I'd brought it along for surveillance use and it mounted easily on my new rifle's Picatinny rail. Shooting from a standing position would be a bit difficult. The optics added nearly two pounds to the front of the rifle.

Looking through the scope, I was amazed as night became day. It wasn't the gray-green I'd been accustomed to seeing through other starlight optics. This was in full color. And even magnified through the scope, the contrast was amazing. It was no different than looking through the Unertl on a bright, sunny day.

I moved the scope around the compound, identifying known positions. I found Weller and Hayes easily enough. Their only real cover was the darkness and this new night optics system stole that away from them. I panned past them to the walled compound.

We weren't high enough. Charity and I would lose sight of them when they moved on the lab. I could only see a portion of it inside the double-stacked perimeter of containers.

"*Señor* Ryan, there is bad news," Miguel said excitedly. He continued in halting English. "A convoy just passed our position. There are three gun trucks like mine and two SUVs headed toward the compound."

"Any idea who's in them?" Weller asked.

"*No se,*" Miguel replied.

I had an idea. "Fall in and hit them from behind," I ordered.

Though outnumbered three to one, the tough little guy would have the element of surprise. I barely heard the sound of Miguel's engine start up when he shouted, "*Cuando me acerque, enciéndelos!*" ordering his men to light them up when he got close.

A moment later, the unmistakable sound of machine gun fire erupted through my earwig. Soon, a second one joined the cacophony, now coming through my comm and from across the water. Then it became silent.

I hung my head a moment. The silence was an obvious indication of the outcome. My only solace was that Miguel had probably gotten at least one of the technicals. When I looked back through the scope, a siren began to blare from the cartel's compound on the other side of the waterway.

CHAPTER SIX

Charity and I looked at one another. She was behind her own rifle, a Barrett M82A1A. It was a semi-auto rifle and almost had to be. It was designed specifically to fire either a standard .50-caliber BMG round or the Raufoss-manufactured Mk-211 incendiary round, either of which would kick like a mule in a bolt action rifle. I'd taught her to use it myself, and she was good. The thing had a range of over a mile.

Charity wrapped her fingers around the bone mic pressed against her cheek. "He knew what he was doing, Jesse. He would have had the same idea a millisecond after you did."

I nodded, though her words didn't lessen my guilt at sending men to fight and die. I settled back in behind the scope, welding my cheek to the stock. I wondered who Maria was and what had transpired between her and Miguel to make him willing to die for her. I'd sensed a deep love in his voice when he'd vowed earlier to carry her into battle.

Weller and Hayes were crouched at the end of the cargo container wall. A guard was moving toward them, weapon at the ready.

"Hold," Charity said, and the two men froze in place.

The sentry was there in the middle of my sights. He wore green fatigues with a yellow T-shirt underneath. I closed out all thoughts and breathed slowly, taking the slack out of the trigger. With the muzzle outside the small room, the roar of my rifle was loud, but not deafening, as it would be if it were fully inside the enclosure. When I reacquired my target, he was unmoving on the ground.

Our two friendlies each grabbed one of the man's legs and dragged him behind the container wall.

"What's going on, Miguel?" Weller asked, though I knew what had surely happened. "Miguel, say your status. Over."

"You got eyes on that party, Jesse?" Hayes asked.

"Negative, and I have more bad news."

"Go."

"We're on the gantry crane nearest the compound." I replied. "The one that's not over a ship. But we don't have a shooting solution for half the target area. The container fortress is blocking a lot of our view."

"Can you move north to the next crane?" Weller asked.

"Negative, Frogman," I replied. "That crane is over a cargo ship and we can't access it."

"Do what you can, Leatherneck."

"We have you now," I said. "But once you move into the stacks, we'll lose you."

"Roger that," Weller replied.

He knew what I was saying. Once they moved forward, they'd be on their own, relying on their wits and skill to get in and out alive. My job was to cover them as best I could and demoralize the enemy. I'd once been very good at it.

Weller ran to the nearest container stack and used it for cover as he and Hayes leapfrogged along the waterfront, covering one another's advance as if they'd worked together many times. They probably had.

Charity's Barrett roared.

"Tango down," she called softly. "More tangos looking for your dead friend."

"Whatever you're going to do," I said, "you better haul ass."

I watched as Weller moved around the corner of a container, jogging toward the office. Then he disappeared behind the wall of containers.

A technical burst through the front gate, disappearing instantly behind the walls of the compound, its headlights illuminating the spot where Weller had vanished just as Hayes reached the same spot.

Suddenly, Weller reappeared, running in the open, back the way they'd come. "I'm bringing the technical to you, Leatherneck!" he shouted over the comm.

"We're ready," I replied calmly, putting my crosshairs on the spot the headlights were coming from.

"Rick?" Weller said, as he stumbled and went down, his KRISS sliding away from him on the pavement.

"I'm here, Usain Bolt. You take care of the tech and I'll blow some shit up."

Weller didn't answer. The technical was closing in, its headlights turning to track him. Leaping to his feet, he made a beeline toward a crane on the opposite shoreline. Right into our field of fire.

The driver made some erratic turns trying to keep Ryan pinned by the headlights, and the gunner in the back nearly flew out. Once the truck was going straight again, he regained his footing and started to aim the M-60 in Weller's direction. He wore goggles and a blue camo gaiter pulled up over his nose.

My mind calculated the difference in distance and the speed of the truck as I breathed out and slowly took the slack out of the trigger. It wasn't a long shot, only 400 yards, but the target was moving fast.

My shot and Charity's rang as one. When I reacquired the target, the gunner and driver were both dead, and the remaining three men in the vehicle were bailing out, rolling across the concrete, then running for cover next to the disabled truck.

Charity fired again as I racked the bolt on my rifle, driving a fresh cartridge into the chamber. A man rising to fire his rifle blindly over the hood took Charity's heavy .50-caliber round in the top of his head, splitting it open and launching the man backward.

I checked on Weller. He pulled the Glock from his holster and ran to the north end of a large mobile crane's wheels. Then he squatted next to the big carriage, aimed, and put half a magazine into the truck. One narco stood to return fire and I pressed the trigger.

Jumping up, Ryan dashed to the truck, slowing as he approached the front bumper.

"I'll drive this guy out," he said, "you pop him." He dropped to his belly, aimed and fired under the truck. The man rolled out from behind it and Charity's big Barrett roared. The man stopped squirming.

"Don't shoot me," Weller said. "I'm running from the truck to the containers."

"Copy," Charity said very coolly. "Don't shoot the cute guy."

Hayes's voice was full of indignation. "Hey, I'm on the net."

"Where are you?" Weller asked.

"I'm trying to breach the drug labs, but your friends have me pinned at the southeast corner."

"On my way," Weller said. He raced through the containers, retracing his steps to where he'd dropped the KRISS.

He found it and after a quick inspection, fired a round to test it, then made his way through the shipping yard, dodging from container stack to container stack before disappearing.

I heard three more shots over my comm from a small caliber weapon; Weller's KRISS.

"Get your ass up here," Hayes said, the comm crackling with gunshots.

Weller's heavy breathing and grunts told me he was on the move again. I scanned the area that I could survey and saw nothing. I could hear the firefight going on across the water, though.

"I need to get to the front gate," Weller finally said.

Hayes's response was immediate and vehement. "Forget about your girlfriend."

I felt helpless, unable to assist. Moving to another nest was useless. It'd be no higher and this would be over before I could get to it. As my scope moved along the office building's glass top floor, I detected movement. There was a man on the roof, but he was behind an air conditioning unit.

"Sniper on the office roof," I said evenly.

"Got an angle on him?" Hayes asked. "He's been making my life a living hell down here."

"We're working it now."

"Please," he said sarcastically. "Take your time."

The distance was over 800 yards—half a mile—and the guy fired and ducked quickly behind an air conditioner, as if he knew he wasn't the only long gun on the battlefield. If he was a trained shooter and using good equipment, we might be in danger. But given the distance, and the fact that we were in complete darkness inside the control room, I was more concerned about the damage he could inflict below.

In the distance, I heard the sound of a large piece of equipment starting—a big diesel forklift or travel crane.

"We need the sniper to show himself," Charity said. "He's hiding behind an air conditioning unit."

"We're working on it," Weller parroted.

Above the wall, I could see the wide arms of a Hyster reach stacker moving toward the gate, carrying a container. It was a monster lift truck with arms that could spread to fit any length container, lifting them by their locking corners.

I could hear the Hyster's powerful engine whining at top speed, which was a little more than a fast jog.

"Ramming speed," Weller called out.

The sound of a collision came over the comm and again, a moment later, across the dividing water. The screech of metal on metal rivaled the sound of the Hyster's engine.

The shooter on the roof appeared and I squeezed the trigger. I knew it was a miss before the round even left the barrel. I'd rushed the shot. I wanted him to take cover, so I could see what Weller was doing.

I shifted my scope to the front gate, where I saw him climbing down from the giant forklift. He'd rammed a forty-foot container against the gate.

"Rick, you good?" Weller asked.

"I'm good," Hayes replied. "We have them pinned in the office. The technical is blocking the door."

The sniper appeared and fired again.

"Take out the freakin' sniper!" Weller yelled.

"Hey, Gunny," Hayes said. "Time to Mogadishu this shit."

I didn't reply and Weller asked if we were still on the net. Charity affirmed we were.

"Rick, I'll meet you on the east side of the container fort," Weller said. "I've got the key to get inside."

"Roger that."

Charity and I waited. The shooter on the roof was cautious, but he was also hell-bent on stopping our guys.

"This place will go up like a rocket ship," Hayes said. "Those barrels have ethyl acetate in them."

Ethyl acetate? I knew it was a powerful solvent and highly flammable.

"What do they use it for?" Weller asked.

"They dissolve the coca base in it, then distill it with heat to get the final cocaine product."

The shooter remained hidden. His targets were inside the lab and I could hear them moving quickly through the interconnecting containers, setting the charges to blow the whole place up.

Charity pulled the drone out of her pack and powered it up. There was no easy way to launch it, but being a hundred feet over the water, she didn't need to. She checked that the controls were working and simply threw it out the window like a Frisbee. Once she got on the controls, the small drone stopped its freefall and jetted across the waterway.

Suddenly, more gunshots erupted from where the wrecked Hyster could be seen over the wall.

"We got company coming through the front door," Hayes said dryly.

"I thought we took out all the bad guys." Weller replied.

"Well, they got more friends."

"What's the situation, Leatherneck?" Weller asked.

"Charity has the drone up. We can see another group of vehicles at the front gate. They can't get in because of your container so they're sending in soldiers on foot."

"What about the sniper?" he asked.

"He's still active," I replied, waiting for the shooter to pop up again. "I'm good, but I can't make a bullet curve around an object."

"We need to blow this popsicle stand," Hayes said. "Literally and figuratively."

There were two explosions, one on top of the other. They came from somewhere near the lab. Suddenly, machine gun fire coming from outside the front gate chewed up the side of the building, spider-webbed several glass panes on the top floor, and then zeroed in on where the sniper was hiding.

The shooter jumped out from behind the AC unit, aiming in our direction. I squeezed the trigger and my rifle boomed. I got the scope back on the man just as my bullet found him, snapping his head back as the round passed through his scope and then his skull.

"Hell yeah," Hayes cheered.

Charity said, "Your friend Miguel is back in the fight."

"Sweet!" Weller said. "Welcome back, *compadre.*"

More machine gun fire erupted at the gate. I moved my scope and saw Miguel, bloodied and battered, hammering away at the cartel's technicals with his M-60. The other trucks returned fire and Miguel went down in a hail of bullets.

"Miguel!" Ryan barked. "Miguel!"

Again, there was no answer.

Charity broke the silence. "Miguel is down. Looks like he joined the party and helped us take out the sniper before he bought it."

A moment later, more gunfire erupted near the lab—a steady stream of single shots and three-round bursts; the unhurried attack of a highly disciplined professional warrior with an attitude.

Hayes's voice came over the comm. "For your next trick, are you going to walk on water?"

"No," Weller replied. "We're going to blast our way into the building."

Though I couldn't see them at the entrance to the three-story office building, I could imagine what they were doing. Doors were easy. Slip a thermite cord through the door opening, above the lock, and it would burn through anything. And I knew Weller had some.

"Don't watch it," Hayes said. "It's a linear thermite charge and will blind you like a thousand suns."

They were blowing the door.

I heard the sounds as the two men breeched the office door and moved methodically through the first and second floors. A few minutes later, there was a loud boom from inside the building followed by the sound of something falling or tumbling. Then came a quick succession of small arms fire.

"Kendra, it's us," Weller said.

"Ryan," Charity broke in. "Sorry to interrupt, but there are more vehicles coming from the south and west."

"More cartel?" Weller asked.

"I don't know."

I could hear Kendra Diaz clearly over Weller's comm. "They are a competing cartel. *Los Patriotas.*"

"The Patriots," Weller said.

"They're not from New England, are they?" Hayes asked.

Moving my scope along the top floor windows, I found them. Weller held Diaz in an embrace and another woman with a baby stood off to the side.

Diaz looked at Hayes. "They have been trying to take over since Guerrero died. Orozco held them off, but with him gone, there is a power vacuum."

Weller pushed her away. "The *autodefensas* were supposed to raid the cartel's other lab sites and Orozco's house."

"They did," Diaz replied, barely audible. "The meth lab blew up and killed most of both forces. Yasmine abandoned the house when she received the news that Orozco was dead. The vigilantes are still on their way to *El Tordo.*"

"Nice to meet you, Yasmine," Weller said.

"Skip the family reunion and get out of there," I barked.

Being on the outside of something and not knowing the players is always a hazard in what I do. There was definitely something I didn't know but was expected to roll with it. Diaz seemed to change sides as often as her underwear.

Weller didn't strike me as a love-blinded fool, and he still seemed to trust her. It was obvious the Yasmine woman holding the baby was a non-combatant. Sometimes, as with Maria and Miguel, I just never found out.

Hayes moved to the door and motioned for the women to stack up behind him. Then the group disappeared through the door as Weller outlined his plan to everyone.

"I want to funnel those guys into the drug lab fort and blast them to kingdom come."

Weller then ordered Hayes to grab an M-60 machine gun from one of the technicals.

Diaz took Hayes's gun and scavenged magazines from dead cartel soldiers while Hayes pulled the M-60 from the smashed technical and hung a spare belt of ammunition around his neck.

When I looked back to Weller, he was backing the black Tahoe into a gap between a container, which rested on top of one of the technicals, and the drug lab fort, sealing off the entrance.

A moment later, I heard Weller say, "Take Yasmine and the baby to the boats."

Diaz asked a question, which I couldn't hear.

"Get the boat started," Weller said. "We'll need to make a quick exit if this doesn't go according to plan. Jesse," he continued, "fall back to the jetty."

"Roger that," I replied, already putting my rifle back in the case.

Charity and I started down, with me carrying all our gear so she could keep her hands free to fly the drone if need be. With no input on the controls, it would hover where it was, dodging left and right, up and down, in sporadic movements designed to keep the enemy from being able to shoot it down. It would do that indefinitely. Until she either took the controls or the battery died.

"All right, Rambo," Weller said. "Let's do this!"

"All I need is the headband and the movie contract," Hayes replied. Then a moment later, his voice was serious. "Good luck, brother."

We reached the bottom and I lowered our gear to the ground, then dropped down off the ladder. A moment later, Charity landed next to me. She looked over and grinned as she controlled the drone.

Looking over her shoulder, I saw Weller's back on her screen, his image growing larger and larger, until the screen filled with gravel, then went black.

"Tie a grenade by its pin to the drone with a six-foot piece of rope," she ordered.

The image on her screen went haywire, jerking and turning, as Weller picked up the drone and turned it over. His face looked grim as he worked. Finally, he turned the drone upright and held it aloft, looking up at it and winking, the grenade in his other hand.

Charity raised the drone, taking up the slack. Then she gave it full power and Weller's image on the screen got smaller and smaller as she flew it to the office building and up around the side, the grenade dangling below.

On the screen, I saw a man slip through the gap between the wrecked technical and the truck. He raised his rifle, the muzzle aimed at the drone. Two red spots appeared on his chest and he went down.

"How many guys are still outside the compound?" Weller asked.

Charity turned the drone. "There are five men standing watch," she said. "I'll use the grenade to blow up one of their technicals and hopefully push them into the kill box."

"I'm ready here," Hayes said.

"Whenever you're ready, Charity," Weller said.

Charity flew the drone high over the fence, watching *Los Patriotas* stealthily move into the compound. She couldn't see the grenade hanging under the drone with the camera at that angle. Moving the quadcopter sideways, she maneuvered it over the shattered remains of Miguel's technical and angled the camera downward. His body lay in a tangled heap on the ground. I felt a moment of deep sorrow for the man. He'd only wanted to make a difference for his people.

Smoothly, Charity dropped the drone down to the truck's bed, looking for a place to wedge the grenade so she could pull the pin with the drone. As it moved along the side of the truck, I saw Miguel's hand move.

Charity stopped and zoomed in on his face. Miguel's brown eyes stared impassively from the screen, then they darted to the right. We watched him make the eye movement three times before turning the drone to see where he was motioning. His fingers clenched into a fist, then opened and clenched again.

I cupped my hand around the bone mic so the others wouldn't hear. "I think he wants to grab the grenade," I said, looking over Charity's shoulder.

She lowered the grenade toward the wounded man's hand. It looked like he had two gunshot wounds to the abdomen and had bled quite a bit. The blood looked black in the low light. Miguel wasn't going to live, and he knew it.

She fought for control of the drone, applying full power to the four rotors as Miguel's feeble hand firmly held the grenade. Suddenly, the drone lifted crazily away. Charity released the controls and it regained a stable hovering attitude. A moment later the video screen flashed a brilliant white, then faded to black.

Gunfire flashed and popped in answer to the grenade blast and a secondary explosion, which I guessed to be the technical's gas tank, rocked the compound entrance.

Our view from the ground was even more limited, but through my monocular, I could see the upper half of the gate and *Los Patriotas* retreating through it to the inside.

"It worked. They're inside the wire," Weller said.

"Copy," Charity replied. "We're heading to our pickup point."

"See you in a few," Weller said.

Charity and I ran to the fence, scaled it, and continued down an alley to the Nissan. After we threw our gear into the backseat and climbed in, I backed out into the street and drove at a normal speed away from the dock. It was only a few blocks to the jetty where the go-fast boat would pick us up. We could hear the sounds of a one-sided battle as Weller and Hayes caught the bad guys in a crossfire, driving them to the safety of the lab.

"Get down," Weller shouted over the comm.

The chatter of the M-60 fell silent, and then there was a massive explosion. In the mirror, I watched as a giant orange and black fireball rolled up into the night sky, the flames illuminating the inside of the Nissan and our surroundings with a dancing orange glow. It looked like hell itself had opened up.

"Rick, fall back to the boat," Weller ordered.

I turned onto another street, driving slowly and heading away from the port's gantries as I listened to Weller and Hayes making their way to the boat. I didn't want to draw any more attention to us than the gunfire and explosions already had. Most of that was on the other side, though.

Hearing the boat's engines start up, I felt a rush of relief. I listened as Weller took the wheel and the engines roared. A second later, I could hear the engines' throaty howl echoing through the streets on this side.

"What are you doing?" I heard Hayes ask when the engines suddenly slowed.

"I promised Greg I'd bring his boat back to him," Weller replied.

I parked the Nissan in an empty lot next to a small public fishing pier, leaving the keys in the ignition. As Charity and I threw open the back doors and grabbed our gear, I could hear the Fountain racing boat's engines coming up to speed again. Across the water, a dark figure was climbing aboard *Kaytlyn*.

The go-fast boat, with the two women and the baby aboard, came close to the pier where Charity and I stood, its powerful engines rumbling. As it edged closer, Hayes put it in neutral and went up onto the foredeck. I fended the boat off the pier as Hayes took our gear from Charity and placed it on the deck behind him. Then he helped us aboard.

In minutes, the boat was headed straight out to sea to rendezvous with John Wilson. He waited three miles offshore to ferry us separately to where *Star of Galveston* would pick everyone up.

I spotted *Floridablanca's* profile in the moonlight and pointed her out to Hayes. Just minutes after leaving the carnage behind, Hayes slowed as we came alongside. I was looking forward to sleeping in my own bed.

"Thanks for the assist," Hayes said, extending a hand.

I took it, pumping it once. "Anytime."

Charity and I climbed over the rail into *Floridablanca's* cockpit and Diaz handed our gear over. Then Hayes punched the throttles, headed for the *Star of Galveston* somewhere ahead. He and the two women would get there well ahead of us, but we'd beat Weller.

"How'd it go?" John asked, when we joined him on the command bridge.

"Hayes and Weller's mission is accomplished," I replied, sounding a bit grumpy. "I'm hungry and tired."

"When did you eat last?" Charity asked.

"This morning," I replied, looking at my watch. "Make that yesterday morning."

"And you've been awake for over twenty-four hours," John said. "There's leftover mahi in the fridge. Eat and get some sleep."

Charity joined me in the galley, and I nuked a couple of broiled fillets. We ate quickly—no utensils—a warrior's meal, eaten fast to stave off the hunger and allow us to sleep for a while.

"Before you offer," Charity said, "you take the big bunk. I'll sleep on the watch bunk up in the pilothouse."

Suddenly, I didn't have the energy to argue the point. I went down to my cabin and was asleep in seconds.

CHAPTER SEVEN

I could feel the Somali heat on my back, but I'd long since learned to ignore physical discomfort. The air was every bit as hot and dry as the blistering sand and rocks all around me. Sweat flowed freely from every pore in my skin. Under the desert ghillie suit, it had to be well over 120° and it wasn't yet mid-morning.

Sergeant Steve Beck lay prone at my side, peering through his spotting scope as he talked quietly on the radio.

"Affirmative, Six," he whispered into the microphone of his SINCGARS-V transceiver. The computer-controlled frequency-hopping radio kept anyone listening from picking up more than a fragment as the transmitter changed frequencies, sending an encrypted message to the receiver, which matched its frequency-hopping. He needn't have whispered, though. There probably wasn't anyone within half a mile of our position.

"Still good, Gunny?" Steve asked, moving the handset away from his mouth. "Six is checking with the old man."

"Yeah, but not for much longer. We know how this turd-fondler operates."

Something unintelligible came over his handset and he put it to his ear. "The target is moving," Steve said into the mic. "But Too Tall says it ain't a problem. The target's dragging a kid, using him as a shield."

I stared unblinking through my scope. The distance was just over a thousand yards. I'd made similar shots many times before. But they'd been on the range, and the targets had been paper and static. This was a man and he was moving, shielding his body with that of the little boy.

Steve and I both knew what the boy's fate would be. The Somali warlord in my sights was a known pedophile.

I'd killed other men, and I'd hit targets that were smaller than what this guy was presenting. I knew I could make this shot. I'd once made two consecutive head shots, on paper, from 1000 yards. It was all about forecasting where his head would be in the 1.2 seconds it would take my round to find its mark. Most people didn't perceive a second being an exceptionally long time. If a person tripped and fell flat on their face, the amount of time between the stumble and the face-plant was normally less than a second. A lot could happen in one second of time: it was an eternity for a Marine sniper.

"Roger that, Six-Actual," Steve whispered. "Standing down."

Steve set the mic aside and looked over at me. "The old man himself said no, Gunny. Said there's too many noncoms in the area for a shot this long."

By that he meant non-combatants, not NCOs—non-commissioned officers—like me and Steve. Everyone in Somalia was a non-combatant, except the warlords. The status of the peasants didn't dictate how the warlords treated them, though. They rained down misery, starvation, rape, death, and destruction without any regard to the status of the people.

Major Franklin sat in a protected bunker and probably couldn't even see the light of day, much less what was happening over on the next ridge. He was up for promotion to lieutenant colonel and planned to retire in two years when he reached his twenty. He seemed to make every decision based on how it might affect his pension.

In Beirut we'd had rules of engagement, but they'd been tossed out the window when our barracks was bombed. We'd had to fight our way back from an early morning mounted patrol. In Panama, the rules were even more stringent. In the desert heat of the Mog, our rules—mine and Steve's—were like straitjackets.

I continued to track the target. He'd been identified as Musa Ali Hassan, one of the bigger warlords in the area. He had a special fondness for abusing kids—boys or girls, it didn't matter—and the younger they were, the more it fueled his bloodlust. When he was finished with them, he killed them.

My crosshairs moved just in front of his face, keeping pace with his lateral movement across the ground and anticipating his path.

My breathing slowed as I took the slack out of the trigger. I knew what I was about to do, and I knew it was career *suicide. Disobedience of a direct order meant a court-martial.*

To hell with the repercussions.

The boom of the powerful rifle split the air.

Before I could reacquire the target, I was sucked into a whirling blackness, tumbling weightlessly through space. There was nothing for my eyes to focus on that would stimulate my brain, telling it which way was up or down. There was a sense of great speed, though I felt no air moving over me. All around, I could hear terrible moans and hopeless sobbing.

Screaming black apparitions swooped past, grabbing at me. Horribly disfigured specters, garbed in black cloaks, zoomed into focus, only to dissolve instantly in a puff of dust. Each cloud of dust had the face of a person I'd killed.

I steeled myself for the inevitable. My subconscious knew it was a dream and also exactly how many there would be. Eleven confirmed kills while I was in uniform would visit me first—the five attackers I'd shot in Lebanon while fighting our way back to our demolished barracks, a soldier in Panama who hadn't even known that he wasn't alone in the jungle, two Iraqi soldiers, two Somalis just outside Mogadishu on my first deployment, and now the Somali warlord whose head I'd just vaporized from a thousand yards away.

But those phantoms wouldn't be alone. Since leaving the Marine Corps there had been others. All worthy of death on the battlefield, but I'd been a civilian when I'd sent their souls to Hell.

They came at me, one by one, clawing and raking at me, trying desperately to rip me to shreds. Each bore the horrible visage I'd seen at the instant of their deaths.

I woke suddenly, drenched in a cold sweat, my chest heaving to get air. I hadn't had the dream in a couple of years and thought it was behind me.

I knew where I was—aboard my boat *Floridablanca*. And I knew where we were going—to rendezvous with *Star of Galveston* and to get Charity's helo.

I also knew there were sixteen other faces that hadn't visited me in my dream—those of the others I'd put down since I'd taken off the uniform. The next time the dream came, there would be a few Mexican faces disappearing in a puff of dust.

Rising from my bunk, I looked through the open hatch to the forward berth. The bunk was empty. I leaned against the port bulkhead and looked out through the porthole. The sea was angry. Not full-on, gonna-kill-you angry, but the chop was a mess, no regimented lines of wind-driven waves. There'd been a sudden change in the wind.

I crossed the stateroom and stepped into the head. After turning the cold water on in the shower, I stripped down and stepped into it, leaning against the bulkhead and letting the cool water cascade down my neck and across my back as the boat gently rocked in the chop.

Floridablanca didn't mind angry seas. She was all steel and very heavy. She was used to just bulling her way past the anger and finding a tranquil, almost mesmerizing balance.

Feeling a bit more like myself, I stepped out of the head and dressed quickly. The old GMC two-stroke diesel engine was droning at a moderate speed. We were going about six or seven knots. Not fast, but we weren't in a hurry now.

When I joined John on the command bridge, he jerked a thumb over his shoulder. Charity lay curled in the fetal position, facing forward. She looked calm and serene. But knowing the woman as I did, I realized that could be a façade. She could be reliving her own nightmare at that very moment.

I also knew she could awaken in an instant, clear-headed and alert, ready for anything. She'd be flying soon, so I didn't want to disturb her. The few hours rest I'd had, though cut short by the nightmare, had still rejuvenated me a little.

The chart plotter showed we were more than ten miles offshore now. We were following a line to a way-point a few miles ahead. A quick glance at the radar confirmed there was a ship out there.

We chugged on in silence.

As we closed in on the large tug, John turned parallel and slowed slightly to match the other boat's speed.

Charity sat up, then pushed off the small bunk, landing lightly on the balls of her feet. "That our ride?"

"We have about ten minutes, if you wanna shower or get a bite to eat," John said.

She only nodded and disappeared down the ladder to the salon.

"Ten minutes?" I asked.

"About how long it'll take us to shadow *Galveston* out to the limit of Mexico's territorial sea. You did just invade a foreign country."

The *Star of Galveston* continued on its course and never hailed us. Just as we were approaching the twelve-mile limit, Charity came back up the steps. She was dressed in her flight suit and her hair was wet and scrunched up.

"You didn't sleep long," Charity said.

I grinned. "I'm a fast sleeper."

John maneuvered us closer, still matching the larger boat's speed.

"Same as before," I said, shaking John's hand. "Weld us to her side for a couple of seconds."

He reached down and switched the closed-circuit monitor to the camera in the cockpit. "I'll see ya."

"Where are you *borrowing* my boat to next?"

"Same as you," he replied. "Belize City. I just bought a little house in Bella Vista, just across from the beach. Includes a slip or a mooring ball. My neighbor doesn't have a boat, so I got both."

"Be safe," I said, as Charity and I headed down to the salon.

We grabbed our things, including a small cooler, and went out to the cockpit. John once again maneuvered *Floridablanca* alongside the much larger boat and when contact was made, I could hear the rudder hydraulics as he turned slightly into the bigger boat, jamming the two vessels together.

Hayes stood above us and we tossed our gear to him before scrambling up onto the rail and hoisting ourselves up to the tug's work deck.

The go-fast boat they'd used to escape the port was strapped down beside Charity's chopper.

"Spoils of war?" I asked Hayes, nodding toward the Fountain as *Floridablanca* pulled away.

"I don't think those guys are gonna miss it," he replied. "Got time to hang around and wait for Ryan?"

Charity kissed the man on the cheek. "Wouldn't that be great? But I'll have to take a rain check. I'm needed elsewhere."

Hayes's face flushed for a moment before he stammered, "Yeah, well, next time, huh?"

She took her tactical bag from his hand and smiled. "Count on it, Rick. Thanks for the fun. And give Ryan a hug for me."

She headed for her bird, giving orders in Spanish to a group of deckhands.

"Appreciate the hand," Hayes said. "We owe you one."

I slapped him on the shoulder. "Next time you're down in the Keys, look me up. You can buy me a beer."

I trotted across the deck. Charity was already going through her preflight as I climbed in and put my harness and headset on. Finally, she started spooling up the turbine.

"What was that 'needed elsewhere' line?" I asked.

She turned toward me with a devilish grin. "I just figured you'd want to get back to Savannah."

"C'mon," I said, as she hit the ignition switch.

The turbine fired and began to whine louder as the rotor gained speed.

"You thought I was flirting?"

"Weren't you?"

"Yeah," she replied, adding more throttle and watching the turbine temperature. "Maybe a little."

"Why?"

"Why flirt?" she asked, then shrugged as she pulled up on the collective. "It's just amusing. And maybe next time, they won't be quite so shy."

The chopper rose from the deck, and she allowed the tug to slide away beneath us before turning and adding full power as she dipped the nose.

I laughed. I was still wrapping my head around this new Charity.

When we flew past *Floridablanca's* bow, we were already moving at eighty knots. I waved at John, though I couldn't see him for the glare from *Floridablanca's* windshield. Getting my feet in a comfortable position, I relaxed a little and looked toward the sunrise.

As we flew across the water, I dozed and reflected on what I'd done the previous night. Men were dead, but they were bad men. Or at least I staved off my own guilt by assuming they were. Choir boys didn't hire on as gunmen for a drug cartel.

I needed to prepare myself for my reunification with Savannah and Florence. The warrior's mask hid a lot, but it couldn't be worn in polite society. Removing it left scars, though. I thought about Miguel, and how he'd fought so valiantly for his Maria, right to the end.

"How are you two getting on?" Charity's voice rang through my headphones, interrupting my thoughts.

I turned to look toward her and wondered if she felt the same way as I did about last night. She showed no emotion; her eyes were calm and bright. It'd been rumored that Charity could turn her mind off to the horrors she'd faced, then turn those memories back on at will, to visit hell upon whoever stood in her path.

Paul Bender, our team's forensic psychologist, had studied her file and talked with her about the things that had happened to her when she'd been held by terrorists. I didn't know what she'd told him or even what she'd told other doctors—those who'd written the file Paul had read—but if it was half what she'd told me, Bender would have nightmares forever.

"It's complicated," I said to her profile.

She grinned and glanced over at me. "No, it's not. She loves you and you love her."

Love? I wasn't sure anymore what the word or the emotion meant. I'd loved my first wife and she'd left. I thought I'd loved the second one, but that turned out to be more lust than anything else. I lost my third wife on the night we were married, murdered by gun runners. Sara and I had known we weren't in love all along. That worked for us for a long while, since neither of us was willing to commit. But Savannah was different. She wore her heart on her sleeve.

"I don't know if we've reached that level of commitment," I said.

She tucked her chin in and spoke with a mocking, masculine voice, "*I don't know if we've reached that level of commitment.*" She turned and actually glared at me. "That's bull and you know it, Jesse. Your worlds have been revolving around each other for nearly two decades. Neither of you is in a real relationship. Of course, you're in love. Both of you always have been."

I was a bit taken aback by her comment. "I'll allow that you might think you know *me* that well," I said. "But you barely know Savannah."

Charity chuckled. "I met Savannah years ago, remember? She's one of only a handful of friends I have outside our circle." She glanced over and smiled, a glint of familiarity in her eyes. "I probably know her better than I know you."

"She told you this?"

Charity allowed her eyes to trail over the gauges before tracking back to the windshield. "Not in so many words. Call it female intuition."

"Female intuition, huh?"

"Do you *trust your gut?*" she asked, dropping back to her comical masculine imitation.

"Well, yeah, but..."

"Same thing," she said. "We just give it a more civilized name." Looking over again, she fixed me with a stare. "She's a keeper, Jesse. Don't let her get away."

We continued in silence for some time, until the coast of Veracruz came into view. Even with the extra fuel bladders filled from a special tank in the tug's stores, the chopper only had a range of 500 miles.

We started our descent toward the beach, zeroing in on the mouth of the Rio Tonala, the border between the states of Veracruz and Tabasco. Just upriver was the sleepy little farming village of Agua Dulce, which is Spanish for sweet water. Charity had a contact north of town who had a small, private airstrip and a good supply of JP-8 jet fuel.

Thirty seconds after we passed over the beach, Charity turned upwind, flaring to slow the bird, then settled onto a concrete apron next to a small hangar.

Once she shut down the turbine, I opened the door and propped it with my foot, letting the cool, salt air fill the cabin. A small fuel truck approached, and the driver got out. Spanish words and American greenbacks were exchanged, and he began rolling out the hose.

Charity climbed in the back and opened the small cooler. "I put a couple sandwiches in here before we left your boat. You hungry?"

"Always," I replied, accepting the paper-wrapped sandwich and digging in.

We finished eating and chugging water bottles before the guy finished refueling. Charity asked him where the restroom was and he pointed to what was basically a modern-looking, concrete block version of an outhouse. We both used the facility and were back in the air less than twenty minutes after landing.

The leg from *Agua Dulce* to Belize City would be over land, almost due east, cutting across the base of the Yucatan Peninsula. It was mostly rugged and inhospitable terrain. We'd rarely see a road or town, even from our high vantage point. Having a problem out there would mean a hard landing and one helluva hike out.

My mind drifted again, halfway between sleep and consciousness. Charity had gotten more sleep than I had the last two nights, but I could tell it was wearing on her, as well. How old was she? Close to forty?

"When's your birthday?" I asked.

Charity looked at her watch and laughed. "Actually, it's tomorrow. I'll be forty at five minutes after midnight."

"Hah," I chortled. "The big four-oh. You could easily pass for twenty-five."

"Only Miss Clairol and I know for sure."

"You wanna stay a while when we get there?" I asked without thinking. "A person should, you know, be with friends on their birthday."

"I don't think so," she said, glancing over again. "You and Savannah should be alone."

"We haven't been since we sailed," I said with a laugh. "Florence would probably like to see you. She's an amazing swimmer now. You could probably give her some pointers."

Charity had been on the U.S. Olympic swim team and had won a bronze medal in Sydney at the 2000 games.

"I'd like to see Flo," Charity said, grinning at the windshield. "It's been a while. I FaceTime with them sometimes, but it's been over a year, in person."

"At least stay the night," I said. "They're at a house on a canal owned by friends of hers, a couple named Erin and Neal Trotter."

"I don't..."

"They have two guest rooms and invited us to stay in their house," I offered. "Florence accepted, but Savannah and I are going to stay on the boat."

"You should call her," Charity said. "Have you talked to her since we exfilled?"

"You're right," I said, digging my sat phone out and plugging it into the antenna port on the dash. "No, I haven't."

Savannah answered so quickly, I didn't even hear it ring after jamming the phone under my headset. "Jesse, are you okay?"

"A little tired," I said, loud enough to drown out the chopper's noise, while checking our location. "We're on our last leg to Belize City and should arrive by 1600."

"What's that in regular time?"

"Four o'clock," I replied, grinning. "Hey, it's Charity's birthday tomorrow. Think your friends would mind one more?"

"I know it's her birthday," Savannah replied. "Flo got her a cute dolphin pendant made of jade. We assumed she'd be staying. Erin and Neal are expecting her."

I had no idea that Savannah and Charity were that close. Then it suddenly dawned on me that Savannah's friends might see it odd that she and Florence had arrived alone and then I came in later with another woman. "What did you tell them about me not being with you?"

I heard the sound of a door opening and closing before she replied.

"I told them you were called away on business."

"And when they asked what kind of business?"

"I'm not very good at this," she whispered. "Neal asked and I wasn't prepared. Then I remembered Charity posed as a magazine reporter and I said you were her publisher."

Oh, great, I thought. Now I'd have to pretend to be something I knew nothing about.

"Don't worry about it," I said. "If I can't baffle them with brilliance, I'll bewilder them with bullshit."

She laughed. It was good to hear her laugh. "So, we'll pick y'all up at the airport at four. I hope you're hungry, Neal is smoking a brisket."

"I'll let Charity know," I said. "See you in a few hours."

I ended the call and turned to Charity. "You're expected. We're having brisket. And Florence got you something for your birthday."

Charity grinned broadly and nodded, all the while looking straight ahead through the windshield. "Okay. One night."

CHAPTER EIGHT

With the sun about 20° above the horizon, we started our descent to Philip S.W. Goldson International Airport and Charity got in line behind a Cessna Caravan. It was the regular ferry flight from Caye Caulker out on the barrier reef, just twenty-five miles away. She kept her bird a good mile behind and slightly above the single-engine Maya Island Air passenger plane to avoid its wake turbulence. Charity matched the plane's speed of ninety miles per hour as we descended toward the runway.

We taxied at about twenty feet off the ground to the fixed base operator, where a ground crewman guided us to a spot on the apron. Charity set the bird down and went through her shutdown and post-flight before opening the door. The crewman was standing outside.

"Do you want to buy fuel, *señora*?" the man asked.

I winced. Charity was unmarried and looked much younger than her years. But she ignored the unintended slight and spoke in fluent Spanish. "*Sí, cada gota que puedas meter en ella. Voy a volar a Grand Cayman por la mañana.*"

English was the official language of Belize, a throwback to the country's former name, British Honduras, and over 100 years of British rule. But many people also spoke Spanish or Creole, as well as English. A third of the population didn't speak any English at all. My Spanish wasn't very good, but I understood her telling him to fill the tanks completely for her next flight.

"How far is it to the Caymans?" I asked, as we walked toward the FBO empty- handed.

"Four hundred and seventy miles," she replied. "I'll be sucking on fumes when I get there."

We cleared customs and followed the agent outside to inspect Charity's bird.

"Is your visit business or pleasure?" he asked her.

"Both," Charity replied, handing him her card. "Pleasure is my business."

The agent's mouth fell open slightly, until he read the card and saw the Tropical Luxury Magazine logo painted on the side of Charity's Huey.

She'd already opened the floor hatch and seats for the inspection, laying our bags on the deck, opened. The floor hatch revealed her expensive array of photography equipment in the custom-made tray. The agent would never suspect what was hidden beneath it. Nor would he be able to find the well-hidden release catch.

He made a cursory inspection and gave Charity a business card while speaking in rapid-fire Spanish, too fast for me to understand. She laughed and took the card, replying at the same pace. The agent left us as the fuel truck pulled up.

"What was that all about?" I asked, as we zipped our bags and pulled them out.

"His brother-in-law is a tour guide at the *Altun Ha* Mayan ruins north of the city. He suggested it might make a good backdrop for a story."

When we reentered the building, Savannah and Florence were just coming in from the other side. Savannah wore a loose-fitting, white, sleeveless blouse over short cutoff jeans, which accentuated her hips and long legs.

"Charity!" Florence called from across the small room, as she ran toward us.

Apparently, my daughter knew Charity better than I'd realized as well.

The two hugged and Savannah stepped into my embrace. "I'm so glad you're back," she whispered in my ear.

Charity strolled over to the FBO's desk, with Florence chattering away about swimming. She gave the clerk her credit card and signed the necessary paperwork for fuel and one days' tiedown.

Next to the desk was a newspaper stand with the local fish-wrap, *Amandala*, in the display window. The headline caught my eye.

Ghoul Claims 7th Victim
Killer Remains at Large

We left together and walked out to where a man stood beside a Scion xB. Introductions were made, and I shook Neal Trotter's hand. I guessed him to be a few years younger than me, but he'd given up on the battle of the bulge a long time ago. His face was deeply tanned, except the area around his eyes. A man who spent time on the water.

We put all our stuff in the back and to my surprise, Florence got into the driver's seat and Neal took the front passenger seat.

"You sit behind Flo," Savannah directed. "You'll have more leg room."

I allowed her to get in first, and she slid over next to Charity. There was more leg room in the backseat than I thought there'd be, but hip room was a different story. Not that I minded my leg being jammed against Savannah's bare thigh.

With Neal giving directions and instructions to Florence, we started out of the parking lot.

"Neal thought she should know how to drive," Savannah explained. "So, he's going to teach her between dive trips."

"An important skill to have," I said.

Some might think a girl of seventeen would have been driving for some time already, but Savannah didn't even own a car, and hadn't renewed her license in over a decade.

Florence turned a little too fast onto International Airport Road, then over-corrected. "Sorry."

"Shouldn't she have a Belizean permit or something?" I asked.

"Not to worry," Neal said. "I'm a private IDP instructor, licensed here and in the States. International driving permits are recognized in 174 countries and a student needs only a valid ID."

I looked out the window. As Charity and Savannah talked, my mind drifted. I knew I was still feeling jacked up from the shootout. In the Corps, the old-timers—guys who'd fought in Vietnam—called it the *jazz*. The moments didn't happen often, at least not in that kind of controlled chaos. But it was something I seemed to thrive on. Could I walk away from it? Did I even want to?

Watching Savannah and Charity talk, I was again surprised at how intimate they seemed. The drive was short, about ten minutes, as Florence navigated her way through the city streets and into a suburb called Ladyville, north of the city.

We finally turned into a residential neighborhood where the main road crossed a series of small bridges every block. Canals extended out both ways from the road to a wider canal at the ends of each block. The roads consisted of a single U-shaped lane that extended out from the main road on either side, creating little man-made "islands" of about a dozen large lots.

Neal's house was on the third little island, a modest, one-story block home built on the main canal. I could see two boats docked behind *Salty Dog's* familiar masts, a smaller sailboat and a nicely equipped center console fishing boat.

"Do you fish, Jesse?" Neal asked, opening the hatch-back so Charity and I could get our packs.

"I have a charter boat back home," I said too quickly, forgetting I was supposed to be a magazine publisher.

"I thought he was a publisher," he said to Savannah.

"Oh, I *own* Tropical Luxury," I replied quickly. "Publisher in name only. Charity here runs things. It's the bread and butter; I kind of dabble at chartering as a hobby."

"Heck of a way to make a living," he said, closing the hatch. "What kind of boat?"

"Rampage convertible," I replied. "And a Winter center console."

"Whoa!" he said. "That's not hobby fishing. We should rip some lips while you're here. The permit bite is on and only getting better."

"I might just take you up on that," I replied, as we entered the home through the front door.

"Come on, Charity," Florence said. "I'll show you our room."

"Flo," Savannah said. "Maybe Charity wants to have the other guest room."

"No, no," Charity said, smiling. "I think it'll be fun to bunk with Flo."

Florence's smile turned up a notch as she led Charity down a hall off the living room.

A woman came into the living room from the kitchen. She wore simple clothes and had a ready smile. Standing at no more than five feet tall, she had short hair and a robust figure.

"Jesse," Neal said, "this is Erin."

"Nice to meet you," Erin said. "Your boat is a floating piece of art. Savannah gave us the grand tour this morning. Such beautiful woodwork."

"Thanks," I replied, shaking her hand. "They don't build them like that anymore."

"Go ahead on out and drop your stuff," Neal said. "Grab a shower if you want. Savannah said you have a water maker, but I went ahead and connected your shore power and water lines to the dock."

"I appreciate that," I said.

"Dinner won't be ready for another couple of hours, but there's a cooler of beer out by the smoker. That's where I'll be, monitoring the smoke temperature."

"Neal has won a few smoking competitions around here," Erin bragged. "He's famous for his brisket."

Savannah and I went out the back door to where *Salty Dog* was tied up, bow toward the sea. She was on a long, decked seawall that spanned the width of the large backyard.

Woden and Finn were lying on the cabin roof and both lifted their heads at the sound of the door opening. Lunging to their feet in unison, they dismounted the cabin.

Finn was first to reach the dock, but only because he jumped over the rail. Labs were good jumpers. I'd seen Finn run the length of our pier, hit the edge with perfect precision, getting his claws barely over it for added push, and leap twenty-five or thirty feet. Then he'd swim back to the pier and do it again, just for fun. When he was younger, he could easily clear a four-foot fence.

But Woden was not built for anything vertical, nor any great, horizontal leaps. The rottweiler was originally bred to pull heavy butchers' carts loaded with meat. Their powerful bodies were built low to the ground to pull heavy loads, and they were well adapted to the task. Or to knocking down an entire NFL offensive line, if the need arose.

Both dogs charged toward us, each weighing in excess of a hundred pounds. The sight of two large dogs running toward a person at full speed would be enough to cause most people to panic.

But Finn melted in front of me, his big rump lying across my boots and his tail swishing the grass like a scythe as he lifted his big head and offered me his throat for a welcome home scratch.

Woden sat obediently in front of Savannah, his mouth open and lips curled back as if smiling, while his little stub of a tail twitched.

We each greeted our dog in our usual way, then Woden performed the meltdown for me, to get his own neck rub and Finn sat grinning before Savannah, awaiting his ear scratch. We both burst out laughing and gave the dogs what they wanted.

"What a pair of moochers," Savannah said, rising and heading toward the boat.

Following her, I looked down the canal to the turquoise waters beyond. The canal was maybe 150 feet wide and looked very deep.

"Have any trouble getting her turned around in here?"

"She's only a little longer than *Sea Biscuit*," Savannah replied.

"And no trouble on the crossing?"

"The channel through the shallows here isn't well marked, but we managed, and Neal talked us through it over the phone. The canal is ten feet deep from bank to bank. Flo was at the helm to turn her around, while I tossed lines to Neal. And no, we didn't pick up any bottom samples coming out of Chetumal or into here, though both had me worried I'd have to buy your boat."

I chuckled. "I think I paid about a hundred bucks for it."

Savannah stopped at the rail. "Really? What kind of sap would sell a boat like this for that little?"

"Charity," I replied, stepping up to the side deck.

I turned to offer Savannah my hand. There was a time when she would have ignored the gesture, but now accepted my hand as a matter of course. Still, her shoes came off as soon as they hit the deck. I was wearing boots, so that'd have to wait until we got below.

"This used to be her boat?"

"Her boyfriend's," I explained. "He was killed and left it to her." I didn't think it my place to explain, so I eased off the subject a little. "So, how are you and Florence adjusting to sail versus power?" I asked, shoving the companionway hatch open and unlatching the double doors.

"Loving it," she replied. "It's very... liberating, I think. But there is something to be said for just turning the key and going."

"No argument there," I agreed. "But crossing the ocean using only the wind for power? Yeah, liberating is exactly the right word."

The dogs went down first, Woden following Finn, as was always their routine. I wondered if they'd weighed one another's abilities and decided on that tactic themselves. In my mind, it made sense for the more agile warrior to breach first and choose a direction based on what he encountered, moving toward an enemy wherever they were hiding. In a breach stack, I always put my strongest man second and he would automatically go in the opposite direction of the first warrior.

Stop it, McDermitt, I ordered myself.

Savannah stepped down beside me. "What's wrong?" she asked, as if reading my thoughts.

I turned and forced a nervous smile. "Nothing," I lied. "Just glad to be home."

She studied my eyes for a moment. It was almost as if she could see in them the things I'd witnessed the previous night. Her features softened and she smiled.

"Home," she repeated, leaning on the counter by the stove. "Where is a boat bum's home, anyway?"

I grinned at her. "You should know. Wherever the anchor drops."

"Until you're called away to save the world again."

There it was. I hadn't figured on having to go off like I had, but my help was needed.

"I'm sorry," Savannah said. Her sweet smile melted away the time since our first meeting. "I shouldn't have said that. It's actually one of your best qualities: loyalty."

She turned and looked down toward the aft stateroom, then looked back at me with a seductive smile. "A shower sounds nice."

"Yes," I replied, tossing my backpack on a chair and moving toward her. "A shower sounds *real* nice."

She pushed off the counter and into my embrace. Her arms went around my waist, pulling me closer as she laid her head on my shoulder. I stroked her hair gently, feeling the warmth of her body against mine.

"I was worried," she whispered.

"There's no need to—"

She looked up into my eyes. "I tell myself that. But I still worry."

Her blue eyes shined, on the brink of tears.

"I can quit," I said.

Could I?

The more I put on the warrior's mask, the harder it was becoming to go back. Could I leave it behind?

Knowing there were people suffering at the hands of tyrants? Could I just give it all up and sail away?

"No," she whispered, looking into my eyes. "I don't think you ever quit anything in your life. Another good quality."

Her lips met mine and we kissed deeply, the unhurried kiss of intimacy. It was almost like being transported back in time to our first nights together. When I was just a guy who'd recently retired from the Corps and didn't have any responsibilities but my own.

Breaking free, she began unbuttoning my shirt as she pulled me toward the aft stateroom and the large shower.

CHAPTER NINE

Casey Jasso walked into a bar on Northern Highway, on the outskirts of Orange Walk Town. He found it easier to find what he wanted in this area, fifty-five miles north of Belmopan, the capital. The right resources were difficult to find and even harder to get.

Actually, what Casey *sought* wasn't really all that hard to find; it was virtually anywhere there were people. The opportunity to *take* those resources without being seen or caught was the difficult part.

Orange Walk Town was the third largest city in Belize and Casey alternated between it and the two larger ones, Belize City and San Ignacio. He prided himself on being only barely visible and he hadn't even come close to being caught before.

His hair was neither short nor long. It was brown, just like his eyes. His skin was neither dark nor light; he wouldn't look out of place in an American honky-tonk or a Mestizo border bar. In short, Casey was forgettable. And it was that easily forgettable look that made him invisible in certain places. Places that were dull and had a lot of people coming and going. Places like subway stations or grocery stores. Or Orange Walk Town bars.

The bar he'd chosen was like many others he'd visited there and in the other two cities. It was attached to a small hotel, which, if judged by the hotel's separate parking lot, didn't have nearly as many guests as the bar had patrons. Yet, in the small, one-room bar, there were only a handful of people, far fewer than the number of vehicles outside would suggest. Some of the cars were rentals— tourists looking for a good time.

Casey moved through the randomly scattered tables, carrying a small lunch cooler. At some of the tables, men sat alone or together, as if waiting for something. Couples occupied two tables; one was a younger couple and the other might be mistaken for father and daughter, except Casey knew they weren't.

He sat at a table and placed his lunch cooler at his feet. A moment later a bored-looking bartender came over with a glass and pitcher, filled the glass with water, and placed it on the table. Casey nodded at the man, knowing how things worked.

The bartender went back to his place behind the long, wooden counter.

Casey waited.

Within a few minutes the door between the bar and the hotel's corridor opened and a man came in. He walked straight through and out to the parking lot, just as a young woman, no more than a girl really, entered from the same corridor. She went to the bar, where the bartender poured her a glass of water and she paid him for it.

The girl was Hispanic, Casey figured, not Maya or Mestizo. She was very small, barely five feet tall. Her hair was long and black, and she wore makeup to accentuate her lips and eyes. Her tight-fitting red dress looked like it had seen better days. She spoke to the bartender for a moment, then moved toward a table where two men sat together.

Casey watched as she talked to the two men, then accepted money from one of them and went back to the bar. She gave part of the money to the bartender and said something to him. The other bills she tucked into a small purse, along with a key he'd handed her. The bartender made three drinks, but Casey saw that only two contained alcohol, American bourbon.

The Hispanic girl returned to the table and sat down with the two men. They talked and laughed as they drank watered-down drinks, and she a plain Coke.

Soon another woman entered and went through the same routine, serving a guy sitting by himself. She looked and dressed similarly to the first girl. Another man came in from the parking lot and sat at a table in the corner. The bartender barely noticed him.

When another couple came in from the corridor, it was the same pattern; the man left immediately, and the girl went to the bar and bought a glass of water. She was taller than any of the women he'd seen so far.

The girl with the two men rose and pulled on the guys' arms, swaying her hips seductively. The men stumbled to their feet and the trio went through the door into the corridor.

The girl at the bar approached Casey's table and asked in broken English if he'd like company. She was very petite, about five-three, and definitely Mestizo.

"Sure, I'm always lookin' to meet new friends," Casey said, with a faked midwestern accent. "My name's Claude."

"I am Sierra," the girl said, sitting close to him and crossing her legs. Her eyes showed a promise of things to come. "Can I get you something from the bar?"

"Yeah," Casey said, nodding and feigning nervousness. "A bourbon and coke would be great, and whatever you're drinking."

"I will get it for you," Sierra said. "It will be seven American dollars or fourteen Belize dollars."

Casey took his wallet from his pocket and handed the girl an American five and three ones and told her to keep the change.

Orange Walk Town bar servers were paid on commission—he knew that. The only employee of the place was the bartender. She'd give the bartender the five and keep the three. The money the girls paid him for the water was their "rent" for an hour in one of the rooms and they alternated, drinking with the men until a room became available.

Prostitution was legal in Belize, but there was a weird bunch of hoops to go through. It was still illegal to offer money for sex, run a brothel, or loiter for the purpose of prostitution, but that's not how things worked.

In places like this, money changed hands through an indifferent third party—the bartender—under the guise of buying a drink or a glass of water. Men could wait for the next girl to become available because loitering in a bar was what bars were for. And the girl would drink with them until a room was available for a quick hook-up. Again, what bars were for.

Sierra returned and sat down. She made small talk as Casey gently prodded her with questions about Belize and Orange Walk Town. She knew quite a bit about both, since she lived just outside of town with her mother and two brothers. When the subject of the hotel room came up, as he knew it quickly would, he thanked Sierra, but said he preferred a woman a bit smaller.

The girl took it in stride and rose from her seat, putting more hip movement into her walk to the bar than necessary, just so he'd know what a treat he was missing out on. She spoke to the bartender, then crossed the room to where the man sat alone in the corner.

The bartender might have been bored, but he at least kept track of who the next customer was. Probably more by where they sat than anything.

A few minutes passed before another couple came out. As with the others, the man went straight for the door, while the girl, obviously Hispanic, spoke to the bartender. She looked over at Casey and smiled, then started toward him. She was slender and pretty, with fingernails and toenails painted to match her purple dress

Casey ordered another drink for himself and one for her, and then the girl—who said her name was Carmen—brought the drinks to his table.

She was barely taller than he was, sitting down. They talked and he again asked about the town. She explained in very halting English that she didn't know it well, she'd only come from Guatemala the week before and was staying in a hostel a few blocks down.

That told Casey a lot. She was alone in a strange country, probably there illegally, and didn't have any family and probably no friends in the area. Nobody who might miss her.

This time, when the subject of the room came up, Casey nodded eagerly. "How much is the room?"

"Twenty-five American," came the reply.

It was easy to do the math. Seven for the drinks meant the girl got two and twenty-five for an hour in a room meant the girl got twenty. The law of averages meant that making change was seldom necessary.

He produced the bills and handed them to her. Then after she stood, he reached into his pocket and palmed something small into his hand.

"Don't forget your drink, *señorita*," he said.

As he picked it up, he dropped what was in his palm into it, then handed it to her. He picked up his own drink and lunch cooler, then followed the girl through the bar and into the corridor.

When they got to the room, there was nothing in it but a single, straight-backed wooden chair, a small bed with an equally small table beside it, and a lamp on the table with a red and gold shade that cast a pseudo-romantic glow about the room. Soft music came from a radio on the table.

"Ooh, I like that music," Casey said, putting his cooler beside the chair.

He turned to the girl and opened his arms. Carmen moved enticingly into his embrace, her body shifting and swaying to the music's tempo as he pulled her close.

Casey wasn't a big man. He was five-nine and a fit 170 pounds, but he dwarfed the diminutive woman. The crown of her head barely reached his shoulders.

Stepping back, Casey sat on the chair. "Dance for me," he ordered, as he took a long pull from his drink and eyed her hungrily.

Carmen moved her body to the music, her dark brown eyes smoldering with notions of what was to come. She took a sip from the glass as her other hand snaked up behind her back and unzipped the slinky purple dress.

Casey lifted his drink to his lips, watching her movements with a look of animalistic lust. He tilted his glass and drained it.

Slowly, Carmen let the dress fall off her shoulders, showing him the tops of her small breasts. As her body softly swayed, she tipped the glass to her lips and drank it down, exposing her delicate throat as the dress slid off her hips to the floor.

Casey smiled. The drug he'd slipped into her drink would knock her out in about fifteen minutes. Though the room was rented for an hour, that's all the time he'd have with her. He had other plans for the last forty-five minutes.

Carmen stepped out of the dress, now a pool of satiny purple around her ankles. She was completely naked. She placed her empty glass on the table, then knelt in front of him and pulled his shoes off. Tossing them aside one by one, she eagerly went for his belt. In seconds, she'd tugged his pants and shorts off as he unbuttoned his shirt and tossed it aside.

Carmen stood, and as Casey started to rise, she put a hand to his chest, holding him in place on the chair. She straddled his thighs and reached over to pull open a small drawer on the table. Then she continued moving to the beat of the music, provocatively bringing their bodies closer and closer as she skillfully opened a condom and rolled it down over his manhood. With a deft movement of her hips, he was inside her. She rocked her body slowly at first, making purring sounds as she wrapped her arms around his neck.

To Casey, the condom was the holy grail. Not because he worried about getting a disease. He was in bed with a Russian mobster. It was more likely he'd die a quick but violent death than waste away with HIV. To him, her using a condom meant she was clean.

She began to move faster, leaning back and holding onto the back of the chair. Casey brought his hands under her thighs, grabbed her ass firmly, then stood, holding her close to him as she wrapped her arms around his neck and squirmed against his groin.

He moved faster, slamming her body against his as he held her in the air. Carmen's breathing began to come faster, her exhalations turning to grunts of pleasure.

Casey arched his back, slamming into her as her body began to fall limp in his arms. He shuddered and thrust once more as Carmen's arms dropped to the sides.

Finally spent, Casey turned and dumped the girl unceremoniously onto the bed. He dressed quickly, then began to carefully examine her body, starting with her arms and finishing between her toes.

No needle tracks. That was good.

She was healthy, though a little underweight maybe. He doubted she weighed more than ninety pounds, but he found nothing else deficient.

She would do.

Rolling the prostitute onto her belly, he admired her body a moment longer. Her dark skin was smooth and unblemished. A faint tan line covered her butt, but nowhere else.

He retrieved his cooler and opened it, producing two syringes. The first was a tranquilizer, which he drove into the meaty part of her butt, depressing the plunger fully. Between it and the fast-dissolving pill he'd put in her drink, she'd remain comatose for at least two hours, even if a tornado tossed the hotel, with her in it, into the jungle.

The other syringe contained a local anesthetic, just in case the tranquilizer wasn't enough. He felt for the woman's ribs, then inserted the needle just below the twelfth one. He did this again at another point a few inches higher, and again a few inches lower.

Casey checked his watch—he still had plenty of time. He removed a small metal box from the cooler and opened it, placing the box between the woman's shoulder blades. A vapor rolled out of the insulated box lined with liquid nitrogen cold packs.

Reaching into the cooler again, he removed a cheap pair of plastic, single-use hemostats, so things wouldn't get too messy. Then he reached in and removed a scalpel, the edge glinting in the light of the lamp.

Slowly, Casey bent over his victim, wielding the scalpel with practiced ease.

CHAPTER TEN

The sun was shining through the trees on the front corner of the property when Savannah and I emerged from the boat. I wore cargo shorts and a T-shirt, feeling almost human again. A tired and worn-out human, but human, nonetheless.

The dogs trotted ahead of us as we walked to the patio where the others had gathered. At the edge of the rectangular concrete slab, a big black grill with a firebox mounted to the side shot a steady stream of gray smoke curling from its chimney.

"What kind of wood are you using?" I asked Neal.

"Three different kinds," he replied. "One for each hour of smoke."

"Is one of them mahogany?" I asked.

"Good guess," he replied, opening a cooler.

"Seems like it'd be a good slow-burning wood and plentiful around here."

I helped myself to a beer as Savannah poured a glass of wine from a bottle in the cooler.

"Smallish chunks of mahogany for the first hour," he continued. "You're right; it burns really slow and maintains a nice, steady pit temperature. After the first hour, I add a good-sized hunk from an allspice tree."

"Allspice?" Savannah asked.

"It lends some sweetness to the meat, along with a peppery first taste," Neal said. "The third hour, I'll toss in a fair-sized hunk from a guaya tree. It's a miniature citrus that grows wild here."

"Guaya?" I asked. "Is that the same as a genip?"

"Yeah," he replied. "I've heard it called that, too. Gives the meat a great finishing flavor."

I noticed a small necklace dangling at Charity's throat with a tiny green dolphin. Florence must have been anxious to give her the birthday gift. I felt bad that I hadn't known it was her birthday.

Charity nudged Florence, who shook her head. Charity nudged her again then smiled at me. "Flo has something to tell you."

"Oh?"

Florence stood. She was wearing a one-piece bathing suit with a pair of khaki shorts. "I wanna challenge you to a race, Dad."

"A race?" I asked, a bit taken aback.

"Swimming," Charity added, trying to hide a grin.

"A swimming race," I repeated, still bewildered.

"Yeah." Florence pointed toward the far side of the canal. "To that boat over there and back."

"Are we missing something?" Erin asked.

Savannah sat down next to her. "Jesse's a great swimmer. He can almost beat Charity."

"Almost?" Neal asked, looking from Charity to me.

"Well," I replied, "she did win a medal in the Sydney Olympics."

"Really?" Erin asked, sitting forward.

I was watching Charity. She looked like the proverbial cat who'd eaten the canary. "You want me to race a seventeen-year-old girl?

"C'mon, Dad," Florence said. "It'll be fun."

"Now, Flo," Savannah warned, "you *know* he's uber-competitive. Remember how he plays Scrabble? He won't *let* anyone win."

"I'm not competitive," I argued, knowing that was a lie. I looked up at my daughter. "You're tall and slim, just like Charity. You know there's a lot more to it than that, right? She had years of training and was coached by the best in the business."

Florence just stood grinning at me. The gauntlet was presented, the challenge made. So, she was a girl. I never cut Charity any slack. I stood and pulled my shirt off as Florence took off her shorts.

With the sun behind the trees and a soft orange light on the water, we walked to the dock.

"You have to touch the boat on the other side," Florence said, laying out the rules. "Then whoever reaches *Salty Dog* first is the winner."

Charity stood beside me. "Remember the second rule of Fight Club?"

I'd seen the movie.

"There was only one rule," I said. "Don't talk about Fight Club—and you just broke it."

"It was an unwritten rule," Charity said, then laughed. "Never underestimate your opponent."

I got the feeling that I was somehow being set up. Florence was a good swimmer—of that I had no doubt; we'd swum together quite a few times. But we'd never raced.

"It's plenty deep all the way across," Neal offered. "Nothing in the water the length of the canal." Then he grinned and added, "I haven't seen a croc up in here in days."

The water was just a couple of feet below the edge of the dock. Tides here rarely exceeded a foot between high and low.

"A diving start?" I asked.

Florence nodded her head, while taking deep breaths and swinging her arms around. At seventeen, she had lost the gawkiness I'd noted when I'd first come to know her, and now strode with lithe confidence to the starting point.

We stood next to each other, Florence on my left and Savannah on my right. Savannah gave a three count and shouted, "Go!"

The water temperature was probably a bit warmer than the air when I knifed into it. When I surfaced and began to swim, I was going full bore. It was only fifty yards to the boat on the other bank.

I breathed every other left stroke to watch out for Florence. She wasn't beside me, so on the next breath I looked back. Nothing.

I heard a cheer from those on the dock, just as I took my next breath. I scanned ahead to see how far it was to the boat. That's when I found my daughter. She'd just surfaced ahead of me and we were nearly halfway across the canal.

Pouring on the coal, I slowly began to reel her in, gaining a few inches with every stroke.

How had she gotten ahead of me?

I'd almost caught her when we reached the boat on the far bank. Florence did a perfect flip turn. Mine wasn't so perfect, but I'd gained back more than half of what I'd lost at the start. I pushed off the boat with all I had in me, hoping I didn't crack the guy's gelcoat.

Opening my eyes as I surfaced, I thought I saw a dolphin before realizing it was Florence rocketing away, using her entire body to kick like she really *was* a dolphin.

I had to resort to taking a breath with *every* left stroke, swimming as hard as I could. Florence again surfaced well ahead of me. This time, I wasn't able to close the distance as fast and she reached *Salty Dog* as I reached her feet.

"What the...?" I couldn't finish the sentence without taking another breath.

"Sorry, Dad," Florence said, smiling, and treading water effortlessly beside the boat. "Are you okay?"

We swam slowly toward the stern and saw the others standing on the dock.

"Who won?" Erin shouted. "We couldn't see the finish."

I took my licking in stride, and lifted Florence's hand in triumph.

"She might be faster than you," I told Charity as I climbed the ladder.

Savannah handed me a towel from the aft locker. "She already is."

"Huh?"

"Great race, Dad!" Florence said. "I'm cold. I'm going inside for a hot shower."

"She beat me for the first time a year ago," Charity explained, as we walked back to the patio. "I've been working with her for quite a while. She's a natural. Flo can be a walk-on at any college in the world that has a swim team, *and* she'll be offered a full ride scholarship. She's ready for the Tokyo games this summer, if she wants."

I collapsed into a chair. I'd been running on adrenaline for a while. The strenuous activities in the shower and exhaustive swim had depleted what little reserve energy I had left.

Who was I kidding? I was just making excuses to myself and I knew it. For a moment there in the water, I really had thought I was watching a dolphin hurtling away beneath me.

The Olympics? College?

I hadn't had much time with any of my kids, something I'd always regret. Eve and Kim had been estranged from me by their mother and were grown before we'd reunited. I'd suspected Florence was my own flesh and blood when she was eight and we'd first met. I'd known it for a fact since she was ten but had waited for Savannah to reveal it to us both. Now *that* time was slipping away.

I looked up at Charity. "She's that good?"

Charity and Savannah both nodded. "Yes," Charity said. "She's that good. I'd like to introduce her to a friend. He's a trainer and NCAA advisor."

"That's a decision for the three of us to make together," Savannah said. "But not right now."

The three of us?

My face must have given away my thoughts because Savannah nodded at me slowly. "Yes, the *three* of us. You have a stake here. You've already set aside college funds; that money can't be used for anything else. Unless you're planning to have another child, her scholarship means you lose that money."

Another kid was out of the question; I knew it and she knew it. So, I was certain she wasn't hinting about that. But she was right about the college fund and the solution was simple.

I grinned at Savannah. "She doesn't *have* to accept a scholarship if one is offered."

Neal's temperature probe beeped. "Brisket's done," he announced.

Erin and Savannah went inside and started bringing the rest of the food out, while I did what I could to assist Neal. I felt like I needed another shower, but at the moment, I just didn't have the energy.

The meal was incredible. The brisket was very tender and had a sweet yet peppery flavor, no doubt from the allspice and genip wood. After the meal, we sat around talking and drinking for an hour.

When it was good and dark, Neil doused the patio lights and we all went out to the *Dog's* big foredeck to watch the sky. It didn't disappoint.

For some, watching TV was the night's entertainment. But for those of us who had experienced it at sea, the night sky was far from dark and endlessly fascinating.

The moon hadn't risen yet and to the south, Crux—the Southern Cross—was visible just above the end of the canal. In the southern hemisphere, Crux had been used to guide early mariners in the southern oceans the same way Polaris—the North Star—had been used in the north.

"How would we go about looking at schools?" I asked Charity, during a lull in the conversation. "You know, schools with a swim team."

"Recruiting starts in July," she replied. "I guarantee she can get into any college she—"

"I wanna be a Gator," Florence interrupted.

Charity smiled. "Great school. And coach."

We watched the stars for a while. I thought about things I'd not thought of in many years. Things like settling down, going to swim meets, and just being a regular guy. I was tired and kept nodding off.

"I heard on the radio this morning that the ghoul got another poor young girl," Erin said, getting my attention. I remembered seeing the headline on the newsstand; the seventh victim.

"Why do they call him the ghoul killer?" I asked.

"Why do you assume it's a man, Dad?" Florence asked.

"Female serial killers are very rare."

"Tell that to Aileen Wuornos or cute little Rosemary West," she fired back. "Ooh, there's one!"

Florence needn't have pointed. The sudden flash of the meteor was impossible to miss.

The tropical night sky was wonderful to watch. It was no wonder early man made up stories to go with the different patterns they saw in the stars.

Once you got away from the city, either on the ocean, in a meadow, or far up in the mountains—anywhere away from all sources of man-made light—preferably dozens of miles from it, you could look up and see what our ancestors saw tens of thousands of years ago. "Timeless and predictable," Rusty often said.

Rusty Thurman owned the Rusty Anchor Bar and Grill in Marathon. We'd served together a few times after meeting on the bus headed to Parris Island. He was my best friend.

"The first victim was found a little over four months ago," Neal said, leaning in conspiratorially. "A young prostitute. Her liver had been surgically removed. Police said she was drugged and just bled out."

I shuddered.

"Since then there have been six more," Erin added, glancing over at Florence. "Same… uh… occupation, except one. All of them had organs removed. They say he's a surgeon."

Seven victims? Six of them prostitutes? Savannah beat me to the obvious question.

"What was the one?" she asked.

"One what?"

"You said all but one were prostitutes," Savannah said.

"The third victim was a college kid on spring break last year," Neal said.

"She died the same way?" I asked.

"That one was a young man," Erin said. "But yes, he had one of his kidneys removed. His friends found him and got him to the hospital, but he'd already lost too much blood."

Why? I wondered. What possible reason was there for a murderer to go to all the trouble to remove one of their victims' organs?

A morbid trophy in a glass jar? Probably not.

Paul Bender made it sound pretty simple; homicidal motivation could usually be attributed to emotion or greed. Emotion could run the gamut from love to lust to rage to hate, sometimes in a matter of seconds. Many other emotions could be added to the list, like shock, surprise, or even curious fascination.

But at the top of the list was greed.

In many parts of the world, money could buy anything. In the sex trade, women and children were bought and sold as slaves. The drug business probably netted in the trillions of dollars world-wide. Having seen how money could corrupt, I had no doubt there was a market for human organs, ready for transplant.

"It's midnight," Florence said. "Happy birthday, Charity."

Everyone chimed in with good wishes. Charity smiled, thanked us, and gave Florence a hug. "I love this dolphin," she said, putting her fingers to the little jade figure. "I'll never take it off."

I tried unsuccessfully to stifle a yawn.

"Y'all can hang out if you want," Savannah said. "But I think Jesse needs to get some sleep."

"I'm fine," I argued.

"Don't listen to him, Savannah," Charity said. "He had a two-hour nap on the boat earlier this morning and dozed off a little on the flight down here. Other than that, he's been going and going."

"The Energizer Bunny only had four hours of sleep the night before," Florence chimed in, her mouth opening wide with a yawn as she said the last word.

Knowing I was fighting a losing battle, I capitulated and rose from my folding chair. I quickly collapsed it, as Savannah did the same with hers and we stowed them in the deck box.

"Get some rest, Florence," I said. "We're sailing out to Ambergris Caye in the morning."

"Be more than happy to take you in the Proline," Neal offered. "Just a little over an hour each way."

"Thanks," I said. "But we'll be doing rebreather dives and *Salty Dog* has an onboard compressor for tank dives. We're doing a night dive on The Wall first. Then we'll be able to dive all day the next day. Y'all are welcome to join us."

"Thanks," he said. "But I gotta work; three students. But we can motor out that evening. This boat's gotta carry a lot of draft."

"Six feet," I replied. "But she's equipped with forward and side-scanning sonar."

"You mean like a depth finder mounted on the side of the keel?" Neal asked.

I shook my head. "Mounted to the keel, yeah. But it's true sonar, able to scan a 270° sweep ahead and to the sides of the keel and slightly abaft."

"That musta set you back a few coins."

"Are you coming diving with us?" Florence asked Charity, as she and the Trotters also folded and stowed their chairs.

"I can't," she replied. "I really do have to leave tomorrow. I'm meeting a friend on Grand Cayman and already postponed it to the afternoon."

With that, we all decided to call it a night. As I went down the companionway steps after Savannah, I paused to look around. It was a habit I'd acquired a long time ago and it had saved my butt more than once.

None of the houses fronting the canal had lights on, and the only man-made lights I could see were the channel markers winking on and off way in the distance.

With my eyes adjusted to the darkness after hours on the foredeck, the stars provided enough light to see peripherally into some of the shadows. I looked up once more.

The Milky Way dominated the sky. Our sun was a small star—a yellow dwarf—one of billions in this vast galaxy, some smaller, many much larger. Sol and our solar system were located way out on one of the spiral bands of the Milky Way. From Earth, it looked like a veil of light across the sky, but in reality, it was more like gazing through a giant pinwheel from the edge. And the Milky Way in turn was but one of perhaps millions of other galaxies, all spinning as they hurtled through the vast nothingness of space. I believed everyone should look up from a dark place now and then. It was always pretty humbling.

Being so immersed in our day-to-day lives—the house, the office, family, and friends—we often forgot that we were far less than a speck of dust in the grander scheme.

But the night sky, when you understood what you were seeing, was a reminder that each of us was small enough to be almost non-existent.

I continued my threat assessment, my eyes finally reaching Neal and Erin's home. Charity had paused at the door after the others went inside. She looked around, also searching for possible threats, before turning in. She saw me and nodded. I nodded back, and not seeing any bad guys hiding in the bushes, I retreated to the cabin.

Savannah seemed nervous.

"What's wrong?" I asked.

"Nothing," she replied, looking out the portholes at the house.

I could tell from her tone that something was amiss. My senses tingled as I surveyed the upper salon. Both dogs were curled up on small rugs on opposite sides of the boat. They were awake, but their heads were down. Neither saw, heard, or smelled anything out of place. If they had, they'd both be on alert.

"Something's bothering you," I said, putting my arms around her from behind.

"It's silly."

"What's silly?"

Savannah turned in my embrace, smiling. "This is only the third night Florence and I will have been apart."

"She returned safely the other two times, didn't she?"

What I could only describe as a look of terror filled Savannah's eyes for a just a moment. Then it disappeared as she again looked toward the house.

"Yes," she replied, staring at the door Charity had just entered. "Yes, she did."

I followed her gaze through the porthole. I sensed a bond between Charity and Savannah, but *anyone* could see the strong bond between Charity and Florence.

"Only the third night? No sleepovers with friends?"

"Once," Savannah sighed. "Several years ago, she spent the night with Charity aboard her boat."

"I never realized how close you were."

She turned and faced me again. "Charity is one of my closest friends. I thought you were tired."

"I was," I said, pulling her close. "Then I realized we had the whole boat all to ourselves."

CHAPTER ELEVEN

O ur first dive was to be our deepest. It was known as The Wall and was located farther north in Belize than any other dive site; right where the Mexican border snaked through the mangrove swamps that made up most of Ambergris Caye. It was rarely visited because of the distance. The only dive operators that dove it regularly were based on Ambergris Caye or Caye Caulker just to the south.

A dive boat from Caye Caulker had been leaving the area as we sailed in. I figured it was hardly ever dived at night. But it would be our best chance of seeing a whale shark.

A full moon in April or May almost guaranteed a time to see them, but farther to the south, off the coast of Placencia. Still, they were known to cruise the edge of the drop-off year-round.

We put the hook down in twenty feet of water an hour after low tide. I'd chosen the time and spot carefully. It was just east of a creek mouth, which served to funnel a current through the mangroves as the trees' roots slowed the tidal flow to either side. I paid out the anchor rode, while reversing the engine toward the creek mouth. Once all fifty feet of chain rode and eighty feet of braided nylon anchor line were out, I backed down hard, setting the anchor deep in the sandy bottom.

Salty Dog was in ten feet of water. For the next five hours, the current would keep her stern toward the mangrove creek and her bow facing the small waves.

A faraway buzzing sound reached my ears. I was hoping the mosquitos wouldn't find us; we were only forty or fifty yards from the mangroves, but the wind felt strong enough to keep them at bay. But the buzzing wasn't coming from the trees behind us; it sounded more like it was from offshore. The sound was mechanical and far off. I looked east and saw nothing, no lights, no boats, nothing but big empty ocean.

The sound went away, so I turned on the bright masthead anchor light, as well as the spreader lights, which flooded the deck, as well as the water around us. It wasn't brilliant, but it was more than enough light to see by and *Salty Dog* was all alone on the sea.

"Do you really think we'll see whale sharks?" Florence asked.

I nodded. "The reef here is known more for pelagic fish sightings than tropical reef fish, and whale sharks are night feeders, like most other sharks."

"How deep will we go?" Savannah asked, stepping up from the companionway in a one-piece lime green and orange Lycra skin.

"No more than eighty feet," I said, admiring her curves in the tight-fitting dive suit. "But the wall drops off here from fifty to over three hundred feet in less than a tenth of a surface mile."

"I wish Charity could have stayed longer," Florence said.

Charity had left early, right after breakfast, to fly back to her boat in the Caymans. We'd left shortly after that on our short, seven-hour cruise.

"We could head that way next," I said. "There are some great dive sites in the Caymans. Besides, she said she wanted to hook you up with a coach she knows, so we'll see her again very soon."

"For real?" Florence asked. "I can go to the Olympics?"

I grinned at her. "Well, that's putting the cart before the horse. Maybe you oughta meet with the coach first."

"If you go to Gainesville," Savannah said, "where would we dock *Sea Biscuit*?"

I'd gone through this with Kim, but my two older daughters had only been in my life for a few years when Kim went off to college. Savannah and Florence had only been apart for three nights.

"Travis McGee's still in Cedar Key," I offered. "It's only an hour away."

"Who's he?" Florence asked.

"Who is Travis McGee?" I scoffed. "How can you grow up on a boat and not know who T. McGee is?"

She smiled at me. "Kidding, Dad—I've read all of Mac-Donald's works."

As she started to suit up, I gazed at her, amazed. Savannah had done a great job raising her. She was bright, funny, warm, and she had her mother's good looks.

I'd pulled out my rebreathers and given both of them a thorough review on how they worked. When we were suited up and ready, Savannah and I ordered the dogs to stay on deck and keep watch. Both knew what the word watch meant. They considered watching to be their job, and it was.

With both dogs alert, we each did a giant stride off the port side, dropping four feet to a loud splash. It was Savannah and Florence's first time using rebreathers and full-face masks. We submerged slightly and swam toward the bow.

"Stay close," I said, switching on the GPS app built into my mask and releasing the tiny float that carried the antenna.

"Wow!" Florence exclaimed. "I can hear you like you were sitting beside me on the boat."

"Is this the kind of stuff you use for your work?" Savannah asked.

"Sometimes," I replied. "But it's not really my *work*. And this is all just personal gear."

With the antenna floating on the surface, the GPS showed the terrain of the sea floor in real time, pulling information from NOAA nautical charts as well as the civilian Navionics app.

I scanned the artificial sea floor displayed in front of my left eye. The farther we got from the boat, the less the lights from the mast illuminated the water.

We swam slowly toward a fissure the mask showed cutting toward shore from the wall's edge.

"Remember, Florence," I said, taking a position on her left, "we'll keep our lights down and outboard, you keep yours ahead."

When we switched on our small dive lights, we could see the edge of the canyon ahead. I left the GPS on anyway. At least until we found a suitable place to watch.

A tarpon the size of a torpedo came up out of the crack in the bottom. The beam from Florence's light flashed off the giant fish's scales as it turned and disappeared along the reef line.

"That was huge!" Florence exclaimed over the comm link.

I thought back to when I was a kid, and the joy I used to find in experiencing the simplest of things for the first time. Like wading along the creek banks catching crawdads, sitting way up in an Australian pine and feeling the wind move the tree back and forth as I looked out over the Gulf of Mexico, pretending I was a pirate in a crow's nest, or snorkeling the grassy flats of San Carlos Bay. Days seemed to go on forever then.

Florence and Savannah were both excellent divers, but they'd mostly dived reefs and wrecks with thousands of little multi-colored fish. The opportunity to see pelagic species, like manta rays, whale sharks, or even whales, was the reason Florence said she'd always wanted to visit Belize.

I'd just blurted it out on Christmas morning, after having spent the night aboard their boat, *Sea Biscuit*. I'd slept alone on the converted dinette that night. But Savannah and I hadn't been apart for more than a few minutes since then.

To my surprise, Savannah had quickly agreed to sailing off with me and we'd spent the rest of that day and the next making plans as we moved her boat to Fort Myers for haul out.

Savannah had called her college friend, Erin, to tell her we were going to come down for a visit. Then she'd arranged to have her boat hauled out for bottom work while Florence and I plotted a sailing course on her laptop with requisite stops for provisions.

I'd spent that night in Savannah's bed and we'd made love like the intervening eighteen years were but a long weekend apart. There was a part of me that missed Sara, but the space in my heart she could never fill was quickly occupied.

I'd borrowed a truck from my friend, Billy Rainwater, promising to return it on some uncertain day when we came back to recommission *Sea Biscuit*. He had several and wouldn't miss the old Bronco, but he'd offered to drive us down because that's just the way Billy was.

Fewer than three weeks after saying she wanted to see a whale shark, I was taking Florence on a dive to hopefully fulfill her wish.

As we started into the fissure, I reeled in my antenna float. The illumination from our dive lights was magnified, bouncing off the different colored corals, rocks, and sea fans, and reflecting back up from the sandy bottom.

The current in the fissure was a little stronger, but nothing a slight kick with one fin wouldn't overcome.

Florence's light fixed on a blacktip shark moving up the crevice toward us. It quickly turned and swam off.

"That was a blacktip," Florence's voice chimed in my right ear. "Do you think there are more?"

"Probably," I said. "Requiem sharks are schooling fish."

I wasn't concerned about blacktips. A big one would be five feet and as sharks go, I always found them to be timid and shy, quickly disappearing like this one had.

We saw a few parrotfish tucked into crevices, wrapped in mucus cocoons for protection. A juvenile goliath grouper, already bigger than Florence, slowly cruised through the coral heads in search of food. What few reef fish there were in this part of the reef line were all hiding out in the coral and rocks, seeking total darkness and confined space to be safe from predators like the shark and grouper. Those who didn't inherit the hiding instinct were quickly removed from the gene pool.

At fifty feet, we suddenly swam straight out into deep water, seeing the bottom fall away almost vertically. The crevice had ended at The Wall, which we then turned to follow.

We moved silently through the water toward our destination. Rebreathers were a closed-circuit breathing device, so there were no noisy bubbles.

Knowing what I was looking for, had made it easy to find the creek and fissure on Navionics Sonar charts, but we were heading to a spot that couldn't be mapped by sonar, unless it was a side-scanning towed array. I'd only been told about the spot once, a long time ago.

"There," I said, lifting my light over Florence's back and illuminating an overhang.

Beneath the outcrop was a wide cavern, just big enough for three or four divers. A friend had told me about this spot and to be frank, I was surprised we'd actually found it. I knew we'd find someplace, but this was perfect.

"Make yourselves comfortable," I said. "I'll go up to the overhang and rig some lights."

Once they were inside, I rose ten feet to the jagged limestone ledge and found a suitable place. Leaving my light on, I positioned it so that the beam pointed out towards the deep, then turned the bezel to change it from a narrow to a wide beam, pointing out and to the left of our position. I did the same thing with my backup light but pointed it a little to the right. Then I swam back down to where the girls waited.

Checking my dive computer, I said, "We have about two hours of oxygen in the cartridges. But we'll never reach that. Let's call it forty minutes."

I worked my way into the small cavern, got comfortable next to Savannah, and switched off the mask GPS. We watched from total darkness, looking out into an illuminated but empty sea.

Inside the cavern it was total blackness, but out toward the deep, it looked like a dark, milky, blank screen. I knew we would see something, but none of us knew what it might be. After just a few minutes, things began to appear, as the creatures of the deep forgot about the strange intruders who'd left the lights and disappeared. Small night foragers came out first; shrimp and tiny crabs could be seen at the cavern entrance. An occasional fish would swim past—a snapper, jack, or small grouper in search of a meal.

The ocean was anything but silent or desolate. Living things were all around, and the sounds they made seemed to come from all directions at once. Since sound travels nearly four-and-a-half times faster in water than in air, and because the human brain is accustomed to determining direction by the time difference it takes sound to reach each ear, it is impossible for humans to determine sound direction underwater. There were clicks and hums and whistles from different animals near and far. I heard a low moan that rose sharply toward the end.

"Was that a whale?" Savannah whispered.

"I think it was," Florence replied softly, her voice full of awe.

Two blacktip reef sharks came into view from our left, gliding into the wide beam of the floodlights. They barely had to make any effort to propel themselves, other than a slight twitch of their muscular flanks. Their bodies were long and slender, with pointed snouts.

They were nearly five feet in length and drifted slowly past our hiding spot before disappearing into the inky blackness to our right.

"Pretty cool, huh, Dad?"

"Yeah," I replied. "Pretty cool."

I've often said that if you were in the ocean, there was a shark nearby. In fact, there was a simple test to see if there were sharks in the water. You took a small amount of the water in question and put it in your mouth. If it tasted salty, there were sharks nearby. Usually, they remained unseen by humans, as most sharks were timid creatures.

I'd read not long ago that a new shark species was discovered in several of the sounds and inland waters of the South Carolina coast. It was a species of hammerhead that had never been seen before and grew to ten feet. If a large species like that, living near shore or inshore, could remain a secret all this time, imagine what else might be down there.

Florence and Savannah were no strangers to shark diving. Over the last several weeks, I'd learned that when Florence was little, they'd spent a year in the Bahamas, where Savannah had done volunteer work for UNEXSO. The Underwater Explorers Society did regular dolphin and shark encounter dives for tourists. Savannah had made hundreds of shark dives, with little Florence helping out on the dive boat.

Savannah hadn't needed a job. Her father had sold off his business and the family's fleet of fishing boats before he died. Savannah and her late sister, Charlotte, had received trust funds after his death and with her mother and sister now also dead, Savannah would never have to work for the rest of her life. Nor Florence, for that matter. There was so much about their lives I didn't know and was learning about more every day.

A dolphin flashed past. It moved so fast, had any of us blinked, we'd have missed it, as it disappeared as quickly as it came. But from the sounds, I could tell there were others.

"We're being watched," I whispered.

The dolphin clicks stopped for a moment, then started again.

"Not watched," Savannah said. "Listened to."

Two dolphins approached, appearing like ghosts at the edge of the light. They moved cautiously straight toward our position. The clicks and whistles were their echo-location sounds and we were the target of their sonar. They were curious about the human sounds they'd heard coming from the rock.

Eighty percent of a dolphin's brain is devoted to interpreting sound. Dolphins can project ultra-sonic waves in a focused beam; then their brains interpret the echo, giving them a three-dimensional *view* that to them is far better than eyesight. They can *see* in total darkness or murky water. They could hear our sounds; not just our voices, but our heartbeats and breathing, as well. Dolphins in captivity seem to be able to hear the rapid fetal heartbeat from a pregnant woman's womb and will treat her differently than others in the water. In fact, a similar echo-location device is used to see what the baby in the womb looks like—ultrasound.

I wondered if a dolphin's sonar could penetrate skin and muscle tissue to see the bones of a person in the water. The thought brought back the images in my dream and I immediately pressed them back down.

The dolphin duo came to within twenty feet. They were probably wondering where all the noisy air contraptions were that they were accustomed to hearing whenever humans were around. With our rebreathers, there were no escaping bubble noises, but I was sure there were sounds I couldn't hear—the opening and closing of mechanical valves and compressed gas moving under pressure.

The dolphins glanced at each other, then turned and swam off to our right, finally disappearing out at the edge of darkness.

"What do you suppose they think of humans?" Florence asked.

"In some," Savannah replied, squeezing my hand, "I'm sure they see a kindred spirit—just trapped in a different shell."

Though I couldn't see it, I knew there was a smile behind her mask. I returned the silent physical expression.

An undulating veil, barely visible, began to appear out at the edge of what we could see. For a moment,

I thought my mask might be fogging up, but when I moved my head, the veil didn't move with it.

"Krill," I whispered.

The tiny crustaceans looked like shrimp and were found in all the world's oceans, swarming and drifting with the currents by the trillions. The name came from the Norwegian word krill, meaning "small fry of fish." They were probably the most important animal on Earth.

As the veil got closer, undulating like a sheer curtain at an open window, another shape appeared. It moved like a giant bird, massive black wings propelling it up into the cloud until it was inverted, exposing its white underbelly to the surface, then banking over to dive through the krill again.

"It's a manta!" Florence squealed.

After a moment, the giant manta ray moved on in the current.

At the mouth of the cavern, a big spiny lobster came trudging over the face of the cliff. It stopped, either seeing or sensing our presence, then shot backward and down, using its powerful tail for propulsion.

I checked my computer. Ten minutes left. Not much time, but there was always tomorrow, or the next day.

Our ascent would be slow, more horizontal than vertical, as we retraced our swim up to the mouth of the little canyon we'd swum through. We'd end at fifteen feet, halfway along *Salty Dog's* anchor rode, where the chain's turnbuckle connected to the nylon line. There, we'd planned to spend three minutes off-gassing the nitrogen that was building up in our bloodstream. Though nitrogen absorption wasn't as much a problem as with open-circuit, compressed air diving, I still thought it a good idea.

Another smaller manta ray arrived. It performed constant loops through the krill, gorging itself on the tiny crustaceans and maybe also having fun, before disappearing from sight. I'd seen schools of these giant rays leap out of the water, wings flapping like an albatross trying to take flight, only to splash back into the sea again. It was known that mostly males did the leaping, hitting the water with a big belly flop, and presumably they did this to attract a mate among the hundreds in the school. Those who jumped highest made the biggest sound when they hit the water and the stronger the fish, the higher he could jump.

The food chain, both below the sea and on land, was in fact many different chains that overlapped and intersected. But there were really only two groups in the chain, producers and consumers, much the same as in business.

Producers were the plants and tiny phytoplankton that turned energy from the sun into protein. They were consumed by larger animals like krill, which were no more than two inches in length. Some krill swarms were estimated to contain hundreds of millions of *tons* of the tiny creatures. In total mass of the species, they outweighed all other living things. Half of them were consumed by still larger predators, which were in turn eaten by bigger fish, and so on, right up the food chain.

Yet, at the larger end of the animal kingdom, where the baleen whales, whale sharks, and manta rays sat, the food chain was very short. These massive creatures fed exclusively on the smallest; krill, phytoplankton, and sometimes the spawn of other fish. Their chain had only one or two links separating them from the producers that turned solar energy into protein. The only purpose of the lowly krill was to eat the phytoplankton and microscopic plants and change light into physical form to provide food for the rest of the sea's creatures. They were even harvested commercially for human consumption.

The veil of krill became denser, as the swarm moved closer. On the fringe, individual krill could be distinguished. The three of us watched in awe as the blanket moved past us.

My dive computer beeped.

"It's time to go," I said, pushing up off the sand. "Sorry we didn't see a whale shark, Florence."

"We'll have another chance for—" Savannah's voice trailed off in the little speaker in my ear.

Just at the edge of my light's reach, well above our depth, something large was moving slowly through the krill swarm. The wide beam of light reflected off its light-colored underside and the intricate pattern of spots on its dark flanks. It was a good twenty feet above us and about fifty feet away.

"It's a whale shark," Florence said, sheer wonder in her voice.

I had an idea. "Come on. We have to go up and it's above us. Let's go say hi to it."

We swam out of the cavern, finning toward a spot ahead of the gentle giant. Whale sharks swim very slowly, conserving energy. In minutes, the three of us were swimming along next to the great fish.

It wasn't big, as whale sharks go, but it was every bit of thirty feet long and probably weighed ten tons. Still, it was likely not even sexually mature yet.

I checked my depth gauge—fifty feet. "Two minutes," I said.

Florence made little gasping sounds of excited dismay as her light played across the great fish's back. We'd sailed over a thousand miles, just on the off-chance of seeing the largest fish in the sea—the largest non-cetacean on the planet—and found one on our first dive. The odds against it happening were enormous, but Florence got what she wanted. I somehow felt that was normal for her.

"Time to go," I said, once the new alarm pinged on my computer. When we turned away from the great fish, I could just see the lights I'd left above the cavern. "This way. Stay close."

Swimming in open water—*deep* open water at night—was risky, but the distance wasn't far.

As we neared the spot where my lights were, I told Savannah to continue on a heading of 290°, staying at fifty feet, and I'd bounce down to grab my dive lights.

I caught up to them as their lights found the crevice and together, we followed its course toward where I thought the anchor was located. The tether on the GPS was only thirty feet long, but I deployed it anyway, and then switched on the mask's chart.

The bottom soon rose up to meet us and we continued in the same direction until we were in less than thirty feet.

"Hold up," I said. "Let the antenna reach the surface so I can get a bearing."

A moment later, the static screen in front of my left eye updated and showed our position as well as the position of the boat. I took a bearing.

"This way," I said. "Keep the lights outboard."

Florence was first to spot the bright orange ball tethered near the end of the anchor chain. It hung a foot below the surface, as I figured it would be. The tide had risen and the heavy chain had held the ball under to provide an easy beacon for our lights to locate.

"Fifteen feet," I reminded them. "Just hang on the buoy line."

"That was great, Dad. Can we do it again tomorrow night?"

"If you want to," I replied. "Now that we know the spot, we can anchor closer if it's calm, and go straight to that little cavern."

Savannah's hand touched mine on the buoy line. "It was like sitting in a theater without knowing what film was going to play. How much more time would that give us?"

"Not much," I replied, checking my watch. "Ten or fifteen minutes. Our bottom time is mostly limited by the oxygen supply. This stop is just a precaution. Staying down over an hour, hypothermia could start to be a problem for some, even in these warm waters."

I checked Florence's gauge. Her oxygen cylinder was low, but not to a dangerous point. It would be too low for another deep dive but could be used again on a shallower reef. I had plenty of cylinders and CO_2 absorbent on board.

I checked my watch again. "Okay, let's head up."

"Good," Florence said, "I'm cold."

Savannah squeezed my hand. "Point taken."

As we started our ascent, following the anchor line, Florence began shaking it, pointing. The only sound she managed was a yelp of delight as a spotted eagle ray swam right past us, illuminated by the lights from the boat.

I hung off to the side as Florence, then Savannah removed their fins, draped them over their arms, and climbed up the boarding ladder. Diving from a sailboat with nearly four feet of freeboard could be a problem. The *Dog* didn't have a swim platform, though I'd thought many times about adding one. So, a long ladder, hung over the gunwale, was the only means of boarding.

Just as I reached for the ladder, movement caught my eye. A blacktip zipped past, its pectoral fins pointed way down, its head up, exposing the ampullae of Lorenzini—sensitive electroreceptors on the bottom of its snout. My head was partially above the surface and I could see that it was moving toward the mangroves in the distance. Something rolled across the sandy bottom and the shark dodged toward it, scooping whatever it was up and disappearing.

Beyond the shore, cloud-to-cloud lightning flashed across the sky. In the distance, the rising sound of thunder rolled across the water like a bass drum note. As the conscious part of my brain registered the threat below, another part began to think about moving the boat if a storm approached.

I knew harboring irrational fears wasn't healthy. Normally, sharks and divers could share the same space with no problem. But ignoring a rational fear wasn't healthy either. Knowing the difference between the typical behavior of a shark and one that was exhibiting aggression wasn't hard to learn. In most species, particularly in requiem sharks, the pectoral, or side fins, were what to look out for. Usually, these fins were out to the side at no more than a 30° down angle from their body. They acted as wings for slow maneuvering, rising and falling over the bottom and reef.

But when high speed turns were required, such as when a shark was agitated or frenzied, those fins would point farther downward, acting more like rudders than wings.

Another blacktip shot past, closer this time. It displayed the same attitude. I quickly grabbed the ladder and hauled myself up, kicking hard, and twisting my body to get my butt up onto the gunwale. My feet were useless on the ladder with fins on.

"What's wrong?" Savannah asked, coming toward me.

"It's okay," I said, pulling my fins off. "A couple of agitated sharks. I figured a hasty retreat was in order."

Florence looked around our anchorage. "Agitated by what? There's nothing to see but water in one direction and mangroves in the other. Could it be the storm?"

"Good question," I said, getting to my feet.

I moved to the stern and shined my light aft. "They were headed toward the mangroves."

Storms on the surface didn't affect sharks or most other sea creatures very much. An intense storm, like a hurricane, with big waves crashing on the reef, could make them seek deeper water. But none of that was going on.

"Go get a shower, Flo," Savannah said, following me. "And put on something warm; you're shivering."

Savannah stood next to me. Her eyes followed my light among the stilt roots of the mangroves. It was in that maze of roots, where only the smallest creatures could reach, that those at the bottom of the food chain could be safe from larger predators. But even the roots weren't completely safe. The sharks we'd seen had probably started life in these very mangroves, working their way up the food chain.

"I don't see anything," Savannah said.

"The mangroves go on for nearly a mile," I said. "Those sharks could be smelling something on the other side of the island in Mexico."

"But the current is flowing *into* the mangroves."

"Good point," I said.

She reached over and put a hand on mine. "I'm cold, too." I looked over at her and she smiled provocatively. "I understand you blow boaters like to conserve water. Share a shower?"

"What shark?"

CHAPTER TWELVE

W e left the companionway hatch open to let the cool night flow through the open forward hatches. The water temperature was probably around 80°, which meant it would be warmer than that inside. We were on battery power, so we couldn't run the air conditioning. We'd have to close the hatches if it started to rain.

Woden remained on deck, lying on the coach roof, as Finn went below with us. This was another thing the two dogs had taken to doing on their own, whenever we were in port or at an anchorage. They'd alternated nights on deck several times when we were in a busy area or took a slip. And a couple of times, at secluded anchorages, they'd actually swapped places halfway through the night. They didn't do it while we were underway at night. Then, they usually stayed below. I guessed it was because they knew one of us had been on deck during those nights. Maybe that was how they'd learned it.

Finn went to his rug on the port side of the upper salon and galley. I could hear the shower running in the forward head, beyond the lower salon.

Savannah pulled me down the aft steps to the master cabin, unzipping and pulling her Lycra skin down and off her arms. She wore nothing beneath it.

Someone—I didn't know if it was the previous owner, Charity's dead boyfriend, Victor, or someone before him—had outfitted *Salty Dog* for some serious long-range cruising. She carried one hundred gallons of fuel between two tanks in the engine room and one hundred gallons of water in a tank under the deck amidships, which the desalinization unit kept filled.

Still, it was best to be frugal with water when on a boat. So, I peeled off my wetsuit and left it and my swim trunks on the deck as I followed Savannah into the big shower stall and clumsily helped her pull the dive skin over her hips and off her feet. Cold water hit my back when I stood and Savannah squealed, wiggling in my embrace until the hot water started running.

Warmth flowed over us as we lathered one another up. I took extra time shampooing Savannah's long, golden hair, letting my fingers caress her scalp, then move on down her slender neck and shoulders.

When she turned to face me, I took the shower wand from the bulkhead and began rinsing her hair. She put her arms around my waist and arched her spine, letting her head fall back as I rinsed the shampoo from her hair. I admired the view as I did so.

With her belly pressed to mine and the slow rise and fall of the boat, our bodies moved together in syncopated rhythm and I allowed a lot of time rinsing her hair.

Our movements were exciting her as well. As Savannah's hands clasped behind my head and she pulled herself up to kiss me, I dropped the wand. It dangled by its hose, and as the boat rocked, the nozzle washed back and forth across us until I turned the knob to redirect the flow to the rain showerhead.

We made love then, holding one another tightly as the hot water flowed over both our heads and down our bodies. Savannah bit softly into my shoulder, trying to stifle her little yelping sounds. She held me tight, riding up and down, and I couldn't hold back any longer. We finally collapsed against the outer hull, nearly slipping to the deck.

We hadn't been frugal with the water.

But that's what water makers were for.

I turned off the spigots and opened the glass door. Grabbing two towels from the shelf, we dried quickly and stepped out into the cabin, wrapping the towels around ourselves.

Savannah grasped my hand and turned me toward her. She put her arms around my neck and pulled me into her embrace.

"Remember that first time on your boat during the hurricane?" she asked, her eyes a little misty.

"Every minute," I replied. "Like it was yesterday."

"That was when I fell in love with you, Jesse."

Love? There it was again. That word that defined relationships.

"It was because I loved you that I had to leave," she continued. "I didn't want to. But you weren't ready to commit then, and my marriage was on the rocks. Letting it go further would have been too painful."

She was right. I wasn't in the right place then. I'd only been recently retired from the Corps and had already had two failed marriages. But I remembered the feeling I got when I'd first laid eyes on Savannah.

I looked into her eyes, now brimming with tears. "I think I fell in love with you the first time I saw you, rowing your dinghy to the dock to bawl me out about your sister."

She laughed and kissed me then, with a passion unrestrained.

"Hey, Mom," Florence called from the forward part of the boat.

Savannah smiled up at me. "She's always had the worst timing."

Breaking free from my arms, she called out through the closed cabin door, "I'm getting dressed. Why don't you start some coffee?"

"Already brewing," Florence shouted back. "And cocoa for you."

I grinned. "She knows us pretty well."

"That, and she's a bean nut just like you," Savannah said, pulling a clean T-shirt down over her bare breasts. "I swear, she'd drink it all day if I let her."

We dressed quickly and went forward. The smell of Costa Rica's finest filled my nostrils.

"Y'all took long enough," Florence said, offering me a mug.

I accepted it and thanked her.

"Well, there's two of us and only one of you," Savannah said, trying and failing to deflect.

Florence looked at me over her mug, her eyes twinkling. "Can we watch a movie before we go to sleep?"

"Sure," I replied, sipping my coffee. "What did you want to watch?"

"I don't know. Let's go look."

I switched off the light, grabbed a bowl of sliced fruit from the fridge, and the three of us went down to the lower salon. The couch on the starboard side was pulled out into a bed, with half a dozen pillows at the head. The forward cabin had been made into an office of sorts, with extra storage, so the lower salon was where Florence slept.

Savannah moved over to the center and I got comfortable next to her as Florence went through the DVD collection next to the TV on the port side.

"We can clear out the forward cabin," I said to my daughter's back. "Turn it back into a stateroom."

"Where would you write your novel?" she asked, without turning around. "Besides, your desk is perfect for me to study."

"Novel?"

"Yeah," she said, looking over her shoulder and grinning. "I bet you have a lot of sea stories you could tell."

I grinned. "Do you know the difference between a fairy tale and a sea story?"

"No. What?"

"A fairy tale starts out 'Once upon a time,' and a sea story starts off with, 'This ain't no shit.'"

Savannah jabbed me in the ribs with her elbow. "You *should* write a book, Jesse. I'd read it."

I grinned over at her. "You'd be *in* it."

"Here's one I've never seen," Florence said, opening a case and putting the disc in the player. "You like Bill Murray, Dad?"

"The Saturday Night Live guy? Sure."

Savannah elbowed me in the ribs again. "He's done a few things since then."

"Yeah," Florence agreed, turning off the light and jumping onto the bed next to her mother. "Like a couple dozen blockbuster movies."

The night's entertainment that Florence had chosen was called *Lost in Translation* and within the first few minutes, I realized it wasn't going to be a comedy. Rather, it seemed it was going to be one of those more cerebral kind of flicks—not what I'd expected from the comic.

Something bumped against the side of the hull and my body reacted before my brain had finished processing the noise.

Time slowed.

When you lived even part-time on a boat you learned to recognize all its sounds, and that hadn't been one of them.

As my left leg swung over the edge of the bed in slow motion, a low rumble started deep inside Finn, who was up in the galley, and Woden started barking up on deck.

I sprang to my feet.

My hand hit a panel next to the DVD stack and it fell open. I lifted a Colt 1911, racked the slide, and turned to Savannah before she or Florence recognized the trouble. "Stay here."

Finn was just rising as I went up the steps, taking all three at once.

"Watch the girls," I told him, as I strode quickly across the upper salon to the companionway.

I didn't have to look back to know that he'd moved to the bottom of the steps behind me and would be on full alert. I also didn't have to look to know that Savannah was getting the shotgun from beneath the mattress at the head of the bed.

With the big Colt .45 leading the way, I went halfway up the companionway ladder. Woden was at the stern, barking. Lightning was still flashing way in the distance as the storm moved away. I scanned the deck and saw nothing out of place, no hidden enemy, no grappling hook, no boarding ladder.

I came up the rest of the way and looked all around, my eyes already adjusting to the darkness. The moon was past full and high in the sky.

Nothing in the water and no boats anywhere in sight.

"*Aus!*" I whisper-shouted, and the big rottweiler instantly stopped barking and stepped back from the rail, fully alert and looking aft. Unlike Finn, who had a good natural instinct to protect, Woden had been professionally trained as a guardian. Savannah had taught me his commands—all German. He knew that when those commands came, he was working. And a working rottweiler guardian was something not to be trifled with.

Our dive gear was hanging from the mizzen boom. I grabbed a light and switched it on. Whoever was out there was about to lose their ability to see, as I narrowed the powerful beam and shined it over the stern rail where I'd heard a splash.

A pale-yellowish thing floated in the water beneath the three rectangular portholes in the wineglass transom. It moved suddenly, bobbing under the surface and away from the boat. When it came up again, it had turned over and was now unmistakable. A small woman, with dark hair and Hispanic features floated beside the dink. She wasn't wearing anything, and she was obviously dead.

I panned the light around the area. There wasn't anything around except the ocean and the mangroves, which suddenly felt much too close.

A splash brought my light and my attention back to the dead girl, as she was again dragged under, the shark thrashing as it tried to saw through her ankle with its teeth.

When the body surfaced again, I saw a long gash in her midsection, running from her navel to near her ribcage, maybe six inches long. There were no other bite wounds around the incision.

A shark grabbed one of the arms and started dragging the body toward the mangroves. Another bit into an inner thigh and the two began a macabre tug-of-war. It ended suddenly, when the first shark rolled and the woman's arm separated at the elbow.

More sharks moved in and frenzied feeding began in earnest.

Hearing a sound, I turned and saw Savannah coming up the companionway. The Mossberg Mariner pump shotgun in her hands was a vicious-looking thing. Coated with a non-corrosive nickel finish and sporting a pistol grip and short barrel, it was the ideal weapon for a boat—a deck sweeper.

"Don't come back here," I ordered, looking behind me to where the dead woman was being devoured.

"What's going on?"

The body was suddenly tugged violently beneath the water and the thrashing ceased.

"Something dead in the water," I replied. "Must've been what the sharks were attracted to when we came up."

"What is it?" she asked, coming closer.

The body was gone now.

"I don't know," I lied.

Savannah screamed as she joined me and looked down. A foot and lower leg, toenails painted a bright purple, was tangled in the dinghy's painter.

CHAPTER THIRTEEN

The sun was already up before help arrived. Savannah and I tried to sleep in shifts, huddled together under a blanket in the cockpit, waiting. What started out as a wonderful evening after a nearly perfect day, the kind that comes along all too infrequently, had turned into anything but that.

I'd used a fish gaff to get the woman's leg into the dinghy before another shark found it. Then I'd called the authorities. I was told they'd have someone there as soon as possible.

Island time.

The first boat to arrive, just after sunrise, was a Belizean Coast Guard patrol boat. The captain took one look in my dinghy and ordered his divers into the water. As they were gearing up, a boat from the Belize Police Department arrived and came alongside with two men aboard.

The one not piloting the boat wore three stripes on the sleeves of his khaki uniform. He looked Mestizo—mixed European and indigenous ancestry—as was more than half the country's population.

"I could come aboard?" the sergeant asked, as the other policeman kept his boat a few feet away.

The sergeant was young, about twenty-five or thirty, and rail thin. He was taller than most Belizeans, at least as tall as Savannah.

"Yes," I replied. "I'm Captain McDermitt, the one who called this in."

The police boat idled closer and the sergeant stepped nimbly up to his boat's gunwale. When the two boats were close enough, he stepped over to the ladder and climbed aboard.

"I am Sergeant Elden Garcia," he said, extending his hand. "Ambergris Caye *Polees*."

His accent was like a Brit's who'd spent half his life in the Bahamas and he used the Belizean Kriol word, pronouncing it po leez, accenting the first syllable.

"Sorry to make you come all this way, Sergeant." I nodded toward the Coast Guard divers now entering the water. "It's doubtful they'll find anything. Sharks dragged the body away."

"And you are sure dat it was a woman's body?"

"You'll have to take my word on that," I said. "A foot was all that was recovered. It's in my dinghy."

I lead him astern and pointed down to the grisly find.

"How did di foot come to be on your boat?"

"We heard the splashing," I recounted. "Something bumped the hull before midnight, and when I went to see what it was, I saw several blacktips in a frenzy around the body. Later, after they'd dragged it off, I used a gaff and pulled the leg into the dinghy."

He studied the leg a moment. "Just by di toenails, I think you are right. And a small woman at dat, maybe just a girl." He straightened and looked me in the eye. "You said 'we,' Captain. You are not alone on di boat?"

"No," I replied. "My girlfriend and our daughter are down in the cabin."

Girlfriend? Is that what Savannah was? The moniker didn't fit.

"Did dey see anything?"

"Come on," I said, knowing that regardless of my answer, he was going to want to talk to Savannah and Florence. "They're down in the cabin."

I went down the ladder first. As soon as the sergeant reached the bottom step, he saw Finn and Woden on either side of the steps going down to the lower salon and he stopped where he was.

"Do dey bite?" Sergeant Garcia asked warily.

"Of course," I replied. "They're dogs. Biting is the only way they have of grabbing something. But these two will only bite a person if told to do so. You have nothing to fear from them."

Garcia hesitantly stepped down, one hand on a holstered semi-auto.

"This way," I said, as the two dogs looked from Garcia to me. I stepped down into the lower salon with the girls. "Sergeant Garcia wants to get a statement."

Savannah and Florence had tidied the room and closed the hideaway bed, putting the shotgun back in its place.

"It's okay, Sergeant," I called up. "The dogs won't bother you."

"How do you know dat?" he called down. "You have not given dem any orders."

"I told them to stay before I went up on deck to meet you," I said, becoming frustrated. "They'll continue to follow that command until I give them another."

Savannah reached up and took my hand, a calming move on her part; she could sense that I was agitated. But it worked both ways.

The man moved cautiously across the deck between the two dogs, then came down to the lower salon.

"Sergeant Garcia, this is my girlfriend, Savannah Richmond and our daughter Florence."

When he looked away from Finn and Woden and saw the girls, he quickly whipped his hat off his head and nodded at Savannah. "My apologies for di intrusion, ma'am."

Savannah and Florence were sitting close together on the couch. Savannah released my hand and took Florence's. "That's all right," she said.

"I must ask a few questions," Garcia said, almost apologetically. "Did either of you see what happened last night?"

"They haven't let me leave the cabin since our dive last night," Florence replied.

"I followed Jesse up onto the deck," Savannah said, nodding. "Last night—when we heard something hit the boat and the dogs started growling. I didn't see anything other than the foot tangled in the dinghy's line. It was like fifty shades of gross."

Garcia and I both looked at her curiously, but she didn't expand on it.

He pulled a small pad from his pocket and scribbled in it. "None of you heard a boat or anything unusual?"

"No," I replied. "We arrived here from Belize City before sunset. One of Frenchie's dive boats from Caye Caulker was leaving when we arrived. It was an incoming tide, which didn't change until well after I saw the body."

"I see," Garcia said, scribbling notes. "And how long after Frenchie's boat left did dis happen?"

I could see where he was going. With an incoming tide, the body might have been a diver carried on the current from one of the dive sites along the reef. At least that would be the logical conclusion—but I didn't think that was where she came from.

I picked up the remote and clicked the power button. The movie was still paused, with a middle-aged Bill Murray flirting with a much younger Scarlett Johansson in a Japanese bar. Pushing the *Source* button, I scrolled to the chart plotter interface and clicked on it.

The chart for the area appeared on the screen, showing our track from Neal and Erin's house the previous day to our current location.

"We've been stationary for sixteen hours and ten minutes." I looked at my watch. "We got here just before 1700 and low tide was an hour before that. High tide was about 2200. It was an hour before the high when I called you guys. So, four hours, at least, after Frenchie's boat left. Far too long for the body to be one of the people from the dive boat."

"You were diving Di Wall?"

"Yes," I said. "As was Frenchie's boat, I'm guessing."

"I see. Is dere anything else you can tell me?"

I turned to Savannah and Florence. "I'll be right back."

Then I motioned Garcia toward the upper salon. "Let's talk outside, Sergeant."

He followed me hesitantly up the steps, Finn and Woden watching him. Both dogs had curious expressions on their faces, but nothing more.

To make Garcia feel more at ease, I gave the dogs another order. "Finn, topside. Woden, *unten.*"

Woden instantly went down to the lower salon and turned around to face the steps as Finn went up the companionway steps ahead of us.

Once we were out on deck, I turned to Garcia. "She was naked."

"Di body?"

"Yeah," I said. "Not a stitch of clothing or any jewelry."

"Di way you talk, Captain? Are you an American *polees* man?"

"Not exactly," I replied. "Retired U.S. Marine and private investigator."

It wasn't completely a lie. I owned part of McDermitt and Livingston Security, and we did do occasional *private* investigations.

"Why do you suppose di woman was naked?"

I looked down at the severed limb in my dinghy. From the heel to the tip of the longer second toe couldn't have been more than six inches, the foot of a child in the States. Most of the people in this part of the world were smaller than average, though. Garcia was at least six inches shorter than my six-three but would be considered very tall among his own people.

"I don't know," I replied honestly. "I doubt she'd been in the water for long. Five hours in this single-knot current means she went in somewhere no more than five miles from here. Wind and current were both coming from the east, and there were no other boats out here."

"You said she had no jewelry? You got dat good a look?"

I turned to face Garcia. "I've seen a few bodies, Sergeant. Believe it or not, this isn't the first severed limb I've recovered. I'm not the kind of man who goes into shock at the sight of a dead person. You might say I'm a skilled observer."

"I see." Garcia wrote on his pad some more. Without looking up, he asked, "Does di toenail paint mean anything to you?"

"Only that the woman had a gaudy sense of style." I shook my head slowly. "Bright purple?"

"That color means nothing to you?"

"No," I replied. "Should it?"

"Was dere anything else?"

I squared my shoulders to the man. "She had a six-inch incision in her abdomen," I said. "Straight. *Not* from a shark bite."

Garcia looked up suddenly, his eyes boring into mine. "Perhaps you are mistaken?"

"No," I replied. "Your Ghoul Killer has taken an eighth victim."

CHAPTER FOURTEEN

A small helicopter with a wraparound glass bubble windshield descended toward a large luxury yacht floating gently on the calm sea. On the yacht's stern was a raised platform with a large H in the middle of a circle.

Casey Jasso guided his Robinson R22 to a near-perfect landing on the yacht's helipad, fifteen miles from the Belizean coast. After shutting down the buzzing engine, he opened the door and climbed out, stretching his back and legs.

Though the yacht was barely outside the twelve-mile limit of the territorial sea, the flight had taken nearly an hour from Casey's base south of Belize City. Casey found the small, lightweight helicopter perfect for his needs.

The rotors slowed as a white-haired man approached the helicopter. He wore creased khakis and a white, long-sleeved shirt unbuttoned to reveal two gold chains. There was a large gold ring on his right hand; the one he used to carry a small cooler just like the one Casey had under the passenger seat. The man was tall, with a face that seemed chiseled from granite.

"Mr. Zotov," Casey said, moving around to the left side and opening the door. "How are you today, sir?"

"You are late," Zotov said, his heavily-accented words both accusatory and questioning.

"Couldn't be helped," Casey said, removing his own cooler from under the seat. "I was almost discovered last night. I had to fly offshore to drop something off."

"Have what ordered?" the Russian smuggler snarled.

Casey smiled at the old *Bratva* boss as he placed his cooler on the deck between them. "Don't I always?"

Before the fall of the Soviet Union, Basil Zotov had smuggled arms, drugs, and anything else of value into and out of the country. Even beautiful Russian women who paid handsomely, thinking they would be taken to a better life in America, only to be sold into slavery and end up in some sultan's harem, ultimately disposed of when no longer desirable or too injured to perform.

Now, though wealthy beyond imagination, Zotov was ostracized from his beloved brotherhood and forced to turn to other means to build even more wealth to maintain his lifestyle and power. The trade in human organs on the black market was very lucrative but considered too morbid, even by Zotov's counterparts in Russian organized crime.

Of course, they'd only thought of taking organs from dead people.

Another man approached the helicopter carrying a briefcase, which Casey knew was full of American greenbacks, totaling $10,000.

"*Otlichno!*" Zotov said, a smile cracking the stony veneer. "Is good! You stay for while, yes?"

"I can't," Casey replied. "Maybe next—"

"*Nyet*," Zotov said, cutting him off. "You stay. You have passenger take back."

Casey removed his sunglasses and looked at the old man. "A passenger?"

"*Da*," Zotov replied, stepping closer, his eyes boring into Casey's like a diamond-tipped drill. He pointed east, out to sea. "Take to same place."

Casey looked to the east. "That'll be extra," he said, looking back and sliding his shades into place.

Zotov nodded to the man with the briefcase, then bent and picked up the cooler Casey had brought. "Come to lower deck when finished."

Zotov went down a level on the starboard side and handed Casey's cooler to a man waiting in a speedboat. In seconds, the boat was roaring away at close to a hundred miles per hour, as Zotov disappeared into the ship's bowels via a side deck.

The man with the briefcase raised it, getting Casey's attention. He held it flat with one arm, unlatched it, then turned it around so Casey could see what was in it. The case was full of small packages of used twenty-dollar bills, each strap equaling $2000. There were ten of them.

Double his normal delivery fee.

Casey smiled at the guy. "Flying's more fun with friends," he said, even though he didn't think the aide spoke English. Considering the old man's instructions, Casey felt certain the passenger wouldn't be a friend, either.

He scooped the bundles into the cooler Zotov had left beside his chopper. Inside it were the battery-powered cryogenic device and surgical instruments he'd need for the next harvest. Casey put the cooler under the helo's passenger seat and closed and locked the doors.

Following the aide, Casey went forward and up a short ladder to the bridge deck. He'd met the aide many times already but had never learned his name. They went down a winding staircase from the bridge to the yacht's main salon, where Zotov was waiting.

A blond woman sat slumped in a chair. Her legs were impossibly long below a clingy white dress that rode up around her hips, exposing the tops of her thighs.

Zotov turned and began to untie the woman's wrists from the arms of the chair. She had a swollen left eye, abrasions on her left cheek, and her lower lip was split in several places, swollen and puffy. The white dress had medium-velocity blood spatter from a beating and there were smudges of blood on her left shoulder that coalesced into an ample cleavage.

Having once been an EMT, Casey could tell her injuries were at least a couple of hours old, possibly from late the night before.

"What happened?" he asked bluntly.

"She is spy!" Zotov said venomously.

"A spy?" Casey asked.

"*Bratva svin'ya!*" he shouted at the woman, though she seemed oblivious. Then he turned to Casey. "How you say? Swine whore!" He smiled broadly at this. "*Da.* Whore pig. You take." Again, he pointed to the east. "Far away. Throw out from high."

"She dead?"

"*Nyet,*" Zotov said. "Give drugs."

Kneeling, Casey lifted the woman's right eyelid, the one that wasn't swollen shut. The vacant orb floated around, barely controlled by muscle movement. The pupil was wide, nearly filling the pale blue iris, though the room was well lit. He put two fingers alongside her throat and felt a weak but steady pulse.

Casey stood and faced Zotov. "She American?"

"*Nyet,*" he replied, removing the last of the woman's bindings. "She is Moscovite."

"Okay," Casey said, taking the woman's right wrist in his left hand and draping her arm over his neck.

Grabbing the inside of her right knee, he stood, lifting the weight of the unconscious woman onto his shoulder in a fireman's carry. She was soft and supple, yielding to his grasp, though he did feel her move gently as he stood and adjusted her weight.

She was over 100 pounds, probably 130, Casey guessed, and very tall. But he carried her effortlessly, following the aide back up the stairs to the bridge and out the back, to his waiting helicopter.

Zotov's aide went to the left cockpit door and waited as Casey fumbled with the key while trying to balance the woman on his shoulder. He finally unlocked the door and swung it wide open. The aide held it as Casey dumped the semi-conscious woman into the seat. She moaned but didn't move. The white dress had now ridden up over her wide hips, exposing her fancy French panties.

Casey rolled her and folded her legs into the cockpit, then pulled her up into a sitting position. One strap of her dress had slipped down, exposing most of her left breast.

Without bothering to strap the woman in, he shoved her over slightly, then closed and latched the door. She slumped against the glass, the injured side of her face pressed to it and her body visible all the way to her knees through the glass.

Stepping back, Casey shook his head. "Damned waste, if you ask me."

He'd fly due east for a few miles, staying down close to the wave tops, then climb to a thousand feet, open her door, and push her out. The impact with the water from that height would kill her instantly.

Probably break every bone in her body, Casey thought. He also knew there would be massive trauma and hemorrhaging.

The sharks would do the rest.

Casey walked around to the other side, climbed into the pilot's seat, and conducted a quick preflight before starting the engine. The aide moved away as the blades gained speed. He engaged the clutch and the blades began to whir even faster.

Glancing over at his passenger, slumped against the door, Casey wondered who she was and what she might've done to piss off the old Russian bear. His eyes traveled up her voluptuous body, then he reached over and grabbed her hair, pulling her around to face him. The left side of her face had received many hard punches, undoubtedly from a right-handed man wearing a ring, leaving it looking like raw hamburger.

Probably Zotov, himself, Casey thought. The man was ruthless, he knew. And more than one whore who was brought out to his yacht went home beaten and bruised.

But the other side of the woman's face, the side that wasn't all busted up was very pretty—beautiful, in fact.

Maybe she doesn't have to take a dive right away, he thought.

CHAPTER FIFTEEN

G arcia had kept us around until noon, though there wasn't anything more any of us could tell him. When the divers finally gave up on finding anything, he cut us loose.

"Where are we going?" Florence asked.

I started the engine, and as it warmed up, hit the button for the anchor windlass. "It's about fifteen miles down to San Pedro," I replied. "We can be there in three hours and anchor in the lagoon for the night."

"Rowdy dive bars?" Savannah said. "I thought you didn't like being around a lot of people."

As the anchor line gave way to the chain portion of the rode, I slipped the transmission into gear for a second. "Right now, I think I want people around."

The chain rode clicked and clacked across the rollers as I watched the chain counter. With twenty-five feet still out, I felt the hook break loose from the sand.

We were free once more.

"I'll get the safety chain," Florence said as she headed forward.

"There's something you haven't told us," Savannah began, once Florence was out of earshot.

"It was the so-called Ghoul Killer and the woman was naked."

Savannah took the news in stride. "Another poor prostitute?"

"Looks that way," I replied, seating the anchor and releasing the switch.

"Got it!" Florence shouted from the bow.

When she returned to the cockpit, I asked her if she'd mind making a few sandwiches, and she took off for the galley, Woden right behind her.

"How do you know it was the same killer?" Savannah asked, avoiding the moniker the press had given the guy.

"There was an incision here," I said, running a finger from my navel to my sternum.

She visibly shuddered. "Who could do that to another human being?"

"Someone who's not human," I replied, still wondering about the cop's questioning. "Garcia kept circling back to her toenail polish, even after I told him about seeing an incision in the woman's abdomen."

"Why?"

"I straight up asked him," I replied. "He just waved it off with more questions."

We motored into the wind until the sonar showed the bottom falling away sharply.

"Want me to raise the main?" Savannah asked, as I started to turn toward the south.

There wasn't much wind. Even if we put up all the canvas, we'd probably only get four knots of boat speed.

"Nah," I replied, as Florence came up with a tray. "I believe I think better with an engine vibrating under my feet."

"Mom likes it better, too," Florence said, putting the tray on the table in front of the helm.

"I never said that," Savannah exclaimed. "I've really enjoyed sailing."

"You said you missed *Sea Biscuit*."

They continued to banter back and forth as I pushed the throttle forward to get us up to six knots. I picked up a sandwich and started eating, not really tasting it.

The scene from the night before kept replaying in the back of my mind, as sometimes happened when I'd overlooked something. What had I missed?

Forefront in my mind was the revelation that Savannah missed her boat. When you lived aboard, your boat was your home. But it was more than that. A boat meant freedom. Aboard *Salty Dog*, I'd found that. On my other boats, there was always an immediate destination: a fishing ground, dive spot, or fuel stop—always a place to go.

With the *Dog*, the journey *was* the destination.

I had a home on land and the *Dog* felt more like my home at sea than my other boats. Savannah's home was wherever her boat was docked. Right now, that was Fort Myers. For all of Florence's seventeen years, they'd probably never stayed in one place for longer than a few months.

This presented a problem.

"Snap!" Savannah said, breaking my thought. "Honey, go get my phone for me, please."

"What is it?" I asked, as Florence hurried off, Woden once more right behind her.

"Weren't you listening?" she asked. "Flo just reminded me that Erin and Neal were coming out this afternoon for sundowners."

Savannah rarely drank alcohol before sunset and even then, no more than one or two. For the last few years, I'd rarely touched the stuff, but obliged her at sunset. She liked to concoct different drink recipes for happy hour. The drinks were collectively just called sundowners.

"Just have them come to the lagoon at San Pedro instead," I offered, as Florence came back up and handed Savannah her phone. "We can anchor just inside the cut to the south. It's deep there."

The cut, I thought, as Savannah made the call. The incision on the woman's body had been in the front. Kidneys are more around to the back and the liver is kind of on the side. What organs were in the front? Stomach? Intestines? Not being trained in medicine beyond patching up a bullet wound, I wasn't familiar enough with human anatomy to even guess at what organs were transplantable, much less where they were.

I was certain that was the reason for the murders. The news reports talked about surgical precision. What other reason would there be for removing organs and leaving the victim to die from blood loss?

Savannah ended her call. "They're just leaving," she said. "Neil has to stop at the marina in town to get gas, but they'll be there by five."

I filed the questions in the back of my mind to look into later. If we couldn't get a Wi-Fi connection in the lagoon, I'd spend a little on satellite time and see what I could come up with on my own. If all else failed, I could check with Chyrel Koshinski, Deuce's computer hacker.

Why was I involving myself, anyway? The sun was warm, but not hot. And the cooling sea breeze, what there was, was on the port beam, making it quite comfortable at the helm. It was fifteen miles to the cut through the reef to San Pedro; three hours, give or take. I should be enjoying my time with my crew.

"Don't you have some studying to do?" Savannah asked Florence, who was idly stroking Woden's muscular flank.

"Yeah, but—"

"No buts, Flo. I said you could change your schedule up a little during this trip and do your schoolwork during free time. Remember? It's three hours of free time to San Pedro."

Florence pouted but went below just the same.

"Sorry for messing up her schedule," I said.

"We do it all the time," she said. "Don't worry about it. The education she gets outside the textbooks is just as important."

"You miss your boat?"

She was seated on the starboard bench, facing forward, stretched out with her feet up on the coaming. She looked over at me, concern in her eyes.

"Not like that," she said. "It's just...well...we've never been away from home before. So, yeah, I'm a little home-sick. That doesn't mean I don't like sailing or being with you, though. 'Cause I do."

"Want to talk about the next step?"

"What next step?" she asked.

"I have a home, or I could live on one of three different boats. Hell, I can live anywhere. Your boat is *your* home."

"Oh," she said, her voice trailing off.

"I'm not talking about moving in, and—"

"I don't want to change your life," she interrupted.

We both laughed.

"Who sang that song?" she asked.

"England Dan, something or other," I replied.

"England Dan and John Ford Coley," she said, excitedly. "What do I win?"

She was deflecting again.

"We should talk about it sooner than later," I said. "Just...you know...let's just be straight up, okay?"

"You never struck me as an emotionally communicative man."

"I've been trying to...evolve," I said, though she was right.

I'd never been comfortable talking about my feelings. I didn't think many men were.

"If things progress," I said, "we should have a plan."

She turned toward me and lowered her sunglasses. "*If*, Jesse?"

Her eyes gave her away, as they sparkled with mischief just before her perfect lips parted into a perfect smile.

"I admit it," I said. "I'm not very practiced at this."

"What you're asking is, where should you keep your skivvies?"

"Well, yeah," I said, grinning. "Or where you'd keep your knickers."

She snorted a laugh and rose, then came over to stand beside me at the helm. "We could both just keep a good supply in a few places."

"But what if we were to—?"

"What?" she said, taking my arm in her hands and giving it a squeeze. "Get married some day?"

My mind hadn't gone quite that far, but apparently my mouth had. "I wasn't thinking that far ahead."

"Our daughter is nearly grown, Jesse." She looked up at me. "She'll go off to college in the fall. I wouldn't rule anything out, but let's just have fun and see where things go."

"I'm probably just overthinking."

"Another good quality," she said.

I looked down to see her staring out across the water. "I have a lot of room on the island," I said. "And it's very comfortable."

"And when you go off again? What would I do?" She looked up suddenly, her eyes full of regret. "I shouldn't have said that. I'm sorry."

"I don't *have* to go off," I said.

There it was again. Did I really want to give up everything I believed I'd stood for my whole adult life? The warrior mask was more than a facial expression. It was more than just the outward reflection of an attitude that burned deep into the soul of those who wore the mantle. And it was more than a simple emotional barrier. The mask was what kept the inner turmoil at bay, pushed deep into the warrior's heart, so that those who are protected by it don't have to actually see it.

I'd helped a lot of people over the years. Was it time to think more of myself? The years had taken their toll—I wasn't a kid anymore. But could I put it all astern? And if I did quit, did that mean the dreams would stop?

"No," Savannah said, putting a hand to my cheek. "It's who and what you are, Jesse. People like you and Deuce and Charity? You're the ones people turn to in a crisis or depend on when there's trouble. You always have been and you always will be. I've been watching you since last night. I can tell you've been thinking about what happened to that poor girl. In your mind, you're playing back what happened, as well as your conversation with the detective, looking for clues to something you're not involved with in the slightest. People are getting hurt and you can't stand that."

The truth must have been written across my forehead.

She smiled and squeezed my arm again. "What is it you're always saying? Improvise and adapt? I can adapt. Flo and I can both adapt. I wasn't really worried about you earlier this week while you were away. I was more worried about what your actions might do to you than the possibility of you getting hurt by someone."

I smiled and pulled her close. "I really don't deserve you."

"You're right," she said, then pulled away. "It's warmed up. I'm going to change into something decadent and get some sun."

She headed to the companionway and down the steps, leaving me alone with Finn and my thoughts.

He looked up at me and cocked his head a few degrees.

"I really don't know, buddy. But she makes me happy."

It was a bit disconcerting, motoring a boat that draws nearly six feet of water within a hundred yards of waves breaking over a reef. But the sea floor rose up sharply along the north end of Ambergris Caye, the coral reef running along the edge at the top. A quick glance at the instruments showed we had over a thousand feet of water beneath us, and the reef ran so straight, we could hug it all the way to San Pedro.

True to her word, Savannah soon came back up wearing a bikini I hadn't seen before. It was small enough that it could have been packed in a sandwich bag. She kissed me, pressing her almost bare body against mine.

"Is that new?" I asked.

She twirled around. "This? Yeah, I picked it up in Chetumal. You like it?"

I didn't try to hide my eyes roaming up and down her body. "Yes, absolutely."

"Don't let me fall asleep," she said, then went forward to the sun pad below the main boom. She tossed her hair and looked over her shoulder, catching me admiring the high cut thong. "No more than an hour."

Savannah stretched out face-down on the one-inch foam padding. It was early afternoon and the sun was high and off the starboard side. The optimal spot for sunbathing just happened to be directly in my line of sight, looking over the bow. So, I relaxed and just enjoyed the view: the barren mangrove landscape passing by to starboard, the open sea flowing past to port, and the magnificent vista directly ahead.

The years we'd been apart didn't seem to have made much difference to her. She was still the same outrageously sexy woman I'd met long ago. Her body was lean and well-sculpted, her skin as smooth as a child's, but firm and tan. When I was close to her, I could see a gray hair or two, but mixed in with all the sun-soaked blond streaks, they simply disappeared.

Savannah's hour in the sun was an hour of frustration on my part. I tried to force my brain to think about other things, but with her lying just ten feet in front of me, that was impossible.

Finally, she went below to change and help Florence with her studies, leaving Finn and me alone on deck.

As we got closer to San Pedro, water traffic increased; mostly dive boats coming and going to the various dive sites along the reef, but there were a few privately owned boats, too. I nudged our course a little farther out to sea, to put more distance between us and any divers who might pop up in the wrong place.

With the cut half a mile ahead, I steered to a spot a good quarter mile out from it, angling still farther from shore. *Salty Dog* was a very capable offshore vessel but maneuvering in a confined area wasn't her strong suit. So, I wanted there to be no doubt of my intention to enter the cut by coming directly toward it from offshore, rather than making a sharp turn right at the cut.

As I made the sweeping turn, Savannah and Florence came up, along with Woden. Finn then went below. The watch change.

Finn had a custom-made insert in the forward shower. It looked like real grass but was very easy to keep clean. He now shared that with Woden. The insert was hinged and could be raised and secured so the shower could be used for its original purpose.

"It's almost like they work as a team," Florence remarked to nobody in particular, as she looked over the bow toward the cut.

"They make a good one," I said.

"How wide is it?" Florence asked, coming back to look at the chart plotter.

"About a hundred yards," I replied. "But we're taking the middle."

She watched a boat loaded with divers power past us on the starboard side, heading in. "Should I call on the radio to warn others?"

"If you want to," I said.

She picked up the mic and checked that the radio was on channel sixteen, then keyed it and identified us as an inbound sixty-one-foot ketch. There was no reply.

"Think anyone heard her?" Savannah asked.

To say the *Dog* was sixty-one feet long was a bit misleading. Her deck length was just fifty-eight feet and the rest was the bowsprit, and her waterline length was only fifty feet. But most of the boats around San Pedro would be less than forty feet. So, anything the size of *Salty Dog* would bring out the curious.

"Not many," I replied. "Some people get lazy sometimes and only turn on their radio if they need to talk to someone."

I slowed to just four knots, plenty fast enough to maintain steerage against the outflowing current, then pointed the bow toward the center of the opening in the reef line. To the untrained eye, it looked like open water all around, all the way to shore. But waves were breaking over the tops of the reef on either side of the cut, showing swirls of white water.

Another boat was heading toward the cut from the mainland. We had the wind and waves on our stern, reducing the *Dog's* maneuverability slightly. I punched the speed back up to six knots and held my course steady. That at least negated the light windage on the hull. The other boat would give way or become a figurehead on the bowsprit.

The dive boat slowed and gave us as much room as possible without getting too close to the reef. We passed about fifty feet apart and the captain waved from the bridge. We all waved back, which got all the divers crowded into the cockpit waving. Glancing back, I saw the name *Leeward to Seaward* across the stern.

Once we cleared the reef and the inner markers to the cut, I turned sharply to port and motored a couple hundred yards along the inside of the reef. We had ten feet under us, but the reef was closer than the sixty feet of scope I'd want to put out. I angled away from the reef until we were a good 150 feet into the lagoon and there, we dropped the hook.

I reversed the engine until we had enough rode out, then backed down to set the anchor deep. The whole lagoon was roughly nine feet deep, getting a little shallower toward shore. We were nearly half a mile from the docks and downtown, and well out of the way of any boat traffic transiting the cut.

"I should try to get some swimming in," Florence said.

"Don't go far," Savannah and I both said together.

While she went below to change, Savannah and I busied ourselves with securing everything that had been needed to move the boat and breaking out everything that was put up while underway. I stretched a tarp over the main boom and bungeed it to outriggers secured to six rail posts. Savannah got the chairs out of the deck box and set them up, and within minutes, we were relaxing in the shade. The tarp wouldn't be much use in a heavy rain or high wind, but on a calm, sunny day, it was perfect.

Florence came back up wearing her one-piece, and I followed her to the port rail. There weren't any boats in our immediate area and the waters in the lagoon were protected by the reef, so there was little in the way of wave activity to worry about. I was more curious than concerned.

"How far are you planning to go?" I asked.

"Why?" she asked, adjusting a pair of tinted goggles to her face. "You and Mom want some privacy?"

I felt my face flush. Having *this* discussion wasn't my intention.

Ever.

She grinned. "You're kind of a prude, Dad."

"Well...er..."

"Relax," she said. "I'm only going a half mile along the reef, then right back. Fifteen minutes, tops."

"A mile in fifteen minutes?" I asked, a bit too incredulously.

"Kicked your butt, didn't I?" With that, she dove head-first into the gin-clear water.

I watched her as she kicked away from the boat, using her entire body, just like a dolphin. The little swirls caused by her up kicks got larger until she finally broke the surface at least twenty yards away.

"No wonder she beat me," I mumbled, sitting back down beside Savannah.

"Charity taught her that," she said, smiling. "Then she taught her to free dive to increase her breath-hold time."

"She stayed under for sixty feet," I said, still not believing it. "A good fifteen seconds with no prep."

Fifteen seconds wasn't a long time to hold your breath. If you weren't moving, that is. But swimming underwater using your whole body burned oxygen fast. And it built up carbon dioxide in the lungs even faster. I could swim freestyle for that long without taking a breath, but my lungs were a lot bigger than our daughter's.

"She must not be pushing hard," Savannah said. "I've seen her do that kick for over twenty seconds."

"Unbelievable," was all I could muster.

"Charity thinks she could win gold."

CHAPTER SIXTEEN

Neal and Erin arrived just before 1700 and we welcomed them aboard. We'd caught several mahi on the trip down the Mexican coast before I'd been called away, and Neal brought a dozen slipper lobster tails to go with the fish.

"Give me a hand setting up the grill, Neal?" I asked, once we had them aboard and everything stowed.

"Sure," he replied, following me aft.

The *Dog's* lazarette wasn't deep, being right over my bunk, but it was expansive. It covered the whole bunk, but left room on the outboard sides to walk around. The same teak was used in the two hatches as on the deck. Except for the two latches, you couldn't tell they were there.

I opened the port side of the lazarette and handed Neal the mounting brackets for the grill as the girls went forward to get out of the sun.

"It's not quite the setup you have," I offered. "That brisket was delicious."

"Well, it wouldn't be prudent to have an open wood fire on a boat, would it?"

I didn't bother to remind him that wood fires on boats were the norm until just the last century. Early explorers had carried firewood with them for the galley and replenished it at every stop.

"What do you know about this Ghoul Killer?" I asked, as we worked to mount the grill outboard the aft rail.

"Everyone's saying he's a surgeon," Neal replied. "But I don't think so. Medical skills, yeah, but I doubt he's a surgeon. There just aren't that many in the country."

"How many are there?"

He held the grill in place while I tightened the wingnuts. "I really don't know for sure, but I'd guess no more than twenty-five."

"Really?"

"It's better than a lot of developed countries," he said. "The healthcare system here is excellent. Back in the States, there are about six surgeons per hundred thousand people. The population of Belize is about 400,000. You do the math."

"I imagine the police have already checked all of them out, then."

"Probably," he said, opening the grill, then looking at me. "You're not a magazine publisher, are you."

He said it flatly; a statement, not a question.

"No," I replied honestly. "That was Savannah's way of avoiding the obvious questions that would come when I arrived with another woman."

"We figured as much," he said with a chortle. "Erin's known her since they were freshmen in college and said she's always been a terrible liar."

"I'm sorry about that," I said. "Charity and I do investigative work for an oceanographic research company. The magazine thing allows us a lot freer access in some places than a private investigator might have."

"And you're looking into these murders?"

"Just curious," I said, tightening the gas line connection. "Well, this is all set."

"I think the guy's an American ex-pat," Neal said. "Someone with a little medical background. But not a surgeon."

"Like regular doctors, nurses, EMTs, or medics?"

"Yeah, maybe even former military."

I laughed. "I was twenty years in Marine Corps infantry—if you get shot, I can stop the bleeding, but if I tried to get the bullet out, believe me, you'd probably end up off on a boat."

"Ah, a Viking funeral," he said. "That's the thing," he paused and looked up at me, "the patient doesn't need to survive the operation."

"Good point," I agreed.

"The medical examiner is a friend of mine. He said a couple of the victims who'd had both kidneys and liver removed had what he called a Makuuchi incision, which is L-shaped. Another indication that the killer has medical training."

"They were prostitutes—did the ME say anything about DNA evidence?"

"Oh, sure," Neal replied. "Lots of DNA, but no way to tell which donor came last. Pardon the pun."

I shuddered at the thought but doubted that the killer would take the time to have sex with his victim before knocking them out and cutting them open.

"What do you know about toenail polish?" I asked.

"Toenail polish?"

"Did Savannah tell you why we returned early?"

"Yeah," he replied. "I hate that she and Flo had to witness that."

"The woman who was killed last night had purple toenail polish and the detective who came out there seemed more interested in the color than the fact that the body had a surgical incision."

"Most of the victims have been prostitutes," he said, shaking his head. "It's kinda sorta legal here. And the girls all wear nail polish to identify who they work for. Being a pimp's illegal, as is running a brothel, or propositioning for sex, but the act of prostitution itself is legal. They work mostly out of bars, usually hotel bars. The color tells the bartender who the money goes to."

"You mean like girls with red fingernails work at the Hyatt and blue at the Holiday Inn?"

"Pretty much, but the hotels aren't quite that high-end. Hell, some of them would make a Motel-6 look good. And the girls will move around, one bar to another. The color keeps the money straight."

"Where would a girl with bright purple on her toenails work?" I asked.

"That I couldn't tell ya, Jesse." Neal arched one eyebrow. "It sure sounds to me like you're investigating."

"No, we're just on vacation," I replied, and we were.

Joining the girls, Neal and I took our seats.

"You really saw a whale shark?" Erin was asking Florence.

"We sure did," she replied excitedly. "And Dad took us out to swim alongside her."

"It," I corrected. "It was a young fish, maybe thirty feet."

"No claspers?" Neal asked.

I saw the light of book learning collide with memory in Florence's eyes. "It didn't have claspers! I remember now. So, it was either a female or an immature male. Oh, and we saw a spotted eagle ray and a bunch of manta rays, and two dolphins even stopped to look at us."

"That's the trifecta," Neal said. "Whale sharks this time of year are scarce, but we still see them sometimes. You're very lucky to have seen those three fish on a single dive."

"Chance favors the prepared mind," Florence said, quoting Louis Pasteur. "The whale shark was high above us. If Dad hadn't put the lights on top of the reef, we wouldn't have seen her...it."

"That's an unusual tattoo," Erin said, leaning forward and looking at my left forearm. "What is it?"

"Marine Force Recon," I replied. "I got that when I was much younger. Not much older than Florence."

"What do the different parts of it mean?" she asked.

"The wings say we're dumb enough to jump out of perfectly good aircraft," I said. "Something I don't recommend. The oars signify small boat operations and the regulator's for underwater. We sometimes employed all three in a single op." Then I grinned at her. "The skull's just for effect."

"When were you a Marine?"

I kind of let the *were* slide. "I earned the title and swore the oath when I was seventeen—neither had an expiration date—and I retired twenty years later."

"Once a Marine, always a Marine," Savannah said. Then she smiled at me. "It's a knuckle-dragger thing they never let go of."

A small powerboat zipped past, heading toward the cut. With the *Dog's* deep, heavy keel, she didn't rock much, but we did bob up and down a little.

"Sometimes," Neal said, "I think the cavemen had it better. If another caveman got out of line, like that yahoo, he got clubbed."

The sound of music began to waft across the water; steel drums and acoustic guitars, amplified. And a sax. It sounded like they were just tuning up and doing sound checks. Florence looked toward shore, and I could see in her eyes that she wanted to go. Kids needed social interaction.

"Would anyone like a sundowner?" Savannah asked, rising and moving toward the cockpit.

Neal patted the small cooler he'd brought along. "I'm good."

"Why don't we go ashore?" I said. "Dance and listen to some music for a couple of hours."

Florence's eyes sparkled. "Can we?"

Savannah stopped and looked at me. "You dance? I don't think we can all fit in the dinghy. And what about dinner?"

Savannah's mind had a way of working on several things at one time. She could carry on two conversations or stories at once, jumping back and forth, one to the other. I didn't know which one to address first.

"We can eat a little later," I said. "I'm still full from lunch."

"The hell with the dinghy," Neal said, putting an un-opened beer back in his cooler and closing it. "We can take my boat. There's usually room at the Sea Star pier and I'm friends with a guy there."

"It's still early," Erin said. "Come on, Savvy. We can eat later."

"Then let's go," I said, smiling at Savannah. "And yes, I've danced before."

Neal made a phone call to confirm we could tie his boat up at the pier, and off we went.

Neal's boat wasn't a whole lot bigger than my dinghy, a little over seventeen feet maybe, with a low gunwale aft and a higher bow. It was probably built local—at least

I didn't recognize the shape and it had no markings—but it did have a reliable Yamaha outboard that cranked up with just a touch of the starter. The girls rode in the open bow and I stood next to Neal at the helm. The boat wasn't fancy, but it was well-equipped and functional.

"Who was the cop that came out there?" Neal asked, keeping his voice low as we headed across the lagoon at just above idle speed.

With the engines burbling behind us and the windscreen in front, the girls couldn't hear us.

"Sergeant Elden Garcia," I replied. "I'd like to talk to him again, but without the whole police department knowing."

"Good kid," Neal said. "His dad used to be the police superintendent here in San Pedro. Want me to have him meet us?"

"Can you do it without it seeming obvious?" I asked, taking my cellphone out of my pocket.

"No problem," he replied. "He works for me on his days off."

While Neal called Garcia, I fired off a quick text message to Chyrel, asking her to dig into what was happening.

Neal ended his call and nodded. "He's still at work, but he said he'll be here in an hour."

It was a short ride to the pier and we quickly tied up in front of one of the dive boats.

The Dive Bar was aptly named. It was the first place you came to when you left the dive boats. It was little more than a framework of beams and a thatch roof over an open-air bar that spilled right out onto the beach, just like a thousand others throughout *El Caribe*. This one had the advantage of proximity to excited tourist divers; a place to unwind after a dive and trade stories and pictures. There were tables and chairs on the beach out front, even a swing set for kids.

The stage was a small, wooden platform, about six inches above the sand. Under the shade, the band—a guitarist, a steel drum player, and a saxophonist—were getting their equipment set up and warming up.

We found a table in the shade and soon the waitress took our drink orders. When the band started, Florence grabbed my hand and said, "It's time to prove you can dance."

Fortunately for me, the band was playing island music, which is perfectly suited for dancing in the sand, as you mostly let the music move you around while your feet just shuffle.

The song ended and we went back to the table. Out on the pier, the dive boat that we'd passed coming in was tying off and the divers were unloading their gear.

Soon the place began to fill up with mostly young people, dive bags stashed beside their tables. There wasn't any dress code and several women wore just their bikinis, some with shorts over the bottoms. Most of the men wore trunks and T-shirts, or no shirt at all. Nobody wore shoes. Island casual.

Savannah took my hand and pulled me up again as the band started a slower tune that sounded familiar. "Come on," she said. "You're gonna dance with me at least this once. Who knows when you'll feel like it again?"

I'd heard the song before, but it was different. I couldn't remember who the artist was or the name of the tune, but it was the same song Rusty and his wife Sidney had danced to when they got married. But these guys were doing it a bit slower, with a sultry, island beat.

With Savannah's arms around my neck and my hands on her hips, we moved together, pulling one another closer. I could feel her hips gyrating in an all-too-familiar figure-eight. I danced her backward in a shuffle step and she stayed right with me. I turned slightly, so we were side by side, but still facing opposite, and I danced her backward in the same short shuffle. When I turned to face her again, I took a slow step back for the song's chorus. Savannah wrapped one long leg around mine and leaned into me dramatically.

A cheer rose up from our table and a few others joined in around the bar. I'd forgotten anyone else was around.

"You surprise me," she said, as we held each other and swayed to the music. "I didn't know Neanderthals could dance like this. Where'd you learn?"

"Dance lessons in school," I lied.

Sometimes, an innocent white lie could alleviate hurt. Dancing was low on my list of pastimes in high school, and later, when I was in the Marine Corps, there were even fewer opportunities. I'd never been much of a dancer. But I'd once spent over a year in a rum- and pot-induced haze, and during that time, I'd met a girl. A much younger girl, who was the epitome of the free spirit. She'd been the one to show me how to dance around a beach fire, and first got me interested in guitar.

She'd taught me other things, too. Things that were sure to put me on a prison bus straight to hell.

"Is that—" Savannah's eyes trailed off over my shoulder.

I turned to look and saw Garcia talking to Neal.

"I wonder what he's doing here?" Savannah asked as the song ended, and we started back to the table.

CHAPTER SEVENTEEN

"**Y**ou have more questions?" Savannah asked Sergeant Garcia.

His dark eyes flicked, almost imperceptibly, from her to me. I shook my head and his eyes went back to Savannah.

"No, ma'am," Garcia said. "I saw Neal and Erin and stopped to talk. I help him give lessons to di younger drivers sometimes."

She looked over at me, and I could tell she'd seen his furtive glance. Then she waved to the empty chair. "Please join us."

He did and we talked about the weather, teaching kids to drive, the dive last night, my boat, the permit bite, and anything else—except the murder—until finally, Florence spoke up.

"Have you learned anything about last night?" she asked Garcia.

Again, his eyes cut to mine before responding. "It is an ongoing investigation," he said. "But no, we learned nothing more today."

Savannah glanced at me and I looked away.

"I'm going to the bar," I said. "Anyone need anything?"

"Yeah," Neal said, draining his beer.

Erin and Florence both nodded, but Savannah said no.

"If you are buying di rum," Garcia said, rising from his seat, "di least I can do is help you carry di glasses."

He was a cool one, but I was already starting to suspect that his being here didn't seem like much of a coincidence to Savannah.

At the bar, I placed the order with the bartender and turned to face Garcia. "You didn't say last night what the toenail polish meant."

He eyed me suspiciously. "Neal said you work as an investigator for a research company. I checked you out but did not see mention of that. May I ask what company?"

"Armstrong Research," I replied.

A slow smile turned up one corner of his mouth slightly. "We know of dem," he said. "What is it dat you do for Mr. Jack Armstrong?"

Though Travis Stockwell had said Armstrong had a lot of pull with many local law enforcement organizations, it was kind of a surprise way down here in the bottom corner of the Caribbean.

Travis was my handler. Before that, he'd been a deputy director for Homeland Security, and Deuce's boss. Before that, he was an Army Airborne colonel. I respected the man a lot.

"I watch and listen," I replied. "Sometimes I fix things that are broken."

"I see," he said, as the bartender brought our drinks. Then he leaned in close as he picked up two glasses. "Can you meet me here later tonight? Alone?"

"What time?" I asked, picking up Neal's beer and tucking it under one arm so I could carry the other two glasses.

"Midnight," he said, and turned toward the table.

Florence was talking to a group of the younger people from the dive boat and soon was dancing with one young man. They danced for several songs while they talked; something I couldn't do if I tried.

When she returned to the table, she said his name was David and he was a sophomore at University of Florida.

"He asked me if I dived," she said, "and when I said I did, he asked me if I'd like to dive with them tomorrow. Can I?"

"You don't know anything about this boy," Savannah said.

My eyes went to the table where the young man sat with his friends. He looked my way and smiled, nodding his head slightly. My eyes shot toward the beach and my head bobbed that way just a little. The smile left his face.

"Excuse me for just a minute," I said, and stood up.

"Dad, no," Florence said.

"He knows what he's doing, Flo," Savannah said, as I walked toward the group of divers.

David rose from his seat as I walked past, and he followed after me. I stopped after we were far enough away

217

to talk over the music and turned to face him. He was about six feet tall, tanned, and trim.

"I'm sorry for asking your daughter without asking you first, sir," David said.

"How old are you?"

"Twenty, just last month."

"Did my daughter tell you she was seventeen?"

"Yes, sir," he replied. "It's just a dive."

"She said you go to UF. Why aren't you in school?"

"My classes are Monday to Wednesday and I work Thursday to Saturday, but this is MLK weekend, so I took time off work to come down here with some friends."

"What's your last name, David?" I asked, my eyes fixed on his.

"Stone, sir," he replied with a gulp. "David Stone. I'm from Florida."

"Where in Florida, David Stone?"

"The Port Charlotte area, on the west coast. A small town nobody's ever heard of."

"Try me," I said.

His Adam's apple bobbed again. "It's called Alva."

"Out on Highway 80?" I asked. "Know where Rainwater 4X4 is?"

"I've been out that way," he said. "The guy who runs the place doesn't seem to like kids hanging around. But he builds some serious trucks."

"I've known Billy Rainwater since I was a kid. My family and his were close. Billy and I are blood-brothers and we served in the Marine Corps together. He knows just about everyone in rural Hendry County. It's a pretty sure bet he knows your dad, David Stone."

"Yes, sir. I understand." He swallowed hard. "Would it be okay if I escorted your daughter on a dive tomorrow?"

"Are you a good diver?"

"Yes, sir." He finally became a bit more animated. "I've been diving since I was fifteen and love the sport. I have a Rescue C-card and I plan to take the divemaster course this summer."

"Morning or afternoon?"

"Uh...Morning."

"Think you can get the boat to stop by my ketch to pick Florence up on the way out and drop her back off on the way in?"

He looked past me toward where *Salty Dog* lay sedately at anchor, the setting sun painting her hull a burnt orange. "That's yours?"

"Yes, she is," I replied. "When you drop Florence off after the dive, you're welcome to stay aboard for a while if you like. I'll see that you get safely back to shore."

He smiled. "Thank you, sir. I'm sure I can get the dive boat captain to do that. There's plenty of room, if you and your wife want to go too."

"No, we'll wait for our daughter's safe return," I said without correcting him. "And stop calling me sir."

"Um...what should I call you?"

"Mr. McDermitt for now."

"Thank you, Mr. McDermitt."

I left him standing there and returned to our table. Sergeant Garcia had left.

"What'd you say to him?" Florence whispered harshly. "Did you embarrass me?"

"If he can convince the dive boat operator to stop by the *Dog*, you can go, and he'll visit for a bit after he brings you back."

"Really?" Florence asked. "I thought you were gonna clobber him or something."

Savannah smiled at me, then turned to Florence and patted her hand, as only a southern lady would. "Now, honey, you know your daddy only clobbers *bad* people. So, I think we can rest assured that young man *isn't* a bad person. And I'd bet the farm that he won't do anything bad tomorrow."

"Clobber a guy for wanting to spend time with a pretty girl?" I said, smiling back at Savannah. "Then someone needs to clobber me."

Later that evening, after sunset, we headed back to the *Salty Dog* for dinner and stargazing. The food was great and, sitting on the foredeck with our backs to the lights from shore, the stars were brilliant all the way down to the eastern horizon.

A gentle breeze out of the east-southeast had the bow pointed in that direction. The wind arrived unimpeded by land for almost two thousand miles and on it there was a faint, tropical West Indian scent. The smell of the Windward Islands.

We talked, but my mind kept wandering to what Garcia wanted to talk to me about later.

Florence looked at her phone for about the twentieth time, then stood and folded her chair. "It's ten o'clock and the dive boat leaves at six. David talked to the operator and they'll pick me up. I should go to bed."

"Yeah," Neal said. "We'd better get home, too."

He and Erin stood, and she hugged Savannah. "Great dinner, Savvy. Thanks for having us. We're still on for later in the week?"

"We'll be there," Savannah said.

Everyone said their goodbyes, then Florence went down below with Woden, as Savannah and I helped Neal and Erin get down to their boat and cast off.

A few minutes later, the little boat puttered toward the cut, both Neal and Erin sitting at the console.

"They're nice," I said, watching them go.

"What time are you meeting that policeman?"

I looked over at Savannah. "I'm—" I could tell in her eyes that she knew, and decided she deserved the truth— "meeting him at the Dive Bar at midnight."

She took my hand and led me forward along the wide side deck. We sat down and gazed silently up at the night sky. She didn't say a word for several minutes—just held my hand.

"I don't want you to quit what you do, Jesse," she finally said. Then she turned her head to face me. "You're a good man; you're smart, very skilled, tough, and loyal. I know that. And I know that you will always come back."

I started to say something, but she placed a finger to my lips.

"Hush now, let me finish this. I know there's a chance that one day you might come back needing to be patched up, and I'll be there to do that. I'm not the same woman you knew before, running from a bad marriage. That woman was weak. And I'm not weak anymore. You go meet Sergeant Garcia. And if you can, you should help him stop whoever is hurting these people. You're good at it. Charity told me. I'll be right here when you get back."

If I had any reservations about her, they were gone now. When we'd first met, Savannah had been any-thing *but* a weak woman. That she was now stronger was self-evident.

We sat and watched the stars for another hour before she kissed me goodnight and went below. Finn followed me to the stern, where I pulled the dinghy around to the port side boarding ladder and tied it off.

I looked down at my dog in the moonlight. I knew I didn't have to tell him to keep guard over Savannah and Florence, but I think he somehow expected me to say it.

"I'll be back in an hour or two," I said quietly, as I climbed down to the dinghy. "Keep watch."

Hearing that last word, Finn stepped back and sat down, his head on a swivel.

CHAPTER EIGHTEEN

I drove the dinghy up onto the beach, killing the motor and raising it just before the hull hit the bottom. Then I climbed out and used the painter, slung over my shoulder, to pull it higher.

I sat on the starboard side and pulled my sat phone out of my pocket. It was close to midnight, but I knew Billy would still be up.

"Aren't you too old to be up this late?" he said instead of hello.

"You're only as old as you feel, brother. How's Leaping Panther?"

"No different," Billy said. "Well, maybe a little. Two girls came to see him a few months ago, a white girl and an island girl with two spirits. They had a dog. A big German shepherd named Whiskey. Dad seemed to connect with the dog for a bit."

"You should get him one," I suggested.

"I did."

That was a full conversation with Billy. The dog incident must have left quite an impression. He didn't usually speak in multiple sentences.

"Do you know a kid by the name of David Stone? Lives over in Alva."

"Good kid," he replied. "Comes from a good family. Why?"

"He's taking my daughter diving."

"Isn't he a little young for Kim? She's what? Thirty?"

"Come July," I replied. "But it's not Kim. Savannah's and my daughter, Florence."

"His dad and I have worked together on some community projects," Billy said. "David helped us build a playground. If I had a daughter her age, I'd allow him to date her."

"Thanks. That means a lot."

We talked a few minutes more, or mostly I did. We agreed to get together in the spring for some fishing, then I ended the call and walked up to the Dive Bar.

When Garcia arrived, I was sitting at the end of the bar drinking a coffee. There were still a few people there; all but one patron sat at tables, and the only one at the bar was at the other end and in no condition to remember anything.

Garcia nodded and sat down next to me, but not too close. He waited until the bartender took his order before saying, "Let's walk," without even looking over at me.

The bartender put the rum drink in front of him. "Put it on your tab, Elden?"

Garcia nodded and without another word to me, headed toward the beach. Apparently, he wanted more isolation than just the two of us meeting alone in a bar. That meant he was worried about being seen talking to anyone.

I gave him a head start while I finished my coffee, then laid a five on the bar. I'd seen Garcia walk to the water's edge and turn north, so I left the bar by a different route and worked my way along the edge of the brush and palm trees, then angled toward the water until I caught up to him.

"Very discreet," I said.

"There is a reason," he explained, but didn't elaborate.

We stopped walking and faced one another in the darkness. "Earlier," he began, "you said you sometimes fix things that are broken as part of what you do for Jack Armstrong."

It wasn't a question, just him searching for a response. "How is it you know my employer?"

"A cousin, who is a policeman in Panama, told me about your organization." Even though we were very alone, he looked around. "Do you also break things that are fixed?"

I couldn't tell if it was an accusation or a philosophically deep question. Break things that are fixed? Fixed in what way? My instinct, after what had happened earlier in the week in Mexico, told me to be wary.

"I'm not sure I understand what you mean," I said.

Though the darkness hid a lot, the light from the moon was bright enough that I could see his features clearly as he studied mine. I tried to maintain a passive expression, but I'd been told many times to avoid big stakes poker.

He sighed, seeming to reach a decision. "There is corruption in my country, Mr. McDermitt. Even in my own small *polees*."

"In what way?" I asked.

"No man should be above the law," he said. "Yet, money and power can sometimes buy it."

"Does this have to do with the murders? You know who's behind them?"

"No," he replied quickly. "I mean, yes, it is about di murders, but I don't know who it is. Dis is the first one out here on Ambergris. All di others have been on di mainland. But I have friends in other *polees* who tell me solving di murders is not very high on der leaders' priorities."

"Because they're hookers?" I asked.

"Not that. One friend said he is sure der is an outside force slowing di investigation. Someone with a lot of money."

For a cop to talk so openly about corruption in his department was unusual, to say the least. Asking an outsider for help was practically unheard of. Yet, I could see that was the direction this clandestine meeting's conversation was going.

"Last night's murder might not have *happened* here," I said, "but the body *was* found here, so at least that scene is under your jurisdiction. Neal said your father used to be the superintendent here. Who is now?"

"I am acting superintendent," he replied. "My father took ill last summer and den two months ago, he was forced to retire. I stepped up until a new superintendent can be assigned."

"And nobody has approached *you* about turning a blind eye?"

"Not yet. But I fear what will happen if and when someone does. I have a family here and being a *polees* is all I know."

A *fix*, I thought. Someone is fixing things, so the investigation is stalled.

"And you want me to help rid the whole Belizean police force of corruption? That's a tall order."

"What do you do when you find a poisonous snake in your garden?"

"Ah, I get it," I said. "You want me to go after the guy who's paying to have the cops look the other way. Cut off the head of the snake?"

"Yes," he replied. "I would go to di mainland and dig around myself. But I am too well-known among my people. As are most of di *polees*."

He handed me a sheet of paper, torn from a spiral notepad, about the size of the one he'd made notes on aboard *Salty Dog* the night before.

"Basic details of each murder," he said. "With notes of where each one happened and who di girl worked for. Or at least di color of di womens' nails. Who a prostitute works for is one of di best kept secrets in Belize."

I looked at the paper, but the light was too low to read it. I folded it once and put it in my shirt pocket. "Is there a way I can reach you?"

He handed me a card while once more looking around nervously. "My official cell phone is on di front. Use di number on di back."

Garcia turned and continued walking toward the north. I added the card to my pocket and fell in beside him.

"Is there a cop in Belize City you can trust?" I asked.

"Yes, but five of di eight murders happened in Orange Walk Town."

He meant the small city to the north, farther inland. It wasn't far from the Hondo River, the western border with Mexico.

"Why do you suppose that is?" I asked.

He shrugged. "There are more prostitutes there."

"What do you know about anatomy?" I asked.

"More than I ever wanted to," he replied. "Di murders were done so di killer could steal organs—human organs. Why?"

"I'd surmised that," I replied. "But the girl last night had an incision in the front. So, unless the killer wanted to wade through her insides, it's the wrong way to get to the kidneys."

"Di pancreas is in front," he said, pointing at the middle of his torso. "Under di stomach. If dat was what was taken from di girl, it is di second one. It's in my notes; a pancreas, a spleen, a liver, and six kidneys."

"That's ten."

He stopped and turned toward me. "Di first three victims would have survived, if they had been found sooner. Di killer only took one kidney from each. Di next two victims had both kidneys removed."

In police terms, that was called "escalating violence." A person could live with just one kidney. After getting away clean the first three times, the killer had become greedy. I assumed other organs brought a higher price for the same reason. Someone could get a kidney donated from a living person, but there was only one of most of the other organs; those could only be procured from a recently deceased donor.

"I'll go up to Orange Walk and see what I can find out," I offered. "But I can't guarantee anything."

"Der is one other thing," Garcia said. "In my notes, you will see dat di seven prostitutes wore three different colors—red, pink, and di one with purple you discovered. But there are two more colors. None of the girls who wear yellow or blue have been killed."

Five colors for five pimps, I thought. And the killer was only preying on three.

"What about the boy?" I asked. "Do you have any idea why he was targeted?"

"He was a young man dat came here with a group of divers back in November," he said. "He disappeared from his group at a bar."

"Same kind of bar?" I asked. "A hotel bar where prostitutes go?"

"No. He disappeared from a bar in Placencia dat allows homosexuals."

I stopped walking. "Allows?"

"It is against the law here," he replied.

"Being gay is against the law? You gotta be kidding. How can a person not be who they are?"

"It is tolerated by many and some even accept it," Garcia said. "But it is still illegal. Belize will not allow a person into di country who is openly homosexual."

That was something I didn't know, not that I pondered it much.

"Was this boy gay?"

"According to his friends, no. The Barefoot Bar caters to homosexuals, but his friends said they did not know that."

"I hear a *but* in there."

"A friend in Placencia was working dat case and talked to di boy's family. Dey knew he was a homosexual but didn't tell anyone."

"Gay," I said. "They prefer the terms gay or lesbian."

"We are not so progressive a country as America," he said, shrugging again.

"Okay, I'll start in Orange Walk. Do you know any officers there who would be trustworthy?"

"If you need help, you can call di *polees* dispatch and tell them you would like to talk to Sergeant JP Menendez. Orange Walk Town is like your Wild West in some ways. JP is di only person out der I trust."

We shook hands and I promised I'd let him know anything I found out. Then we parted.

Tiny waves washed silently onto the sand as I walked slowly along the beach. I was thinking about how I would approach this and how much I should tell Savannah. I'd be going to bars and would be talking to known prostitutes. That could never be a good thing for a relationship.

My phone vibrated in my pocket and I pulled it out. I had an email from Chyrel.

CHAPTER NINETEEN

The sounds coming from the basement fell on deaf ears—both literally and figuratively. The only two people who resided in the sprawling ranch house northwest of Dangriga were Casey Jasso and his Mestizo cook, Juan, who'd lost his hearing to meningitis when he was a small boy. Juan had come to work for Casey just a year earlier and couldn't hear the cries for help coming up from below. Besides the two of them, there wasn't anyone else around for miles.

There was only Casey to hear the screams and wails emanating from the basement. And Casey enjoyed such sounds.

After taking off from Zotov's yacht, Casey had flown very low, going due east for five minutes, and covering more than eight miles. To anyone watching from the high bridge of the big yacht, he'd simply flown over the horizon and beyond their sight.

There, he'd climbed steeply to 1000 feet, knowing Zotov would be watching on his radar for Casey to follow his instructions to ditch the girl from high altitude. Then he dove again and hugged the water as he made a beeline for home with his prize. He didn't think the Russian's radar could pick up anything as small as a person's body falling from a helicopter.

At least, he hoped not.

The Russian woman had awakened as they'd neared the coastline. Though still groggy and in pain, she'd begun to struggle weakly and thrash about. That wasn't good in a small, two-seat helicopter going ninety miles per hour just above the waves. But Casey had been prepared and plunged a syringe into the meaty part of the inside of her bare thigh. Her struggles became weaker and she'd once more slumped against the door. Casey had reached over with his left hand and fondled the woman roughly, until his hand was needed on the collective to land the helo.

It'd been Juan's day to go down to Placencia for supplies and Casey hadn't expected him to return until just before dark. He'd had no trouble carrying the woman into his home, then down the steps to the basement. There, he'd unlocked a door that led into a deeper, second basement.

This deeper part of the basement had been excavated two years earlier, by a team of four Guatemalan workmen, using only picks, shovels, and hand tools. Blasting through the rock wouldn't have been possible with the house directly above. It was hard, back-breaking work, and at first, had been performed in cramped quarters. The digging had progressed much faster once there was room for all four to work. Each morning, rock and dirt from the previous day was hauled out, using yokes and five-gallon buckets.

He'd paid the men well and had worked them hard. So hard that they hadn't bothered to go into town to blow their pay on cheap women and cheaper booze. He'd fed them and given them a place to sleep at night in the bunkhouse, where they drank beer and tequila. So, they had stayed at the ranch throughout the project. If they weren't eating, drinking, or sleeping, they were working. He'd promised a bonus for every day the basement was completed ahead of schedule and gave them a month to complete the excavation.

It only took three weeks to dig out and shore up the lower basement, creating a room about twenty feet by fifteen. He'd explained to the men that it was going to be a wine cellar, and indeed, the room stayed a constant 65° down there, day or night.

When the men were finished with the job and had poured a new concrete floor, Casey'd put a bullet into each one's head as their "bonus." He also took back the money he'd paid them, and dumped their bodies, one at a time, far out to sea.

Casey had then finished the interior work himself last winter. There was an old-fashioned stockade in one corner and a table with manacles at one end as well as at the bottom of the legs at the opposite end. Next to it stood a Saint Andrews cross with leather restraints at the four corners of the X-shaped wooden beams.

An electric hoist was mounted to the ceiling and hanging from it was a steel beam with four more leather restraints attached at one-foot intervals. Casey was particularly fond of the hoist because of its versatility. It could easily hold the weight of two people, dangling above the floor like sides of beef, helpless and at his mercy—a quality Casey didn't possess. Or all four restraints could be used on the wrists and ankles of just one slave, dangling her by all fours, exposed and vulnerable.

After unlocking the door to the lower basement, Casey switched on the light. He heard a frightened gasp from the Russian woman and grinned as he took a slow step down. Day or night, if the light wasn't on, Casey's dungeon was thrust into absolute, numbing darkness.

"Being in the dark and strapped to a table," he called out, as he continued slowly down the steps, "yeah, it can be pretty scary, huh?"

"*Poshol nahui!*" the Russian woman shrieked, then struggled against the bonds that held her wrists to the tabletop. Her arms were stretched to their limits.

Oh, we're going to get to that, Casey thought. He'd intentionally not violated her yet for a reason. The breaking began with being observed as a mere object. Sex would come later.

He was surprised at her endurance. For the last four hours, she'd been screaming almost non-stop. Juan had returned, his truck loaded with a week's worth of supplies, and then gone about his business, completely oblivious to the high-pitched wails coming from below. While the two men had eaten dinner, Casey had marveled at the woman's energy level and vocal range while conversing with Juan, who read lips.

Casey knew a little sign language. He'd learned it to impress a deaf girl in high school, who had a really hot body. The closest he'd ever gotten to reading lips, was when she'd used hers on him.

Everyone had a breaking point. Even the hard-as-nails Russian spy. And Casey knew how to find it. For some it was the darkness, for others, it was humiliation. Occasionally, one would require the administration of pain. Casey was quite capable of doing any of that.

And more.

When Casey reached the bottom of the stairs, he crossed the floor slowly, admiring his work as he approached the table. He hadn't bothered to straighten her clothing when he bound her to the rough-hewn tabletop. Fear and humiliation were also part of the training. Waking up in total darkness, bent over and bound to a table, clothes disheveled, and unable to do anything about it was usually enough.

Casey glanced down at the Russian woman's feet. She'd lost one of her expensive high heels somewhere, so with one stiletto on and her ankles strapped to the legs of the table, her bare hips were tilted slightly. Uncomfortable, but that too was part of what he had in mind. The woman wasn't going to know comfort until she broke.

Casey knelt and took the woman's hair in one hand, yanking her head up to face him. "What is your name?"

"*Poshyel k chyertu!*" she spat venomously.

"Unusual name," he said. "But Posh it is."

Casey knew enough Russian to understand that she'd told him to go to hell, not given him her name.

She struggled against her bindings, but it was useless.

"Do you speak English, Posh?"

"*Nyet!*" she hissed, though in answering, she'd conveyed that she did at least understand.

Casey stood and looked down the length of her body. The white, blood-stained dress was bunched around her narrow waist and the high-cut lacy black underwear she wore below it was twisted to one side.

"Here's how this is going to work, Posh," Casey said, as he took a small device from a shelf.

The device was long and had a forked tip at one end and a leather handle with a trigger at the other.

"I'm going to ask you some questions," he said, turning the device on.

It made a whining sound, increasing in pitch. He touched the tip to the top of a metal chair in front of his prisoner and pressed the trigger. It created a buzzing, electrical spark as electricity arced across the forks.

Fear. Apprehension. Anticipation. Submission tactics, which Casey had learned from the best.

The low whine of the prod increased pitch as it recharged.

"Every time you refuse to answer a question, lie, give me the wrong answer, or hell, anything I don't want to hear, I'm gonna give you a jolt."

"*Yest' steyk iz trubki!*" she yelled, shaking her head vigorously. Her blond hair flew in all directions as she flexed every muscle in her body in an attempt to break free.

Casey laughed at the vulgar tube steak expression and at her futile struggling. Then he touched the prongs to her side, just above her left hip. When he pressed the trigger, her body spasmed and jumped for just a second before the charge was depleted. Then she screamed at the top of her lungs, fury pouring from the depths of her soul.

Nearly a full day she'd been immobilized on that table, and she still had some fight left in her. Casey was impressed.

"Do you speak English?" he asked once more, moving around the table to her legs.

The device made the whining sound again, growing steadily higher.

"*Za cyun v shopu!*" the woman shouted, trying to turn her head to look back at him.

"Stick it in *my* ass?" Casey roared, laughing in response, as he placed the prod's handle between her cheeks, sliding the two-foot long shaft slowly back and forth like a handsaw. "No, baby, that's not the way this game is played."

With one quick move, he pulled the handle back until the tip found its mark and the woman's back arched as her ass rose and quaked violently. When the charge was spent, her hips thumped back onto the table. She began sobbing.

"One more time," Casey said, turning the device's dial. It made an audible click as the whine intensified. "That click you just heard was me turning the voltage up. Now, do you speak English, Posh?"

"*Da*," she mumbled.

"What was that, Posh? I didn't quite hear you."

The whine continued to rise as the device recharged.

"Yes," she whimpered between sobs. "My name...is not Posh...and you know it. Please don't hurt me."

"So, you lied?" He put the prod against the tender flesh of her inner thigh and hit the trigger.

The woman's right leg tensed and shook violently. She turned her ankle, breaking the heel right off the only red-soled shoe she still had on.

Laughing, Casey put the prod back on the shelf and pulled her head up by the hair again. Once the first barrier was broken the rest came easy.

He studied her face. The swelling around her left eye had subsided a little, but she was going to have one helluva black eye. Still, nothing seemed broken and what had once looked like hamburger was only clotted blood from small cuts that would heal easily.

She was unusually beautiful. Someone somewhere was going to miss her. He'd have only a short time to make as much as possible with her. Then he could "retire" her to the deep or sell her overseas.

"You're going to live by my rules now," he said. "When I think you're ready, you can leave this room. But we still have a long way to go, don't we? What is your name?"

"Yelena," she moaned.

He released her hair and her face dropped to the table. She slowly rolled her head, so her injured side was off the rough surface.

Casey walked around to her side and lightly caressed the spot he'd first shocked. She flinched uncontrollably, which made him laugh once again.

"Now see?" Casey said, going to a desk and opening a drawer. "That wasn't so hard."

When he turned back to face her, he was holding a woman's jar of nail polish. "Now, if you hold real still and don't cause me to mess up, I won't have to get that prod down again. Do you understand?"

Yelena nodded her head slightly.

"Say it."

"*Da*, I understand."

"*Da, ser*," he corrected her. "You will always address me as sir or master. Is that clear?"

"*Da, ser*," she whined, her breathing wracked with sobs.

Casey pulled the chair over and the scraping sound on the floor caused her to flinch.

"After this," he said, placing the chair in front of the table where her hands were bound, "I might clean your face up a little and see to those cuts."

Within minutes, Casey had painted her fingernails and toenails a bright yellow, then stood back to admire his handiwork. If anything, the color seemed to deepen her tan. She was tough, but sooner or later, they all submitted. Eventually, they all thought that he was the only person in the world who understood them.

"What is your last name, Yelena?" he asked, placing his right hand on her bare shoulder, just above her dress.

"Kotova," she moaned. Her shoulder muscles twitched at his touch. "My name is Yelena Kotova."

Casey leaned on the table, as if he were surveying an all-you-can-eat buffet to figure out where to start.

"So nice to meet you, Yelena Kotova," he said, running a hand down the small of her back and over her rump. He gave it a sharp smack. "But you know what? I think I like Posh better."

He lifted his hand and her whole body began to quiver with the anticipation of another smack.

Without warning, Casey grabbed the material at the top of her dress in both hands and violently ripped it apart. The zipper gave way but stopped at the bottom. Yelena screamed as he moved lower and continued to savagely rip the dress from her body. He yanked furiously at the thin straps, which dug deep into her skin before breaking. Then he jerked the dress from beneath her body and threw it across the room.

"Why you do this?" Yelena cried out, as Casey moved back into her line of sight.

"Like I said," he replied, pulling his shirt off. "We're just getting warmed up here."

CHAPTER TWENTY

Savannah woke me, caressing my back. I blinked my eyes open and could see through the aft portholes that it was just starting to get light. I rolled onto my side and she curled into my embrace.

"What time are you leaving?" she whispered.

There was no avoiding it. She knew.

"After the dive boat gets here," I replied. "I'll be back by midafternoon."

"That's why you wanted that young man to stay, isn't it?"

"That's part of it," I admitted.

"This is kind of Flo's first date."

"Really?"

"Well, if you count going diving with a young man as a date, it is. She's hung out on the beach with boys, always in a group setting, though."

Once more, she was deflecting by talking about something other than what was on her mind.

"Are you sure you're okay with me looking to see what I can find out?" I asked.

"Of course," she replied, but I detected a bit of apprehension.

"I promise," I said, kissing her forehead, "I'm just going to have a look around Orange Walk."

She rose up onto an elbow. "Orange Walk? I heard it's one of the most dangerous—"

"Bad people look for *easy* targets," I said, pulling her back into my arms. "Always remember that. Appearing vulnerable makes you a target. I'm rarely seen as a target, much less an easy one. Unless I want to be."

"I want to believe that," she said. "If only half of what Charity's told me is true, I shouldn't worry in the least. But I'd be lying if I said I wasn't."

"Worry's good," I said. "It keeps a person alert. Just don't let it consume you."

"We'd better get up," she said, pushing me away. "The boat will be here soon to pick up Flo, and I need to make breakfast."

I held her in place, my arms tight around her back. "Are you sure we don't have a few minutes?"

"I'm sure, Captain. Now let go of me and get your ass up."

"Aye, Admiral," I said, releasing her.

She rolled toward the edge of the bed and I followed. We dressed quickly, her for a day of boat chores, and me for a day of street walking.

Florence was already in the salon when we came up.

"Good morning!" she announced excitedly, while whisking eggs in a bowl. "What are y'all going to do all morning without me?"

Savannah glanced up at me and I nodded.

"I have a lot to do here," Savannah said, moving toward the stove and taking the bowl from her. "Let me do that. You have to make the bacon first, so you can cook the eggs in the grease. Jesse has some things to look into on the mainland."

Florence was used to her mother's way of talking about several subjects at one time. She looked up at me, worried, as Savannah set the bowl aside and dropped half a slab of bacon into the hot skillet.

"What things do you have to look into, Dad?"

I shrugged. "I'm just going walkabout. Maybe ask a few questions."

Florence looked from me back to Savannah and must have read the concern on her face, then put two and two together. "Don't worry, Mom. You remember what Charity said: 'If he could be hurt, he'd be dead ten times already.'"

I laughed. "Did she really say that?"

Florence's head bobbed. "Uh-huh. She said you've been shot, stabbed, blown up, and even smoked. But I don't get that last one."

"It was a long time ago," I said. "And being tied up and locked in a meat smoker with no fire going isn't the same as *being* smoked."

247

Savannah put two slices of bacon on each of two plates and scooped the rest onto mine. I picked up a piece and munched on it as she poured the whipped eggs into the pan. She stirred quickly, until the eggs were fluffy, and then doled out the same portions—a little helping of eggs on their plates and a lot on mine.

"I don't know where you put it," she said, handing me a plate.

"I weigh as much as the two of you put together," I said, moving toward the dinette.

"No, you don't," Florence said.

"You're what? Barely a hundred? I'm 225. The bigger the engine, the more fuel it needs."

Florence reached over and took a slice of bacon from my plate. "And I'm still growing."

Later, while Savannah and I washed the dishes, we heard a diesel-powered boat approaching. Up on deck, Woden barked once. Finn rose and trotted up the steps.

"Did Woden just call for backup?" Florence asked.

"It's crazy how the two of them behave together," Savannah said. "It's only been a couple of weeks and they already act like they think with a single mind."

I picked up Florence's dive bag and shouldered it. "Do you have everything?" I asked her, pulling my money clip out.

"Yeah, David said they have snacks and sodas on the boat and he already paid for my dive."

I peeled off five $20 bills and held them out to her.

"Pay him back," Savannah said. "Never allow a man to do for you if you can do for yourself."

I cocked my head toward Savannah. "What she said."

Florence glanced back and forth at the two of us. "Talk about thinking with one mind. Will he be embarrassed or offended?"

"Here," I said, taking her hand and putting the money in it. "If he is, that's his shortcoming. But I kind of think he'll appreciate it for what it is. An independent young woman settling a tab."

"Yeah, but I'm not really the one doing the settling."

"How do you figure?" I asked.

"It's your money, not mine."

"You worked hard helping sail down here," I said. "Good swabs are hard to come by."

Savannah covered a smile with her hand and shook her head. "Jesse and I both have more than we'll ever spend," she said. "You stand to inherit quite a fortune one day. Anything you get from either of us is coming out of that."

"And trust me," I added, "you won't be able to spend all you'll get, either. So, keep that in mind when you think about college. Do what you love to do, and your work will never be a job."

The three of us went up on deck. The sky was clear and light, though the sun hadn't risen over the reef yet. A red dive boat from Sea Star was approaching. David Stone stood on the starboard gunwale, one hand on the flybridge frame. The captain of the boat stood and waved, then expertly reversed his engine, stopping the boat just a few feet away.

Someone tossed a line, which I caught and used to pull the two boats closer together. Then I tied it off to the midship cleat.

"When you bring her back, can you stay a couple of hours?" I asked David, while handing him Florence's dive bag.

"Sure thing, Mr. McDermitt. What's up?"

"I have to take the dinghy somewhere," I said. "But I'll be back by three o'clock to get you back to shore."

"Dude," one of David's friends said, "we're going back out at two."

David glanced over at his friends, then back up at me. "No problem, Mr. McDermitt. Glad to do it. You can count on me."

With David's help, Florence hopped down to the other boat, and I untied the line.

"Be careful," Savannah said.

"Have fun and take lots of pictures," I added.

One of the crew coiled the line and David pushed the boat away with his foot. The captain put his vessel in gear and idled ahead slowly until he was clear of the *Dog*, then turned toward the cut and brought the engine up to speed.

I was anxious to get going. It was twenty miles to the mainland and then I'd have a four-mile hike to the nearest town.

The email Chyrel had sent me the previous night contained all the files from the official database of the Belizean Police about the murders, such as they were. Very little information had been entered about any of them, except the first girl. It was obvious, even to a layman like me, that the murder investigations were being quashed.

I'd replied to Chyrel's email asking what Armstrong assets might be in the area and she'd responded instantly, asking me what I needed. When I told her what and where, she'd written back to say that it would be waiting when I got there. With the contacts in Jack Armstrong's network, I had no doubt that it would be. But it was still a six-hour round-trip once I got going.

"The earlier you leave, the sooner you'll get back," Savannah said, reading my mind again.

I glanced at my watch—it was 0600. So, at the most, I'd have three hours to find out whatever I could in Orange Walk. That wasn't much time, and every minute I spent not moving was a minute less time poking around the town's seedy underbelly.

I shuddered.

"Don't worry," she said. "I texted Erin. Neal's working today, but she said she'd come out and keep me company for a few hours. If we need anything, she can take me into town."

"When did you do that?"

She smiled. "Before I woke you."

"You knew I'd be gone today?" I asked. "Even before you asked?"

"It's what you do, Jesse. You're inquisitive." She stood on her toes and kissed me. "That's a polite way of saying you're a nosy busybody and easy to predict. I'll get your go bag."

I watched her walk to the companionway steps, where she turned her head and smiled before going below.

I shook my head. "Unbelievable."

Finn and Woden both looked at me, cocking their heads toward one another.

"You guys wouldn't understand," I told them, then went to the stern to pull the dinghy over to the port side.

Was I simply a busybody sticking his nose in where it didn't belong? I didn't like thinking of myself in those terms. I didn't like to see innocent people victimized. And what was that about being predictable? In all things, I'd always strived to be just the opposite. Predictability could get you killed.

Savannah came back up with my light-weight tactical backpack. The one with the concealed bottom that held a Sig Sauer 9mm pistol.

We kissed and said our goodbyes. Minutes later, I was zipping across the lagoon to the southwest.

CHAPTER TWENTY-ONE

I found a tidal creek that I could run the dinghy up into a ways, then pulled it up onto shore between some overhanging mangroves. I covered it with a few dead palm fronds, then pulled my phone out. The GPS showed where I was, and the compass app gave me a direction to work toward. I set off, slogging through a primordial tidal marsh. The ground became firmer after a quarter mile, and when I got to dry sand, I kicked and scraped my muddy boots on a log.

Half an hour later, I reached a road of sorts. The GPS indicated that it was Old Northern Highway and the town of Lucky Strike was to my right. I started walking that way. When I came to a tree with a branch that hung out over the road, I stopped and opened my backpack. In one of the pockets was a roll of yellow ribbon. I cut off a short piece and tied it to the branch before continuing.

To include the word *old* in the name of the road didn't just mean there was another, newer Northern Highway somewhere.

And the word *highway* in the name should've just been tossed.

The road I walked on was a patchwork of long-ago repair jobs, cracks, and potholes. It was barely a lane wide and there was a nearly continuous rut on both sides, where vehicles had pulled over to pass one another.

In the tropics there were only two seasons—wet and dry. The wet season ended in November, so it probably hadn't rained very much in this area for over a month. The ruts were in dry, crumbly mud, meaning cars hadn't passed one another here since the rainy season. Maybe even the one before that. I'd have been surprised to see any kind of vehicle.

A short, five-minute walk got me to the outskirts of Lucky Strike, which was barely more than a wide spot in the jungle. Apparently, when they'd built the new Northern Highway, this little settlement had been nearly abandoned.

Ahead, parked on the shoulder, was an ancient Land Rover. When I reached it, I went around to the right side and opened the door. As I lowered the sun visor, a single key fell onto the seat.

"Thanks, Chyrel," I said, tossing my pack across to the passenger seat and climbing in.

The old truck smelled musty, but there weren't piles of trash in the floorboards. The floor was covered with a rubber mat from one side to the other, bare steel below it. The seats were worn but not ripped.

I hope the thing starts, I thought, inserting the key in the ignition.

The engine caught and I revved it a couple times. It settled into an even idle and the oil pressure gauge was reading well into the nominal range.

A manual transmission on a car that was right-hand drive could take some getting used to. Fortunately, though the driver's position was on the wrong side, the gear pattern and foot pedals were the same. Still, shifting with the left hand was awkward.

I put the truck in gear and started through town, quickly reaching the other side and continuing through the forest. Due to the condition of the road, I only occasionally got into second gear.

About ten miles up the road, I entered the town of *Maskall* and the road condition improved a little. In some places, I was able to get the speed up to almost forty miles per hour in third gear without breaking any teeth.

Crossing a bridge over a dark river, which my GPS identified as New River, I went a few miles farther and reached an intersection. Old Northern Highway ended at Chan Pine Ridge Road, on the southern outskirts of Orange Walk. I turned right and drove slowly through the town, identifying four hotels that seemed to have bars, either inside or attached.

When I reached the other side of town probably four miles later, I turned the Land Rover around and drove back to the last hotel bar I'd seen. I glanced at my watch when I pulled into the nearly empty parking lot beside the place. It was 0930. Still early, but it had taken over three hours to get there. If I left now, I'd be back about the same time Florence returned. That meant any time I spent in Orange Walk took away from time with my daughter.

I drove toward the back of the lot, as was my habit, and that was where I found overflow parking behind a small English-style tavern, probably a throwback to British colonial days. The Brits had ruled what was then British Honduras for nearly 120 years, but Belize had gained its independence in 1981.

The tavern's parking lot was nearly half full. I parked in the nearly empty hotel lot, anyway.

As I got out of the truck, a man came out of the bar. He seemed in a hurry as he strode quickly across the lot and got into a car. Shouldering my pack, I walked toward the hotel's front entrance.

Inside, the lobby was sparsely decorated. A table in one corner had a dormant water feature on it, something like what used to be popular back home when I was a kid. It and the table were covered in layers of dust. I took three steps to the counter, beside which a darkened hallway disappeared into the building.

There was no one behind the one-inch thick glass. The barrier had a hole, about chest level, that a child might be able to get a hand through, and below it was one of those scooped trays where money or papers could be passed back and forth.

I touched a small desk bell beside the slot, which emitted a half-hearted clang. Everything about the lobby seemed abandoned. I heard the twin thump of two feet hitting the deck in a back office beyond the glass.

An old man stuck his head out. "What you want?"

"I'd like a room, please," I replied. "Three nights."

I had no plans to stay in this hotel, or any other. And I definitely wasn't going to register or leave my name anywhere. There were ways to get a room without giving a name. Every hotel had empty rooms that weren't making a penny. It was all about how well a person could negotiate.

The old man came slowly toward the counter, scratching at a gaunt, stubbly jaw. He was white, with a face that looked like tanned leather.

An ex-pat? There were a lot of Americans and Canadians living in Belize, as well as people from all over the world.

He looked over the desk, down toward my feet, then out to the lot. I saw his eyes focus quickly on the Land Rover, probably recognizing it as the only strange vehicle out there.

"That all the luggage you got, mister?"

I nodded.

"Hell, you don't need ta get a room," he said. His accent was American with a country twang. "Just go into the bar there and one of the girls'll take care of ya."

He started to turn away.

I slid a hundred-dollar bill into the tray. "One room. Three nights."

He stopped and his head turned, eyes shifting down to the tray. His body followed the motion of his head, shoulders first, then torso, hips, and legs, like a spring slowly unwinding.

"What is it you want here?" he asked.

I turned on my own country accent. "Just need a place to sleep at night, that's all. This is a hotel, ain't it? I mean, that's what it says on the sign outside."

"You runnin' from the law," he asked, "or a woman?"

Early in my career as a Marine, I'd lived in a squad bay with other junior enlisted men. We were infantrymen—a rowdy bunch, to say the least—and we had guys in our platoon from everywhere. Over the years, I'd probably met several people from every state in the country. This guy was straight up Ozark—an Arkansas Razorback.

I lifted one corner of my mouth in a slight grin. "Could be both."

"It's thirty bucks, American, and I ain't got change."

"Change for what?" I asked.

"I can't break no hundred, mister."

"Break a hundred for what?"

The old man eyed me curiously. "For the room, ya damned fool."

Grinning, I pushed the bill farther into the slot. "What room? Who are you talking to?"

He stepped closer and studied my face through the glass. My eyes flashed over to a rack with keys hanging from it. Then his lips parted, showing a tobacco-stained grin. He quickly took a key from the rack, snatched up the bill, and slid the key under.

Negotiation complete.

I paid ten bucks over the rate for a room I had no intention of staying in and he pocketed the hundred without his employer ever knowing. The important part was that there was no record of the transaction.

"Guess I musta been talkin' to myself again," he said, with a wink. "Ain't nobody a'tall come in here all day."

I nodded and took the key, which had a metal tag on it with the number nine. Or was it a six? I started to turn back to ask the old man, but he'd already disappeared.

I walked into the hallway, scanning the door numbers; even on the left, odd on the right. I could see a glass door at the far end of the hall that opened into the tavern. When I got to room six, I tried it, but the key didn't turn. When I pulled it out, the door suddenly flew open.

A small Hispanic woman looked up at me, her face showing obvious irritation. She was slim and moderately attractive, with a dark complexion, long black hair, and chocolate-colored eyes. She wore a loose-fitting blue tank dress made of a light material that clung to her body. I took all this in, as well as the interior of the room.

"Sorry," I said, holding up the key. "Guess this here's a nine, not a six."

She pointed down the hall. "Nine over there." Her nails were painted blue— one of the two groups of prostitutes that hadn't had a girl killed.

Inside was a sparsely decorated room. A young, dark-skinned man sat on a bed, shirtless, tugging his pants up.

"Sorry," I repeated, turning away.

I went one room down and across the hall to number nine and unlocked the door. The room looked just like number six but flipped around with the bed on the opposite wall. Besides the small bed, there was a table with a lamp on it and an armless, straight-backed wooden chair beside it, like the kind you'd find in a school back in the Sixties.

No closet, no dresser, and no television. Not that I planned to watch TV, and I damned sure wasn't going to lie on the bed. This would just be a fallback position.

I dropped my pack on the bed and opened it. Moving everything aside, I found the manufacturer's tag and pulled on it, lifting out the false bottom.

The Sig felt good in my hand when I pulled it out. Racking the slide slightly, I insured there was a round in the chamber, even though I knew there was. Old habits were hard to break and that was one I didn't plan to lose. I laid the gun on the bed and reached back into my pack for the holster, then pushed the stiff plastic bottom back into place.

I holstered the Sig and slid the holster into my pants behind my back, clipping it to my belt before moving back over to the door. I listened for a moment—nothing.

Retracing my steps to the lobby, I noticed the old man sitting back in his little office, so I went quickly through the small room and out the door. Then I walked around back and entered the tavern, as if I were just another patron coming in from the parking lot.

I remained in the doorway for a moment after I'd removed my sunglasses, to allow my eyes to adjust. A guy behind a bar to my right didn't even look up. Except for him, one guy sitting alone at a table, and another guy drinking with a woman, the place was empty.

As I crossed the room, the guy sitting alone glanced up, but nervously looked away. He was white—American, maybe—hard to tell at a glance. I chose a table by the wall and sat where I could see both the door I'd just come through and the one leading to the hotel. A jazz number was playing from somewhere, a song I'd never heard before. Local maybe, judging by the recording quality. Jazz was very popular in Belize.

The bartender, if that's what he was, looked in my direction, then got up from a stool where he'd been reading a newspaper. He turned his back, then did something behind the bar.

My eyes drifted to the couple. He looked local, dressed in work clothes. They seemed to know one another. She wore a blue halter top and white shorts. Her nails were painted blue.

I glanced over at the guy who sat alone. Beside his chair was a small cooler, something a working stiff would carry. He was looking at me, but quickly averted his eyes, which I would consider a normal reaction in a place like we were in. He wore jeans and a work shirt, with boots on his feet.

The bartender came over, carrying a glass and a water pitcher. Without a word, he filled the glass and placed it on the table, then retreated to his perch.

I scanned the room. Aside from the two doors at opposite ends, there were four pairs of stained-glass windows—a pair on either side of the exterior door and another pair on either side of my table. They were fixed panes and couldn't be opened. They *were* points of emergency egress, just the same. You just had to send something, or *someone*, through one of them, ahead of your leap.

A dozen or so tables were scattered haphazardly around the room. They had an odd mix of chairs around each, two here, four there, three at most of them, but very few of the chairs matched, and I knew why.

I'd been in a few rough, third-world bars. They all seemed to have that one thing in common—when a chair got busted, usually over someone's head, it got replaced with whatever worked, if it was replaced at all. This place was nowhere near as bad as some others I'd been in.

A woman entered from the hotel's hallway. She spoke to the bartender for a minute, then went over to the guy sitting alone. She hadn't even reached his table when the couple who'd been drinking together stood and moved toward the door to the hotel.

They almost ran into a man coming from the hallway, who also seemed hurried and nervous. I watched the girl who'd just entered talking to her prospective client. She also looked Hispanic and wore a tight gold dress. She also wore the same blue nail polish.

After a moment, she laughed at something the guy said and took money from him. She went to the bar, where she placed their order and paid for it. I noticed that she hadn't given the bartender all the money the guy had given her. She gave him one bill and stuck three into a small purse. The bartender reached into a top-loading cooler and placed a bottle of water in front of her, along with a key.

So that's how it worked.

When she went back to the guy, she leaned toward him with her back to me and whispered something to him. I looked over at the bartender, to see if he was keeping an eye on her. He wasn't. She sat at the guy's table and they talked. It soon looked more like an interrogation, though. I couldn't hear either of them, but I got the sense that he was asking her questions.

The kid I'd seen in room six came into the tavern and headed straight for the outside door without looking around. A moment later, the girl I'd seen him with came in and went to the bartender. They said a few words, then she looked at me and smiled.

The woman in the gold dress and her new client at the other table got up from their chairs. He picked up his lunch cooler and they went into the hallway as the

Hispanic woman in the clingy blue dress did her best to walk seductively toward my table. Because of her small size, I had a hard time buying into it. I like women who don't look like kids.

"*Nos encontramos de nuevo, hombre grande.*"

"*Esperaba eso,*" I said. "*Habla usted Inglés?*"

"Yes," she replied. "My English is very good. Would you like a drink from the bar?"

"A lot better than my Spanish," I agreed. "A beer, I guess. If you'll have one with me. It's still early."

"I don't like beer," she said. "A glass of wine?"

"*Si,*" I replied. "*Perfecto.*"

"Your Spanish is very good," she said, putting a hand on my shoulder and moving it down to my chest. "I think that is not all, too. I am Lupe Robles."

"My friends call me Stretch," I said.

"It is five American dollars for the drinks," she said, getting down to business. "And twenty to drink them alone in my room."

I looked around the barroom, even though I knew there wasn't anyone else except the bartender. Then I took my money clip out and peeled off a ten and a twenty.

"Tell him to keep the change," I said, handing her the bills. "He's been a load of fun to talk to."

She laughed and went to the bar. A moment later, she returned with our drinks. "Come with me."

I stood and she looked up at me again. Closer, the difference in height seemed greater, at least fifteen or sixteen inches.

She smiled and took my hand. "I have my own room here," she said, leading the way. Then, almost whispering to herself, she added, "*Disfrutaré montando este caballo.*"

Sorry, Lupe, I thought. *Only one lady rides this horse.*

Then she led me into the dark hallway.

CHAPTER TWENTY-TWO

Zotov had sent an early-morning email to Casey demanding another delivery, and he wanted it fast, today if possible. Only this time, he needed four items.

Casey had, for a brief moment, considered taking them from Posh's perfect body. But dollar signs flashed in his eyes when he thought about what she could be worth, fully intact. How often was one just handed a gift like her to do with as he wished?

Besides, it wasn't that much more difficult to harvest from the local communities. A girl strapped to a table in front of him, or one lying unconscious on a hotel bed a few hours later—it was simply a matter of time and distance.

Casey had the time and his helicopter meant the distance didn't matter. He could be anywhere in Belize in an hour.

He had no doubt what he'd be able to get out of Posh in a very short time. More than Zotov would pay for having her sliced and diced.

A lot more.

But not in Belize. His stable of girls in Placencia were cheap Brazilian street prostitutes, brought in to be used and abused by the migrant farmers. Some were addicts. All were expendable. Posh could bring in more in one hour than they could all earn in a whole weekend.

Two weeks, he decided. Once she was completely broken and properly trained, he'd send her to a handler in Shanghai for two weeks of intense filming. Madam Tseng had a lot of very high-end clients and was always looking for new talent. Her clients would collectively pony up a hundred grand for two weeks of filming. Posh would be at their mercy for up to ten hours a day, one man or group of men, after another. He was certain she could take anything they could dish up. And by the time he finished training her, she'd relish it.

If she truly was a spy for the Russian mob, once the footage was released on the dark web, Yelena Kotova would be exposed. In the long run, it didn't really matter. She had the looks and he had her. Casey wasn't planning to take the risk, anyway. He'd just get rid of her once the movie clips went public; palm what was left of her off on someone else. Which would also be profitable.

The commercial on the radio ended and a jazz number started. It was a local soft jazz trio he'd seen play in the city. Casey swirled the water in his glass as he continued thinking about what the Russian might bring.

The demand on the dark web was like dangling fresh meat above a school of hungry sharks. Madam Tseng's production company made the best high-definition videos of the worst of human depravity.

Within minutes after the videos flooded the super-secret side of the world wide web—hours and hours of footage, in little fifteen-minute clips, selling for ten dollars a pop—the bids to buy her would start coming in.

Casey knew the potential from past experience, and he didn't think any of the others he'd sent to Madam Tseng had been nearly as exquisite as Posh. But then, Casey had a thing for tall, blond Russian women.

He also knew there were people who would gladly pay well into six figures to have her for their own plaything and do to her all the things he'd done the previous evening and would continue doing until she craved it.

The door to the bar opened and a tall man stepped inside. He removed his sunglasses and looked around before making his way across the room. He glanced at Casey for a moment, but Casey turned away. When his eyes darted back, the man had also looked away and moved to a table on the far side of the barroom. He was a white guy, but then so was Casey. He wore faded jeans and muddy boots, also similar to Casey's own attire. But in places like this, men minded their own business, even if they obviously had something in common. The man took a chair and looked in his direction briefly. Casey quickly averted his eyes again.

The bartender served the tall man his glass of water and went back to his paper at the bar. Casey thought he was a tough-looking guy, but already going gray on his chin and the sides of his head. Just another boat bum who'd trekked through the marsh to get a little action. He studied the man's features a moment longer, without making it obvious. There was something about the way he moved, with the confidence of a much younger man. Casey dismissed him as harmless. But he couldn't help thinking he'd seen the guy around somewhere.

Casey had been watching this place from a car parked across the street. Stopping by every few days for the last month or so, he'd hung out and observed who came and went.

Maybe the guy was a regular, and that was why Casey thought him familiar. But he'd been paying more attention to the girls coming and going than the johns. Usually the girls stayed for four or five hours, but their tricks always less than an hour.

He'd learned a little about some of the whores, particularly two that he thought looked a bit cleaner than the others.

That was what had brought him to the north side of Orange Walk. Casey knew that delivering an item that would prove tainted when tested would quickly come back on Zotov and by extension, on himself. But he'd learned enough about both of the girls that he felt certain neither used drugs, and if he was lucky, one of them would be working the bar.

Shortly after he'd arrived, Casey saw one of the two girls go to a room with a local young farmer. He waited his turn.

The next girl to come out of the hotel hallway was one of the girls he'd dismissed quickly after having seen her snorting coke with a john. She'd gone to a man Casey knew he'd seen around. There, she'd waited her turn for a room, drinking with her customer. Now that a room was available, she and her new "boyfriend" for the hour disappeared down the long dark hall.

Soon, the other of the two girls he had in mind came out, and her john left immediately afterward. She went to the bar, got a glass of water and came over to where Casey was sitting. She was dressed in gold and had amber eyes.

"Would you like a drink and some company?"

"A bottled water, if that's okay," he said sheepishly. "It's kinda early for me."

"I will get it for you," she said. "We could go somewhere?"

"Yes, we can," Casey said, nodding very agreeably. "For a *couple* of hours, if you have the time."

She smiled at his offer, probably thinking he wouldn't last twenty minutes. Guatemalan girls were good at getting their hours' worth in less than an hour. And Casey was good at getting his two hours' worth.

"Bottled water is very expensive in Orange Walk Town," she said. "Fifty American dollars a bottle, I am afraid. But you will have all the time you need to enjoy it."

Casey grinned. "Oh, it'll be worth it, I'm sure." He handed her two twenties and two fives, knowing that the bartender would only get five bucks.

She laughed and took his money, placing her water glass on the table beside his. When she turned toward the bar, Casey moved her glass to the other side of the table, dropping the fast-dissolving tablet into it at the same time.

Returning with his water, she leaned over so the flimsy straps of her dress hung down and he could see her breasts.

He grinned up at her.

"I am Larissa Cortez," she said. "I have seen you watching. Touch me so I know you are not *polees*."

Casey's grin broadened as his hand made its way up the inside of her thigh "Those will have to come off," he said, eyes staring hungrily at hers as he groped her through the thin material of her underwear.

She pushed his hand away and pulled the other chair closer. "You think two hours?" she said. "I think ten *minutos, mi gran semental blanco.*

"The first time, baby," Casey growled, loving the white stallion reference. "But I'll be going for four."

He almost laughed at his ridiculous joke, then began asking his usual questions, though he'd already learned a little about her.

The other of the two girls he'd been following entered the bar, trailed by the young farmer, who continued out to the parking lot. After talking to the bartender, she went over to the tall, white guy.

Larissa pulled him to his feet and he picked up his cooler, then allowed her to drag him toward the hotel's rooms.

Once they were in the room, Casey placed his cooler beside the chair and turned toward Larissa, handing her the water glass she'd left at the table.

He opened his bottle and held it up. "We're both going to need to be well hydrated for what's to come."

He slowly drank from the bottle, watching the little *puta* do the same from her glass. Then he smiled at her, knowing that in ten minutes she'd be out cold and, in an hour, or so, she'd just be cold.

She came at him aggressively then, intent on satisfying Casey's lust and getting him out of the room as fast as she could. She pushed him down onto the bed and tugged his pants loose, pulling them down over his hips. Without removing her dress, she climbed on top of him.

It'd only been an hour since he'd been with Posh, but Larissa's efforts soon had him ready. She got her ride on her big white stallion, as she'd called him, but it didn't last long enough for either of them. In fact, the drug had started to take effect after just a few minutes and soon her movements slowed, until finally she'd just collapsed on top of him.

Pushing her up to a slumped sitting position, still straddling him, Casey considered finishing, but he didn't have a whole lot of time. Holding her upright with one hand, he pulled the gold dress up to her face, exposing her body.

Casey shook his head. "Should've booked three hours."

He rolled her off and stood, pulling his pants back up. Retrieving his cooler, he placed it beside the woman, now lying on her back, face covered by her dress. He

273

rolled her onto her belly and pulled the back of her dress up as well.

Casey opened the cooler and withdrew the two syringes. He jabbed the first into the meaty part of her butt and plunged the handle. There was enough diazepam in the syringe to keep her unconscious for six hours.

After a moment's thought, Casey put the other syringe—the one with the local anesthetic—back into the cooler. There wouldn't be any need for it. She would bleed out and die before the two hours for the room were up, and definitely before the sedative wore off. That is, if she even survived what was about to happen to her. He'd have to work fast to collect all four.

Removing the cryogenic device from the cooler, he placed it beside the woman and picked up his cordless harmonic scalpel. Usually, he'd use a throw away blade but getting all four required more time. The battery powered instrument would cauterize the blood vessels using high intensity sound, as he cut through flesh.

Suddenly a scream came from one of the nearby rooms. He'd heard screams in these kinds of hotels before, so he ignored it and turned back to his *patient*. Just as he was about to make the first incision, there was a loud bang just outside the room, followed by the splintering of wood, and more screams and shouts.

"Shit!" Casey cursed under his breath and quickly started putting his things away.

He wanted to be ready in case he had to make a quick getaway. He reached into the cooler and withdrew a small .38 caliber revolver, then went to the door.

He listened for a moment and was just about to open it when he heard a man shout, "Don't move!"

It sounded like he was right outside Casey's door. The doors didn't have little peep holes, so he couldn't see what was going on.

"Back up!" the man outside the door ordered, but it now sounded like he was a bit farther down the hall.

Casey took a chance and slowly turned the doorknob, cracking the door open enough to see what was happening.

The bartender had his back to Casey, pointing a shotgun at the tall man he'd seen in the bar.

"I heard a scream," the man said. "I thought someone was being hurt."

"Shut up!" the bartender barked.

The tall guy looked at him over the bartender's shoulder. Beyond the man, Casey saw other doors opening.

"Everyone out!" the bartender ordered. "The cops are on their way."

Casey backed up, put the gun back into his cooler and closed it. After grabbing the handle, he patted Larissa's rump. "Maybe next time, *chica*."

When he returned to the door and opened it wider, he saw the two men and one of the girls in the hall just outside his room. Beyond the tall man, who was again staring right at him, were other people hurrying toward the hotel exit. Nobody wanted to be there when the cops arrived.

Casey suddenly recognized the guy. He'd seen him in San Pedro at the Dive Bar the previous night with two hot blondes, a dumpy older couple he'd seen around many times, and the tall cop who lived on Ambergris.

Casey grinned at the old boat bum and opened the door fully. He followed the others down the hall and into the bar, letting them hurry ahead. Then he slipped quickly behind the bar and grabbed a bottle of rum, so the trip wouldn't be a total loss.

A moment later, Casey was out the door and getting into his car. There was another blue bar just down the road.

CHAPTER TWENTY-THREE

I really didn't have a plan for when I got to the room with the prostitute. I only wanted to ask the woman some questions, see if she knew about the murders or maybe knew one of the victims. It was doubtful, as they'd been from a different group than hers.

What do I know? I thought. Maybe they move from one to another, traded like ball players.

As we approached my room, I was debating taking my key out and pulling Lupe Robles in there when I heard a scream coming from room twelve, which we'd just passed.

My reflexes and training took over. For the majority of people, the sound of turmoil—gunshots or screams—triggered their natural instinct to move away from the source of the commotion. But in the immediate cerebral choice of flight or fight, I'd been trained to ignore the former and even more trained to embrace the latter.

Without conscious thought, I stepped across the hall, turned, and planted my size twelve boot heel right above the doorknob. The door splintered inward, revealing the couple from the bar who had seemed as if they knew one another.

They were on the bed.

He was on top of her.

The woman screamed again, but this time the scream was one of anger. I suddenly realized the earlier scream had been one of delight, not pain.

I held both hands up, palms out. "I'm so sorry," I said. "I heard a scream."

The man had rolled off the woman and both were huddling on the far side of the bed.

"Get out!" the woman shouted.

I didn't know what to do. I looked to Lupe for help, but she was already at her door, hurriedly trying to unlock it. As she disappeared inside, I heard the unmistakable sound of a pump shotgun chambering a shell.

Behind me.

A chill ran down my spine unlike anything I'd ever experienced.

"Don't move!" a voice yelled.

I froze stiff. I'd had guns pointed at me before and some of those times I'd been without backup. Savannah and Florence popped immediately to the forefront of my mind. I had a lot to lose now.

"Turn around real slow, mister."

I did as I was told and found just what I expected; the bartender staring at me down the long barrel of a 12-gauge pump-action shotgun.

He was ten feet away.

There was zero chance he'd miss, and the distance was too great for me to get to him before he could fire.

"Back up!" he ordered, stepping toward me.

The door to room thirteen opened and I saw the white guy from the bar peeking out.

"I heard a scream," I said, stepping back from room twelve. "I thought someone was being hurt."

"Shut up!" the bartender barked, as he glanced into the room.

Just over the white guy's shoulder I glimpsed the girl in the gold dress. She was lying on the bed on her belly, a cooler beside her.

Her dress was pulled up over her head.

She wasn't moving.

I saw all of that in about half a heartbeat before the guy closed the door. My senses were on full alert, and I could feel the adrenaline coursing through my veins. Behind me, I heard other doors opening and people talking. But my focus was on the bartender's trigger finger. I didn't want anyone to get hurt and I sensed people had come out of rooms and into the hallway behind me. They were in the line of fire.

If the bartender increased the pressure on that trigger just a little, I'd have no choice but to roll backward and come up shooting. Shotguns were messy and indiscriminate, but once fired, the pump action had to be worked to eject the empty shell and load a fresh one. In that time, I could get off two or three rounds. Anyone behind me was on their own.

"Everyone out!" the bartender ordered. "The cops are on their way."

The guy from room thirteen had looked familiar. I'd seen him somewhere before but couldn't place him. He came out of his room and hurried toward the tavern, carrying the cooler he'd brought with him.

Everyone was in a hurry to get out. With the police on the way, I didn't blame them. I was screwed and I knew it. The cops would arrive in a matter of minutes and the bartender's deck sweeper was pointed right at my midsection. When they arrived, they'd find my gun.

"I'm serious," I said, taking another slow step back. "I heard a girl scream and my instincts just took over."

"Doors cost money, asshole. Real slow now, I want you to get down on your knees."

This wasn't going the way I wanted. I figured that if I just did what he said, he might relax, and I could get the drop on him. I went slowly down to one knee and then the other.

"Turn around," he ordered.

Had he seen my gun?

Awkwardly, I turned my back to him, trying not to pivot on my knees too fast. I could hear his feet on the floorboards as he moved closer.

"Lupe! Get out here!" he shouted, as he pressed the muzzle of the shotgun against the back of my neck.

Another cold chill went up my spine. I'd faced worse situations. There were even a few times I'd thought I wasn't going to get out alive. I don't remember ever being afraid. But this was different. Savannah and Florence were waiting for me to return.

I involuntarily shivered as the door to room six opened and Lupe stuck her head out.

"Here," the bartender said, as something flew over my shoulder. "Know how to use that?"

A nylon flex cuff landed on the floor in front of her and Lupe looked down at it. "Yes," she replied.

"Figured you did," the bartender said. "Behind his back, and make sure you pull that strap real tight."

Lupe came out of the room and picked up the cuff.

"Hands behind your back," the man ordered. "Make one wrong move and your head's gonna come clean off."

Lupe moved around behind me and put the band around my wrists. I obliged her by moving my hands away from my back. Mostly it was to keep her fingers from bumping the Sig under my shirt. She quickly tightened the cuff and moved back to her door.

"I can keep the money?" she asked.

"Probably best if you just go in your room."

Just then, I heard the door to the tavern open.

"*Polees!* Don't move!" another man shouted.

"Name's Kent," the bartender said, the barrel of the scatter gun still against my neck. "I work the bar. This guy just kicked in one of my doors. I think he's the Ghoul Killer."

"Lower di gun and step to di side," the cop ordered.

Kent did as he was told, and I heard the rushed footfalls of two people coming up behind me.

"I'll take that," a woman said.

I heard the sound of the shotgun's butt on the wood floor, as whoever took it from Bartender Kent leaned it against a doorjamb or something. It should have been unloaded and cleared.

"On your feet," the woman said. "Kent, you go back to the bar."

"But he's—"

"He's not going anywhere," the woman said. "You got him trussed up real good."

Slowly, I went to one knee, then pushed myself up into a standing position.

"Turn around," the woman said.

I unhurriedly turned to face her. I didn't want a jumpy cop to get the wrong idea.

She was a black woman, tall and athletic-looking, with a broad nose and high forehead. The Beretta 9mm in her hands wasn't moving off the middle of my chest.

"Who are you?" she asked. "And why did you kick down the door?"

"I heard a girl scream," I said, thinking fast. "I'm in room nine—just checked in—and heard the scream. The key to my room is in my right front pocket."

Without a word she jammed a hand into my pocket and fished out my door key. She looked at it, then stuck it in the lock and turned it, as her partner, a Mestizo man a few inches shorter than her, covered me. She flung the door fully open and swept the room with her gun.

Then she turned back to face me. "I am Sergeant JP Menendez. You still haven't told me who you are."

JP Menendez? The only cop in Orange Walk who Garcia said he trusted.

"I'll tell you after you reach in my left shirt pocket and read the business card that's in there."

"Watch him, Renaldo."

Sergeant Menendez moved quickly to her right, crossing between me and her partner, who dutifully raised his weapon as she passed. He squared it back on my chest as soon as she was clear.

Menendez pulled the card Garcia had given me out of my pocket and looked down at it.

"Flip it over," I whispered, so her partner didn't hear. "He told me to contact you if I needed anything."

Menendez looked up at me, studying my eyes.

"Step into your room, please," she said, then turned to her partner. "Renaldo, go take Kent's statement."

"But you shouldn't—"

"Because I am a woman?" Menendez said, more than a little irritation apparent in her voice. "Do as I say."

I stepped into my room. Menendez followed me and closed the door.

"The walls are thin," she said. "Who are you and why did Elden send you here?"

I figured I'd give it a shot—Garcia had heard the name.

"Are you familiar with Armstrong Research?"

A light came on behind her smokey brown eyes. "You are investigating the prostitute murders?"

It didn't escape my attention that she hadn't said *Ghoul Killer*. The media liked scary names to sell headlines. Most of the cops I knew hated them.

"My name is Jesse McDermitt," I said. "You can call Elden. By now, he's checked me out through Armstrong."

"Sit in that chair," she ordered, taking a phone out of her pocket.

I complied, but with my hands behind my back, it wasn't very comfortable. I pulled my elbows up, and sat down, certain I looked like an albatross trying to take flight. One of the pitfalls of being a knuckle-dragger.

Menendez made a call. After telling Garcia what was going on, she listened for a moment, then ended the call and holstered her gun.

"Have you learned anything?" she asked.

"I only just got here, but I think your killer might have been in the room two doors down—number thirteen."

"Come with me," she said.

"Um—" I turned slightly and pulled my hands around.

Menendez pulled a switchblade from her pocket. "Turn around."

I did and heard the click of the blade. I once more extended my hands as far back as I could. The nylon strap parted easily with a flick of her blade.

"You know there aren't many *polees* who can be trusted," she said, folding the knife and returning it to her pocket. "Including my partner. But if you tell Mr.

Kent you'll pay for the damages, Renaldo won't ask questions."

"Someone with deep pockets is behind this," I said. "If I can find the source of the money that would help end the problem."

"There is corruption everywhere," she said. "It will still be here and someone else will come along and feed the money to the politicians so they will look away."

"That's for people like you and Elden to fix," I said. "We try to stay out of politics."

"I have heard how you people operate," she said, opening the door and stepping into the hall. I followed her. "It is probably better if I don't know your plans for when you find the source of the money."

Menendez opened the door to the room the white guy had been in with the girl in the gold dress. I followed her in.

The girl was still lying on the bed, face down, her dress pulled up. Menendez rushed to her side and put two fingers to the woman's neck.

"She's alive," Menendez said, then started to roll the woman over. "No cuts or bruises."

"There," I said, pointing at her thigh.

Menendez let the woman roll back onto her belly and looked closer. Then she used the bed sheet to wipe a small drop of blood away.

"She was injected with something," she said. "Very recently. What did this man look like?"

"Are you really going to investigate?"

Menendez turned and glared at me. "I take my job very seriously, Mr. McDermitt." Then her face softened. "But you are right. If I push this too far, it will not be good."

"It was probably just a sedative," I said. "Transplant-able organs have to be harvested from a live or recently deceased donor."

CHAPTER
TWENTY-FOUR

Knowing that the killer was spooked, I told Menendez that I'd be wasting my time in Orange Walk—he was long gone. She called an ambulance for the girl and convinced Kent not to press any charges if I paid for a new door. I obliged and offered the guy a hundred-dollar bill. He snatched it from my fingers. I knew the busted door jamb would just be hammered back into place with a few pennies' worth of nails and maybe a piece of scrap wood trim.

I drove slowly as I headed back through town, scanning the sidewalks and places where men loitered, looking for the man I'd seen. He was probably miles away.

Or parked behind another bar.

On the other side of town, I turned onto Old North Road, not relishing the long, bone-jarring ride back to where I'd stashed the dinghy.

An hour later, I nearly missed the yellow ribbon hanging from the tree branch. I backed up and shifted the truck into four-wheel-drive.

Land Rovers were iconic off-road machines. They'd crossed deserts, mountains, and streams and were very reliable in the bush. So far, this one had lived up to that reputation. But now it'd really be tested.

I turned off the road and drove the vehicle east toward shore, dodging around palm trees, clusters of sea grape, mature gumbo limbo trees, rocks and holes.

Soon, I found a place where I could stash the truck before the going got too muddy and slippery. I parked behind a large sea grape, left the key over the visor where I'd found it and marked the spot on my GPS. If I didn't need it again, I'd give the coordinates to Chyrel to give to the owner.

From there, I continued on foot, angling toward the coast until I found my tracks in the mud. Then I followed them to where I'd hidden the boat.

I checked my watch. Almost noon. Florence would be back soon. I wanted to talk to David about the guy who'd been hanging out with them the night before.

The dinghy ride back to *Salty Dog* took another twenty minutes. As I approached, I saw Savannah and Erin on the foredeck, and Neal's little center console tied off to the stern.

"You're back earlier than you planned," Savannah said, grabbing the painter from my outstretched hand and holding the dinghy alongside the boarding ladder.

"Yeah," I replied. "I kinda wanted to be here when Florence gets back from her first date."

She eyed me suspiciously for a moment but didn't say anything as I killed the engine and climbed up the ladder.

I took the line from her hand, kissed her, then went aft to tie off the dinghy.

Savannah followed me.

Out of earshot from the foredeck, she whispered, "You found out something, didn't you?"

"Maybe," I replied. "I might know more after the kids get back."

"What do they have to do with it?"

"The killer was at the Dive Bar last night."

"What?" Savannah stepped back, a look of terror in her eyes.

"Don't worry," I said. "He wasn't on the dive boat."

Savannah turned and looked out over the reef, searching for the boat our daughter was on. "You can't possibly be sure of that."

I took her shoulders and turned her toward me. "Calm down. He wasn't on the boat. I saw him in Orange Walk."

Her eyes stopped the frantic search and she looked into my eyes, then melted into my arms. "Thank God," she said. "I don't ever want to go through that a—"

I pushed her back to arm's length. "Go through what again?"

Savannah's head turned toward the sea once more. "Oh, nothing. It happened when she was little. She got lost in a store once and I nearly lost my marbles."

It was my turn to look at *her* suspiciously.

"There they come," she said, pointing toward the south.

I followed her gaze and saw the familiar red and white boat about two miles away, making for the cut.

A few minutes later, the dive boat turned through the opening in the reef. Once clear, it turned our way and slowed. I counted heads, even though I knew the guy couldn't possibly be with them. There had been four men and two women in David's group at the Dive Bar. I counted only four other divers besides Florence and David, two men and two women, plus the divemaster and captain. The typical six-pack charter. David's group consisted of him and two couples, Florence rounding out the six. So, it *was* the guy I'd seen them with.

The boat maneuvered alongside, and I caught a line from the divemaster, once more pulling the two boats closer. Florence was beaming. David looked worried.

"Stay for a bit, David?" I called over.

"Clean and stow my gear for me, Perry?" David called to one of his buddies, the guy who had whined about the afternoon dive.

"Yeah, bruv," he replied. "No problem."

David handed Florence's dive bag up to me and I laid it on the cabin top. He held her hand as she stepped up onto the dive boat's gunwale, then up the ladder.

"You'll never believe what we saw, Mom!" Florence said, hugging Savannah.

David climbed up quickly, and I released the line. In seconds, the dive boat captain moved his vessel away, then turned toward the dock.

"Try us," I said, shaking David's hand.

"A whale!" David said, his eyes widening with the kind of wonder only the young can exhibit. "Flo said it was a fin whale."

"*Balaenoptera physalus*," Florence added. "The second largest animal in the world, after the blue whale. It breached about a hundred yards from the boat as we were boarding after our last dive."

"I've never seen anything like it," David added.

"Did you see it underwater?" Savannah asked.

"No," Florence replied. "The captain said he saw it surface about a quarter mile away as we were boarding, then it breached, and half its body came out of the water."

"Once we were on board," David added, "it spy-hopped us even closer."

"There have been a few sightings of them along the reef," Erin said. "Orcas as well."

Florence started for the companionway. "I'm going to get a quick shower."

"If your dad can show me where the hose is, I can rinse off your gear for you," David offered.

Florence smiled and disappeared below. David might have seen it as an oversight, but Savannah and I both knew she was a stickler about maintaining her equipment. She was testing him.

"I need to get going," Erin said. "Neal will be home soon."

The women said their goodbyes, and David helped me pull her boat up to the ladder.

Once she was aboard, I grabbed Florence's dive bag and nodded toward the bow. "Hose is forward," I said to David. "You can rinse the salt off there, too. We have plenty of water."

He followed me up to the bow and I pulled the wash-down hose out of the large anchor chain locker. David took Florence's dive gear out and carefully laid it on the deck.

"You and Flo's mom should have come," he said, arranging the equipment for easy rinsing. "It was an incredible dive, and seeing that whale was like, insane." He stopped what he was doing and looked up at me, realizing I wasn't focused on chitchat about the whale.

I decided to get right down to business. "Tell me something," I began. "Last night? There was another man in your group. A slightly older guy?"

"Huh?"

"You were sitting with the two couples who were just on the dive boat with you and one other man, who *didn't* accompany y'all on the dive."

"Oh, yeah. He was just a guy we met somewhere else."

"You didn't know him before last night?"

David shook his head. "He said he was traveling alone, so since he was an American, we invited him to join us. What's this all about?"

"I think I know him," I lied. "Did he tell you his name?"

"KC something," David replied. "Kind of a foreign last name. Is that it?"

"You don't remember the last name?"

"It started with a J," he replied. "Jasa or Jasso, something like that. You know him?"

"Lunch is on," Savannah called from the cockpit.

I looked back at her. "We're on our way."

As he finished rinsing the gear, I said. "I wasn't truthful with you, David. I'm sorry. I don't know him, and I think he might be someone dangerous."

"You're kidding, right?" David said.

I could see the change in his eyes. When a person realized they'd come close to being involved in a dangerous situation, their mind made connections quickly. I knew the killer had taken the life of one man and seven women. If I hadn't caused a ruckus earlier, it would have been eight women. Had he been cruising the bars looking for another victim last night? Had he had his eyes set on one of those in David's group? I didn't want to tell the kid everything I knew. That would involve telling him who I was and how I knew it, but I wanted him to be wary.

"Wait," he said. "He seemed okay to me. What makes you think he's dangerous?"

"Remember the tall Mestizo man who was sitting with us last night?" I said. "He's a cop here in San Pedro."

"And he told you something about KC?"

I measured my words carefully and decided on a partial truth. "In a roundabout way, yeah. That guy you were with was the reason Sergeant Garcia was *at* the Dive Bar last night."

"Did he say what the guy's done?"

"No," I replied. "But he's a person of interest in a crime committed in Orange Walk." Then I nodded toward the cockpit. "Don't say anything to the girls, okay?"

"No, sir," he said. "You can count on me. What should we do if we see him again?"

"Just call me Jesse," I said. He smiled and nodded. "If you see him, steer clear, and call the police. Ask to be patched through to Sergeant Elden Garcia, nobody else. Tell Garcia you saw the guy who Sergeant Menendez missed this morning in Orange Walk."

"I'll keep my eyes open," he said, as we started aft. When I stepped down into the cockpit, my sat phone buzzed in my pocket. I pulled it out and saw that it was Chyrel calling.

"I need to take this," I said. "You go on down and tell Savannah I'll be just a minute."

I answered the phone and headed to the stern.

"I saw a police report just a few minutes ago," Chyrel said without preamble. "An attempted kidnapping at a brothel."

"Brothels are illegal in Belize," I said.

"But I read that prostitution was okay there."

"It is," I replied. "But everything associated with it isn't."

"Yu-uck," she said, making the word two syllables in her Alabama accent. "Anyway, your fingerprints were all over that report. What's going on down there?"

"What do you mean?" I asked.

"According to the report, a tall, white American man was held temporarily after breaking down a door. No name given."

"And you just assumed that it was me?"

"Well...yeah," she replied. "Wasn't it?"

"It was," I admitted. "But I can't be the only tall, white man in Belize."

"True, but I bet the number of those who make a habit out of kicking down doors is pretty slim."

I chuckled. "Touché. Look, I want you to check something out for me. See what you can come up with on an American ex-pat living in Belize who goes by K. C. Jasa or Jasso, or anything like that."

"The name Casey, or the initials KC?"

I hadn't thought about that. David's intonation made it pretty clear the guy went by his initials. How many names started with K?

"The way it was said, it sounded like initials, so check for first names that start with a K and middle initial C."

"I'll get on it," Chyrel said. "How was the vehicle?"

"Right where you said it would be," I replied. "But I left it somewhere else. If I don't need it again, you can give the owner the coordinates."

"Did it run okay? I know it was an old truck, but you didn't give me much time."

"Thanks," I said. "It was the perfect truck for this area. Now, if you could do something about the roads."

She laughed. "That's stuff in the real world, Jesse. I operate in the cyber world. Sorry. But if it's any consolation, the road looks real flat on my screen."

She laughed again and ended the call.

Savannah and Florence both looked up expectantly when I went down the companionway a few minutes later.

"Do you have to go somewhere?" Florence asked.

"No." I gestured with my hands, wondering how much about me she'd told her new friend. "No, that was just the office. Chyrel wanted to tell me about a report she'd read."

Lunch was, of course, heavy on fruit and light on meat. I knew full well that nothing quenched your taste buds after a dive like fresh pineapple or mango. Breathing dry air from a tank for an hour left your mouth parched all the way to the back of your throat.

We ate and talked. David told us that he was planning to take classes through the summer and get his business degree early.

"Won't you miss out on some of the 'college experience?'" Savannah asked, making little air quote signs.

"If you mean the frat parties and all that, no," he replied. "I mean, I won't miss not being a part of it, that is. I was approached by a couple of houses, but I'm just not interested in that."

"So, you're living in a dorm?" she asked, continuing the subtle third degree.

"My parents arranged for a little apartment over a garage owned by this nice lady. She's a widow and her late husband was one of my dad's professors when he went to Florida."

"Your own place?" Savannah asked. "What do you like to do in your free time?"

How David couldn't see what Savannah was needling at was beyond me. Every answer he gave, she was sorting and filing in her mind, making tick marks on a mental chart to see if this young man was good enough.

"I pretty much work whenever I'm not in class," he replied. "And I have a pretty heavy class load to cram four years into three. In my free time, I take care of my landlady's yard and anything else that needs doing to cover the rent."

"What kind of work do you do?" I asked, impressed that he was so independent at such a young age. Kids usually learned this by example. What Billy had told me explained that.

"I work for a web developer," he replied. "Mostly maintenance stuff, finding bugs and fixing them. I do a few other tech jobs when I find something interesting and challenging. I work out of my apartment, so a quiet place is sort of necessary."

"It doesn't sound like you have much time to have fun," Savannah remarked, leaving the trap set for David to step into.

"My work's fun for me," he said. "Some of my friends think it's boring, but I don't care. I like what I do. Writing and fixing code is a challenge, the pay's good and I don't need much. I'm saving for a down payment to buy a house when I graduate. My parents paid for me to come down here with my friends. They thought I needed a break and I don't have any classes scheduled, so here I am."

A homeowner at twenty-two?

David smiled at Florence. "If I'm not in class, I'm at home. Boring, huh?"

"It doesn't sound boring to me at all," Florence said. "You have your own place and pay your own way. You're independent."

My sat phone pinged and I pulled it out of my pocket, looking at it under the table.

It was an email from Chyrel.

"More work?" Savannah asked, gathering dishes and moving them to the sink.

"What kind of work do *you* do, Mr. McDermitt?" David asked.

I read the first line of the email and looked up at him and Florence sitting across from me. "I do security work," I replied to David. Then I glanced over at Savannah. She was looking back at me, waiting. "That was an email from Chyrel. She found out who he is."

CHAPTER TWENTY-FIVE

Savannah's eyes darted to Florence and David.

"Found out who who is?" Florence asked.

"Who who?" Savannah absently commented, without breaking eye contact with me. "You sound like an old barred owl."

I grinned at her. Sometimes, Savannah dropped right back into the homespun Carolina-girl accent of her youth.

"Can you just call the local authorities with the information?" Savannah asked, as I rose from my seat.

"What's going on?" Florence asked.

This was it. The Mexico thing was bad enough. But to get involved in two operations in the span of a week would tell me if I'd made the right choice in telling Savannah all about what I did. If she and Florence couldn't handle it, I'd quit. We'd hoist anchor right then and sail away from this trouble.

But could I really break all ties? Could I just ignore the pain and suffering of others? Just walk away and finally retire to do things that brought me contentment instead of pain and guilt? Would I ever be able to put the mask and what it stood for away for good?

If not, every time I'd get a phone call or email, Savannah and Florence would wonder if I was going to be called away. That had never been a problem with Sara; she usually knew about my assignments before I did. Savannah was right, in a way. I *was* good at what I did, but more importantly, I had an excellent team and an organization that could provide state-of-the-art support and logistics.

Savannah *had* changed. Though she'd called herself weak, anyone who'd known her back then knew she wasn't timid. What had caused the change in her I had no way of knowing. Raising a child alone on a boat? No, the Savannah I'd known before could have done that with one hand tied behind her back.

This *new* Savannah had the kind of quiet, assured confidence I rarely saw in others. Florence had it, too, but not to the degree of the woman standing before me.

She smiled, then turned to David and our daughter. "I'm sorry, David, but Jesse hasn't been entirely forthcoming with you. He owns a security company, that's true. But that's not his job."

We sat down at the table across from the kids.

"Will one of you tell me what's going on?" Florence demanded.

I wanted to see just what kind of support I had, so I looked over at Savannah and nodded toward the kids, urging her to continue.

"The *errand* your father had to run this morning..." Savannah began. "He's working with local authorities to find the man responsible for the recent murders."

David remained silent.

Florence looked from her mother to me and back again. Finally, her gaze settled on me. "Is that why you wanted to come down here?"

"No," I replied. "The first I heard about the killings was a newspaper headline I saw at the airport, when you picked me and Charity up."

"And this has nothing to do with what happened in Mexico?"

"No."

She looked over at Savannah again. Then both turned toward me.

"What can Mom and I do to help?"

"I don't think I'm following this conversation at all," David said.

I turned and looked into David's eyes. "Remember yesterday, when I asked if you knew who Billy Rainwater was?"

He nodded.

"I could tell you knew more about him than you let on." I decided to cut him some slack to see how much he'd divulge. "I'm guessing it's because you know him through your dad. Am I right?"

"Yes, sir," he replied, somewhat meekly. "He and my dad served on a couple of county and civic boards. They're friends."

"Yet you didn't shy away from asking my permission to see Florence," I said, with a halfway grin. "You don't have any skeletons in your family closet, do you?"

"No, s—no," he replied a bit more forcefully.

"David's nice, Dad," Florence said. "He doesn't have anything to hide."

My eyes moved slowly from my daughter to the woman I loved. Then I turned and held David in a hard stare.

"I know. But we do."

"I don't know what you mean," he said.

"I'm going to tell you some things, David. The only reason I'm telling you is because I need your help and I feel that I can trust you."

He sat up a little straighter and glanced around the table. "Do I have to do anything illegal?"

"Legality sometimes depends on the situation," I said. "If that guy last night had pulled a gun and shot Sergeant Garcia, that would be illegal. If that same guy pulled a gun and threatened to shoot you, but Garcia beat him to the draw and shot him, that would be in the line of duty."

"What guy?" Florence asked.

"The man who's been committing these murders was at David's table last night," I replied.

"What?" all three asked, almost simultaneously.

"He was there," I said. "This morning, I saw him again, way over in Orange Walk, near the Mexican border. He'd been interrupted before he could kill another prostitute. So, you see how the situation can change whether something is illegal or not?"

"But I'm not a cop," David said. "I can't do anything illegal. I won't."

"What if someone took a swing at you?"

"That's self-defense," David said. "I might not win, but I won't let anyone hit me without fighting back. At least I'd hope not."

David looked from me to Savannah and back again.

"I think what Jesse's trying to ask, is—" Savannah looked at me for a brief moment, "—and I think it's a very sexist question—would you stay here and protect me and Flo, while he goes after a killer?"

"You're a cop?" David asked, incredulously.

"It's not sexist," I said to Savannah, with a bit of a smirk. "There's safety in numbers."

"What can we do to help?" Florence asked again.

"Wait a minute!" David said forcefully. "Are you with the police or something?"

"Or something," Savannah replied.

"Look, David," Florence said, "Dad's a good guy. He used to be with the government, but now he does the same thing for a private company."

"What do you mean by the same thing?"

"I'm a fixer, David," I said, leaning forward. "Just like you. I find bugs and fix them."

"I still don't get it," he said.

"The bugs I fix aren't in computers," I explained. "They're cockroaches in human form. You've heard how certain people get away with doing bad stuff, just because they have the clout to rise above the law? I work for an organization that can't be bought. We fix things that are broken in this world."

"And you need *my* help?" he asked. "A guy who studies business and works with computers?"

"The email I mentioned?" I said. "It came from a woman in Key Largo. She has a business degree and fixed computers to pay her way through school. When we hired her, she was an analyst for Homeland Security and before that for the CIA. She's one of our most valuable assets.

"Come with me," I said, reaching a decision. "All of you."

I made my way down to the lower salon and over to the flat-screen TV. They followed me.

"Have a seat," I said, then pushed against the foresail of a sailboat that was carved into the wood panel next to the TV.

The carving depicted a Formosa ketch, just like *Salty Dog*, under full sail. The foresail gave slightly and the whole panel folded down like a desk, a computer keyboard attached to the inside. In the exposed recess were a series of switches and a small computer monitor. I activated the satellite modem and turned on the TV interface. The monitor and TV screen flashed blue for a moment, and then the Armstrong logo appeared on each.

The logo was an inverted triangle in horizontal blue and white stripes, the blue lines getting thicker and the white ones thinner, going toward the point at the bottom. It gave the illusion of deepening water, accentuated by a pair of fish in the middle and a research boat on top of the triangle. A circle of words surrounded the triangle: Armstrong Research at the top, and Mobile Expeditionary Division at the bottom.

David's mouth fell open and even Savannah and Florence looked a bit surprised. Though they'd been aboard for two weeks, the *Dog* still had a few tricks up her sleeve.

The logo faded away and the static blue background changed to a young man sitting in the darkened control room aboard the research vessel *Ambrosia*, thousands of miles away. She was headed toward the Med, then through the ditch to the Red Sea.

"Hello, Captain McDermitt," the man I only knew as Scott said. "What do you need assistance with?"

"Hey, Scott," I greeted him. "I'm sure Chyrel has brought the colonel up to speed on what's going on here in Belize."

Another face leaned into the picture, the chiseled jaw, hard eyes and salt-and-pepper crew cut of none other than retired Army Airborne Colonel Travis Stockwell, head of security aboard *Ambrosia* and former deputy director at Homeland Security.

"She has, Gunny. Who is that with you?"

It was against protocol to bring anyone into the loop from the outside, but I needed this connection to be able to do what I had to do.

"This is my family, Colonel. Savannah and Florence Richmond and Florence's friend, David Stone, a computer expert at University of Florida."

"I see," Stockwell muttered.

"I'm leaving shortly," I said. "I'm going to have a couple of local cops—people I trust—meet me in Dangriga, Belize, to find a man who has already killed eight people."

Someone handed Stockwell a tablet, which he looked at for a moment. Then he tapped Scott on the shoulder and the young man rose from his seat and stepped aside. Stockwell took his place.

"I have Jasso's file," he said. "Before this goes any further, why are we communicating with others in the room?"

"David has agreed to stay here with my family," I said. "Jasso saw me. I can't operate without knowing they're safe and I want them aware of everything going on."

Stockwell's head fell for a moment. "First Snyder and now you," he muttered. Then he looked up at the screen. "What is it with you guys always wanting to be honest with your women about everything?"

"I know that's a rhetorical question, Colonel. But I can't operate without knowing what's going on with them. So, they need to be fully read in."

"Great," he said, muttering once more. Then his brows narrowed, and his nostrils flared. "Why don't we just have them aboard with Alicia and get it all done at *once*. While we're at it, let's change *Ambrosia's* name to the

Love Boat, then we'll all sit around a campfire, roast marshmallows and sing friggin' Kumbaya. It was bad enough with you and—never mind."

I felt bad that Sara was probably just outside Stockwell's control room on the bridge.

"How is she, Colonel Stockwell?" Savannah asked, moving up to stand beside me.

Stockwell's eyes flicked back and forth as he looked from me to Savannah on his screen. "She understands how to separate work from private life, Miss Richmond. I won't even bother to ask how you know my name."

"Can it, Colonel," I said flatly. "She has a need to know."

Stockwell didn't take kindly to anyone dressing him down, but he'd get used to it. Our relationship went back many years.

"I need your help with this," I said. "If you don't want to, that's fine. I'll bring Chyrel in, and then when I get back, we can schedule my boats for a retro-fit."

Travis and I had a long history. He knew that I never bluffed. I'd yank all of Armstrong's equipment out of my boats in half a heartbeat.

Though we'd chewed some of the same sand in the Middle East, he and I hadn't met there. We'd met soon after Charity and I took Jason Smith down in the Turks and Caicos Islands, and Travis took over as Deuce's boss. Later, after the team was broken up, he'd "retired" and I'd hired him as first mate on *Gaspar's Revenge*. We'd gotten to know one another quite well during that time. What

I hadn't known at the time was that he wasn't retired at all. He'd been Charity's handler for the CIA.

Stockwell looked over his left shoulder for a moment, then nodded.

"You win," he conceded, when he looked back to the screen. "This time. What do you need?"

Jack Armstrong must have been in the control room.

Stockwell was a crusty old soldier, single for more than half his life now and he had no kids—at least none that I knew of. He'd probably forgotten the hell he'd put his wife through when he was a young paratrooper. He was pushing sixty-five now and had been in service to his country in one form or another for over forty-five of those years. His outlook on soldiers with families was that if they needed one, they'd be issued one.

Jack Armstrong, on the other hand, had lost his wife and their only child on 9/11. It was that tragic event that had brought about the creation of Armstrong Research's new Mobile Expeditionary Division a few years ago. Wealthy patriots like Jack joined forces and organized a group of skilled operators like me, who had the ability to move around by land, sea, or air. Sort of a civilian version of the Marine Corps.

And nearly as big.

"I need a fast boat," I replied. "I'm anchored in San Pedro and need to get to Dangriga in a hurry. I'm twenty miles east of the mainland and then it's ninety miles south on some seriously piss-poor roads to get there.

Or I can go straight there in my dinghy. Either way, it'll take me several hours to get there with what I have."

"You know Jasso's there?"

"No," I replied. "But that seems the place to start."

Stockwell turned to his right and spoke to someone else. "Get me a go-fast in Belize. I want it in San Pedro, ASAP."

"Thanks, Colonel," I said.

"What else do you need?" he growled.

"Patch the *Dog* into my telemetry," I replied. "I want Savannah to see all comms at all times."

"You'll need someone on that end to operate the com—" he began. "Ah, Mr. Stone, is it?"

David stood quickly. "Yes, sir?"

"Do you know anything at all about AES 256-bit encryption?"

David's face literally came alive for the first time in several minutes.

"The so-called military grade encryption?" he replied, as Florence joined him by the keyboard. "Yes, sir. I sure do."

Stockwell again spoke to the person to his right. "Get on channel six four alpha," he said. "Walk Mr. Stone through the setup process. Then monitor Jesse's comm and add the transcription to his bravo console. Make yourself available on that feed to answer any questions his family has while he's on this op."

Stockwell turned back toward his console. "Anything *else*, Gunny?"

"The roads here are terrible," I said with a crooked grin. "Can you get someone to fill in the potholes?"

The corner of his mouth twitched. About as close to a smile as his granite features would allow.

"Six out," he said, then the screen went blank.

"What's he mean by six?" Florence asked.

"Think of the hands of a clock," I said, "and how you point to something on the horizon while on your boat. Six o-clock is behind you, at your back. You've heard the expression, 'I've got your six?'"

"He has your back?"

"Reluctantly, sometimes," I said, putting an arm around her. "But there aren't many I'd rather have with me in a fight. You can trust and count on Stockwell."

The three of us watched David working at the keyboard, only occasionally glancing up at the screen, where another person was doing the same. Finally, he looked up at me and said, "It should be done."

I crossed the room and pressed another panel—the same one that hid my Sig—and it dropped open. I removed a small box from the bottom of the hiding spot and opened it. There were three small communication devices inside.

"These are called earwigs," I explained to my silent audience. I took one out, turned it on, and put it in my ear, adjusting the bone mic. "Test-one."

My words immediately appeared at the bottom of the blank blue screen.

"This is incredible," David said.

The blue screen on the TV dimmed to black and the control room appeared behind an empty chair.

Then Sara Patrick sat down.

CHAPTER TWENTY-SIX

"Jesse?" Sara said. She looked a bit surprised, but quickly recovered as she adjusted her headset. "And how are you, Savannah and Flo? Who is that with you?"

This isn't awkward at all, I thought. But Sara was a professional, so there must be a reason she'd been called in. Or was Stockwell just that kind of prick?

"Sara?" Savannah said, then glanced at me. "What are...? She suddenly turned on me. "Did you know about this?"

"No," Sara said. "Mr. Stockwell just now ordered me to take over an admin console. I didn't know who I'd be working with until I saw you."

"Wait," I said. "You're first mate; second only to Captain Hansen, and he answers only to Jack."

"Mr. Stockwell is now the CSO for all of Armstrong."

"What happened to Bishop?" I asked.

William Bishop had been the chief of security for Jack Armstrong's organization ever since the beginning. He was the head of Jack's first oil exploration company's small security team decades before 9/11.

"Bill retired," Sara said. "And Nils will be retiring soon."

"Old salts like him never retire," I said. "But the question still stands; why is the first mate doing a logistics job?"

"Cross-training," she replied. "You'll be doing it one day, too."

"Not likely," I muttered.

"Why do you think Jack had you get your unlimited papers?" she said. "You'll be captain of *Ambrosia* one day."

What? This was news to me.

"Savannah," Sara continued before I could say anything, "please don't allow the past to influence your future. Jesse was never mine. He has always been yours." She straightened in her chair and smiled. "Now, will one of you introduce me to the young man I'll be working with?"

"This is my friend, David," Florence said.

Savannah nodded toward the upper salon. She wanted a private word, and I knew what it would be about. We both stepped away from the screen as Sara very efficiently got David familiar with the technology he'd be working with.

"Nice to meet you, David," she said. "I'm Sara Patrick, and as I said, I'll be your logistician until this is over. I assume Jesse has told you what's going on?"

"Yes, ma'am," David replied, as Savannah and I went up the steps. "I'll help any way I can."

Moving to the aft part of the upper salon, out of earshot, I turned to face Savannah and in a hushed voice, said, "Honest, I didn't know this would happen."

"But you knew she was there," Savannah hissed.

"Which you *also* knew," I said, exasperated. "I had no idea she'd be on the comm. It's always been Scott or Stockwell."

Slowly, a mischievous grin turned into a smile. "Gotcha!"

The image of the cartoon character Goofy from the Mickey Mouse cartoons popped into my head. As a kid, I'd always wondered why Goofy—a dog just like Pluto— wore clothes, talked, and walked on two feet, while Pluto did what dogs do. Moreover, I could never understand why they'd made him so tall. He was nearly twice as tall as Mickey and the others. Standing there with my mouth hanging open, I realized why. Tall guys looked goofy sometimes.

Savannah snorted a laugh, then covered her mouth. "I'm sorry. I couldn't resist. I'm not a jealous woman, Jesse. You're a grown man who can decide for himself who you want to be with and you're with me. That's that."

I took her in my arms and pulled her close. "I really do love you. I hope you know that."

She turned her face up to me and smiled. "Yes, I do. Now go hug your daughter so you can call the cavalry and get going. If these people are as good as you say, a boat will be here for you any minute."

"That's it," Sara said on the screen, as we stepped back down to the lower salon. "Now you're all set up."

"Yeah, I can handle this," David said.

"Jesse," Sara said. "A boat is headed your way." She leaned over to her right, looking at the next person's screen. "Should be there any minute. He's coming from Caye Caulker."

I turned to Savannah. "You know where everything's hidden?"

"We won't need it, but yes. Go after him, Jesse."

"I'm just going to have a look around," I said.

How many times had I said those words? As a Recon Marine, having a look around meant something altogether different. Recon was short for reconnaissance. Our motto was Swift, Silent, Deadly. We'd spend days, sometimes weeks, in the field, moving under cover of darkness like ghosts, then remaining stationary most of the day, never moving more than a few feet. Watching and waiting.

In the distance, I heard a buzz that quickly grew to a roar.

I hugged Florence and kissed Savannah, then put the box with the other two earwigs in my pack.

"I'll be in constant contact with Scott through this," I told Savannah, pointing to the comm in my ear. "Sara will be assisting him and will pass on to you everything that's going on, including where I am and what I'm doing. I'll be back in a few hours."

When I mounted the steps to the upper salon again, I found Finn and Woden were waiting there.

"Watch the girls," I said. "*Bewachen.*"

They rose and stood shoulder-to-shoulder in front of the steps, over 200 pounds of devoted loyalty, fierce tenacity, and flashing teeth and claws. Only a fool would try to get past them.

Up on deck, I could see the boat approaching. A dark blue go-fast boat. It didn't have the gaudy paint job you saw on a lot of these types of boats. It slowed, then turned into the cut. Coming down off plane, it turned toward me. A moment later, the sleek-looking Donzi 38ZR came alongside, its twin racing engines rumbling.

It never ceased to amaze me how fast Jack Armstrong could get things done. For nearly three decades, he'd built a network of business associates and contacts all over the globe. And those people had networks as well. Since 9/11, he'd focused on a different kind of relationship-building—wealthy patriots. Given time, he could get anything he needed delivered anywhere in the world. A go-fast boat was nothing in a country with as many boats as Belize.

A man rose and stood between the front seats. "You the guy needs a lift?" he asked.

American, I thought. There was a touch of east Tennessee or Kentucky in his voice.

The man was tan and lean, about thirty-five, wearing shorts, an open shirt, and wraparound Maui Jim sunglasses.

317

"Appreciate the quick response," I said, pulling my phone out to call Garcia. "Name's—"

"Don't need to know, friend," the man said. "Come aboard."

I stepped down the ladder as the guy nudged the boat toward me. When it was close enough, I stepped lightly onto the bow and moved quickly back to the cockpit.

"Head for the Sea Star pier," I said, settling into the right seat as he got behind the wheel. "We're picking someone up."

"If you gotta call, do it now," he said, jerking a thumb to the rear. "Those beasties back there only get louder."

I called the number Garcia had written on the back of the card and he answered instantly.

"It's McDermitt," I said. "I know who and where. Meet me at the pier."

He said he could be there in five minutes, and I ended the call.

"Where to after we pick up your friend?" Maui Jim asked.

"Dangriga."

"I can get ya there in about forty minutes," he said, putting the boat in gear and bumping the throttles up a little. "Or sooner if ya ain't scared."

"What do you have for power?" I asked.

"Mercury Racing 860s," he replied. "Top speed's eighty-eight knots."

I let out a low whistle.

CHAPTER TWENTY-SEVEN

The incident in Orange Walk had been a close call. The second one since Casey had started working for the Russian. It put him in close contact with more people than he preferred. That was dangerous.

Casey always took steps to keep a low profile and relied on his average looks to melt into the background. Given a choice, he'd avoid people altogether, eliminating any risk. But what Zotov wanted meant he had to interact with people. It was easy with the whores; they even provided a private location. But being American, he stood out in those places.

That was why he hung around with tourists. There just weren't a lot of white Americans in Belize. He'd tried a few times to get one of a group alone—that's how he'd gotten the kidney from the gay kid. Another time, it was a group of three couples. Getting one of them alone wasn't so easy and he'd abandoned the effort when one of the guys thought Casey was hitting on his wife.

The group of American college kids he'd met two days ago were easy to fall in with. They were scuba divers and he'd tagged along with them to a couple of dance clubs, arranging to meet up with them at the Dive Bar the next evening after their dive. One of the girls he was sure was clean; she'd said no to a joint they'd passed around, as had the one solo diver of the fivesome, a kid named David. He would have been easier to cut from the herd, since Perry never let his girlfriend out of his grasp. But then David had started flirting with a young tourist girl.

When the tall boat bum took the kid out on the beach to read him the riot act for messing with his daughter, another guy came and sat at his table.

Casey had seen that guy quite a few times and knew he was a cop. So, he'd given up on the college kids, faded into the background, and decided to go to Orange Walk the next morning.

He was certain the guy that caused all the commotion at the whorehouse was the dad of the hot little blonde David had been dancing with. The meddlesome old guy had recognized him. Of that he was certain. But what was he doing there? His old lady was plenty hot for an older woman. Maybe the guy just liked variety. Or maybe she was frigid. Or his sister.

Orange Walk was known as the place to go in Belize to get some cheap action.

He hadn't waited around to find out how long it had taken for someone to find the unconscious whore. It was doubtful the cops would connect her with the guy breaking down a door—they were in different rooms.

And what if they did? Casey thought, as he chewed a bit of his food.

With any luck, they'd go after the tall, white man from the ketch. He knew the bartenders paid little attention to which whore went with which john to which room.

An abandoned farm a little over two miles west of Orange Walk had served him as a safe place to land and take off without being seen. The road to the farm was long abandoned and overgrown, and a gate with a rusted chain and lock blocked what was once a driveway. The jungle landscape around the area absorbed the sound of his helicopter once he dropped below the tree line. In a pinch, he could have gotten there on foot in just fifteen minutes.

He'd briefly considered making the short walk to the next hotel, where he could find another victim, but decided it would have to wait. When Larissa was discovered, the heat in Orange Walk would just be too much.

Zotov's money could only make the authorities look the other way *after* the fact. Getting caught in the act, *with witnesses*, would be too great a risk to take.

Zotov would just have to be patient, not one of the man's strong suits.

Occasionally, Casey could hear Posh down in the basement as he finished his late lunch. She was finally broken now; it'd taken three days. But there was still a lot of training to do.

The lower basement was well-stocked with provisions and there was a sink and toilet that he let her use when he felt like it. There was also a drain in the floor for when he didn't. Soiling oneself was the ultimate in degradation.

Her whimpers were growing less exuberant. Over the next week, she'd learn to relish her new role as a play toy and Casey would become the center of her world. Physically, she needed little improvement beyond a little makeup and wardrobe. For now, she'd wear only what she was born with.

Casey knew he was taking a great risk keeping her. If she really was a spy for the Russian mob and they or Zotov found out that he had her, Casey knew what his life expectancy would be; almost nothing. And he'd never see it coming until it was too late.

Maybe it was time to move on—cut loose from the old Russian bear and get the hell out of Dodge. Posh could be his ticket to do just that. With the cash she'd bring, he could live like a king in the Philippines or Malaysia.

Juan rose and took his plate to the sink.

"I was just thinking, Juan," Casey said to the deaf man's back, loud enough for Posh to hear. "Thanks to that boat bum, I didn't get to slice and dice that little Guatemalan hottie. I *still* need two kidneys by tonight."

Then, with an accent similar to the native Mestizo's, he said, "You should kill di Russian and sell her heart, too."

The chains of the hoist rattled and Casey laughed loudly. "I don't think Russian women have hearts," he said, enjoying the little mind game. "But yeah, that's still an option."

Juan turned around and raised both hands, palms facing him, then turned them out, like he was flicking something from them. He was asking Casey in sign language if he was finished eating.

Casey nodded and Juan took his plate, scraping the crumbs into a bucket to be fed to the pigs. Then he turned back to the sink.

Rising, Casey left the kitchen and headed to the basement door in the living room. Once down the first flight of steps, he crossed the main basement floor and opened the locked door, then flipped on the lights. He listened for a moment before starting down, his footfalls on the rough wooden planks echoing as he slowly descended.

Juan knew about the second basement, but he'd never asked anything about it and had only ventured into the upper basement one time. Without any windows, he got very anxious before getting halfway down the steps, then turned and ran back up. Casey knew the man was claustrophobic, but Juan had explained it away, signing that the basement was too close to the devil.

If he only knew.

Posh hung from the hoist by her wrists, head slumped forward. With her back to him, and her feet barely touching the floor, she was a very enticing distraction.

Casey's new slave had a black bag over her head and a gag in her mouth. Though her sobs and screams on the first night had fallen on deaf ears—Casey just didn't care and Juan couldn't hear—the noise *did* keep Casey up that night. He preferred to sleep with the windows open in total silence.

So, about 3 AM, after taking her once more while hanging from all fours, he'd let her feet down to the floor. Then he'd lashed her with a leather strap, frayed at the ends. It left red welts but didn't bruise or break the skin. After that, he'd gagged her and covered her head before going to bed. He'd left her standing in the darkness like that, while he'd slept soundly in his very comfortable bed. She'd remained in that position when he'd flown to Orange Walk and back.

Twelve straight hours of standing would be hard on anyone. Doing it in the dark, with a bag over your head, gagged, and dangling naked, he was sure would drive anyone insane.

Casey walked up behind Posh and took his phone out of his pocket. His hand stroked her stretched ribcage, then moved down to her hips. She didn't flinch. He smacked her on the ass. That got a squeal.

"Now, what was on that order again?" he muttered as he touched the keypad on his phone so it would make noise. He watched the woman carefully. "Hmm, oh yeah, here it is; two kidneys, a pancreas, and a spleen."

Her body trembled as he slowly turned her, punctuating each word by touching her in the area where the organs were located. Even if she had no knowledge of human anatomy, she understood the implication.

"Anph," came a sound from under the hood.

"What was that, Posh?"

Casey put his hands on her narrow waist and turned her to face him, then whipped off the hood.

Posh's eyes blinked at the sudden bright lights. The side of her face was looking a lot better. The bruising had gotten smaller, but it was now darker, concentrated all around the orbital socket. Her left eye, though now open, was unusually bloodshot. Trails of salt residue streaked down both cheeks.

She'd cried.

"Were you asking permission to say something?" he asked, his voice cold and even.

She nodded her head, long strands of blond hair bouncing on her bare breasts.

Casey stepped closer, pressing his body against hers, so he could reach around her upstretched arms. He unclasped the gag and removed it from her mouth, dropping it to the floor. Then he stepped back just far enough to not be in contact with her body.

"You may speak," he said, a quiet, confident tone in his voice. "But keep in mind that you are nothing but a thing in here."

Her blue eyes locked on his, tears again streaming from them, but she was no longer sobbing.

"Please do not kill me," she whimpered. "I will do anything you say."

"Anything I tell you?" he asked.

"Yes."

He watched her face to gauge her reaction to what he was about to say. "I kill people and cut out their organs, Posh. Then I leave them to die and sell those organs on the black market."

She didn't break eye contact. "I will help you," she said, legs trembling.

Casey laughed. "You will?"

She nodded again, the light of hope shining in her eyes.

"What do you want most right now, *thing*?" he asked, looking down at her exquisite body.

She gulped. "To please you."

He stroked her face and let his hand roam down her body. She moaned softly as he cupped a breast, hefting its weight. When he smacked it, she squealed again.

"Well," he said, moving his hand lower, "I guess I might get what I need from the boat bum's girl on the ketch. Poetic justice, right?"

Posh's head went back between her raised arms as she moaned louder.

CHAPTER TWENTY-EIGHT

The Donzi racing boat idled toward the dock. Garcia was already there, waiting. He wasn't in uniform, but he did have his shield and sidearm on his belt.

"Can Menendez meet us in Dangriga?" I called to him as we approached.

"I just got off the phone with her," he replied. "She's in di City."

I fended us off the dock as Garcia stepped down.

"Call her and tell her to get to a pier," I said. "We'll pick her up."

"Another stop," Maui asked. "I thought you were in a hurry."

"Who's he?" Garcia asked.

"I don't know," I replied. "And he doesn't know us."

Garcia made a call, then turned to the driver, who was backing the boat away from the dock. "Radisson pier, Fort George."

Maui turned toward deeper water, headed for the cut. In seconds, he had the boat up on the step and we blasted through the cut at what I guessed to be close to fifty miles per hour. Then he turned south and opened the throttles up a little more.

I didn't know how fast we were going; the speedometer wasn't at an angle where I could see it while pinned into my seat.

Judging from the spray to either side, only the aft ten feet or so of the thirty-eight-foot boat's Deep-V racing hull was in the water as it easily skipped across the light chop.

It took just over half an hour to cover the forty miles to Belize City, including the slow approach in the busy waters around the city. A quick calculation in my head told me we had to have been going nearly eighty miles per hour. And I don't think Maui Jim ever pushed it to wide-open throttle.

As we neared the pier, I recognized Menendez standing at the end, a black backpack at her feet. She, too, was dressed in street clothes, but unlike Garcia, she wasn't wearing her weapon or badge. She tossed her pack down to Garcia in the back as I held the boat off the pier.

"Whose boat is this?" Menendez asked, stepping down.

"His," Garcia said, nodding toward my Maui Jim-wearing cohort.

"Nice boat," she said. "I am—"

"Gonna fall out unless you sit down," Maui said, putting the boat in reverse.

Garcia explained what we'd both assumed—that he didn't want to know our names, nor us to know his. Anonymity was fine by me, as long as the man did what he was supposed to do.

I studied a satellite image on my phone of the area around the target, then handed it to Maui Jim and asked, "Do you know this creek?"

He looked at the screen and zoomed it out a little. "Yeah, but it ain't navigable."

"How far can you get us in?"

"Not far at all," he replied. "There's shifting sand bars all up that creek, like most creeks around here. There's only a couple feet of water once you get just a little way in from the coast."

"Good enough," I said, punching the coordinates into Maui's chart plotter. "Put us on the south bank, as far in off the beach as you can get. We'll find a spot you can land or tie off."

The sun was already behind the trees when Maui slowed and made the turn toward the coast. I stood and watched the water ahead as he mostly kept his eyes on the chart plotter.

The natural channel, created by eons of runoff water from the creek, meandered away from the coast. Or maybe the channel had once been the creek bed itself, at a time when sea levels were lower, during the last ice age. Either way, it was narrow and winding.

Small waves washed over coral heads on either side as we navigated the channel. Maui did an amazing job keeping us centered.

Palms and mangroves lined both sides of the creek as we moved upstream. Ahead, a small sandbar jutted out from the first bend in the creek.

"That's about as far as we can go," Maui said, pointing to it. "After this bend, there ain't enough water to float anything but a canoe."

"Can you beach us on that sandbar?" I asked, pulling the box out of my pack.

"Yeah, I think so," Maui replied, standing and looking over the windshield. "It looks deep on the inside of the bar," he concluded, pointing the bow toward it.

I opened the box and took one of the earwigs out. Turning it on, I handed it to Garcia, then did the same for Menendez.

"With these, we can stay in contact if we get separated," I explained. "My logistician is on there, too."

The two cops put the devices in their ears and adjusted their bone mics as if they'd used similar equipment before.

"Comm check," I said.

"Loud and clear," Garcia replied, nodding.

"I hear just fine," Menendez added.

"Roger that," Scott said over the comm. "If you need anything, let me know. Just call me Scott."

Garcia grinned. "I could use one million dollars, Scott," he said. "Belizean or American, makes no difference to me."

Scott chuckled. "I'll see what I can do. But I meant more in the way of information."

"Worth a try," Menendez said. "We playin' out of our league, cousin."

"You two are related?" I asked.

"By marriage, of course," Menendez said.

Maui told me where the dock lines were stored, and I took one with me to the foredeck. The pool behind the sandbar was indeed deep. The bow was already over the sand before the keel made contact.

Jumping down, I found a sturdy, overhanging palm tree and tied the boat off to it as the two cops joined me on the sandbar.

"How long can you wait?" I asked Maui.

"Right now, I'm all yours until midnight. But that can be extended with a little more gas in the tank, if you know what I mean."

He was obviously not a part of the Armstrong team. Maui Jim might know someone who knew someone who was connected to the organization, but Maui Jim worked for cash.

"We won't be that long," I told him, then turned to the others. "It's going to be dark soon. I have one set of night vision optics and a spotting scope. So, stay close."

I shrugged out of my pack and opened it. Pulling out my lightweight Pulsar Edge goggles, I switched them on and perched them on my forehead.

Then, using my phone's GPS, I got a bearing on the target. "The house is only a quarter mile from here," I told them, pulling the goggles down and looking in the direction indicated.

We were too low to see any lights from the house directly, but there was a distinct glow in that direction.

I turned on the spotting scope and handed it to Garcia. "You can see the glow of the house's lights from here. Once we get up on solid ground, we should be able to see the house."

He peered through the scope, then handed it to Menendez.

"This guy has already killed a bunch of people," I said. "I'm guessing more than we know. But he's just a stepping-stone. I want the guy who's buying from him."

"We'll arrest this guy," Menendez said. "Then we'll find out who's paying him."

She started to turn toward the creek bank, but I put a hand on her shoulder to stop her. "*I'll* be the one who finds out," I said. "You two are sworn police officers."

"What's that supposed to mean?" she asked.

"Once you take him into custody," I began, "he's gonna lawyer up and the money man is going to bolt. There's no allegiance among these people. Then the money he was using to buy off your bosses will go away. Do you wanna be *that* scapegoat?"

"We have to arrest him," Garcia said.

"You can," I replied. "After I get the information from him."

"What makes you think he'll talk to you before us?" Menendez asked.

"Because I'm not a cop," I replied. "I'm not bound by your rules."

"Now, wait!" Garcia said. "What do you plan to do?"

"You said you knew how our organization does things," I said. "We don't wait for the courts or due process. If a turd's a turd, it gets flushed."

"That's vigilantism," Menendez said.

"We don't like that word," I said, lifting my goggles. "Nor do we like the term 'mercenary.' Vigilantes have a vested interest and are fueled by emotion. Mercenaries don't care about anything but money. Armstrong Research is only interested in results and making the world a better place."

"And you can't be bought?" she said sarcastically.

"Jack Armstrong's net worth is way into the billions," I said. "As are all of the organization's board of directors. I don't know who's funding your corruption, but whoever he is, he can't buy Armstrong."

"And you?" she asked.

"Even if I were still just an enlisted U.S. Marine, he couldn't buy me."

"How do you know this is the right man?" Menendez asked, taking a different tack.

"I saw him come out of that room where you and I found the girl. I assume a doctor saw her. What was in her system?"

"Diazepam," she admitted.

"The same as the others," Garcia added.

"The guy I saw coming out of that room was carrying a cooler. He had that same cooler last night when Garcia and I met at the Dive Bar. One of the people he was with last night identified him as Casey Jasso, an American ex-pat who lives in that house just over the rise. Before he left the States, he was an emergency medical technician and trained nurse. Shortly after each murder, Jasso made sizable deposits to a numbered account in the Caymans. Did I miss anything, Scott?"

"He was a person of interest in a kidnapping and assault case in Montana," Scott added over the comm. "The victim nearly died and one of her kidneys was missing. He disappeared after that."

"Okay, so he's probably the guy," Menendez conceded. "But if Elden and I aren't here to arrest him, what are we here for?"

"You can have him after I'm through. But I *am* going to find out who's paying him."

"He still has to stand trial," she countered.

I'd had about enough. I yanked the goggles off my forehead and glared at her in the gathering gloom.

"He just did," I growled.

"Okay," Menendez conceded. "But most of the murders took place in my town. I will be with you when you question him."

She returned my stare and I could see the determination in her eyes. I suddenly realized that Savannah and Florence were reading my words.

"That's fine," I said. "My methods are more psychological than physical."

If I needed to, I could just turn the earwigs off. There were some things Savannah and Florence didn't need to know.

"Let's go," Garcia said. "It's dark enough now to get across the open ground without being seen."

Pulling the goggles down, I proceeded to lead the way, and the three of us scrambled up the bank and quickly reached the high ground. There were trees along the bank; mangroves down at the water, palms hanging over them, and tropical hardwoods up at the top.

When I peered through the trees, the gray-green optics were overpowered by the lights from the windows of a ranch house on the other side of a broad field. I scanned the open ground, and once the bright lights of the house were out of my field of vision, the optics adjusted. It looked like a pasture for cattle, but I didn't see any animals.

"The field looks clear," I said. "No angry bulls or dogs."

"Perfect," Garcia whispered unnecessarily. "We can get to the back of the house in complete—"

The sound of an unmuffled engine starting up interrupted him. Not a car or a truck engine. It increased speed and I heard the unmistakable whine of helicopter rotors spinning.

"Hurry!" I shouted, spotting the flashing light on the chopper.

I broke out of the tree line at a dead run, pulling my Sig from its holster behind my back.

Halfway across the field, I watched as the chopper rose and flew off toward the north. I raised my Sig, following it, but I knew it was way out of range.

We'd wasted too much time arguing on the sandbar.

"Dammit!" I said, slowing to a walk and holstering my gun.

"What happened?" Scott said.

"He got away," I replied. "Or someone did. A helicopter just took off, headed north. You didn't tell me he was a pilot, Scott."

"Stand by," Scott replied. "I'll pull up BZE's flight control."

"Let's check the house," Garcia said.

I looked to where the helo had taken off, seeing a square of asphalt with a big H in the middle of it. "There's a helipad."

"Jasso still might be here," he argued. "Maybe the helipad is for visitors."

I was certain it was Jasso in the chopper and didn't expect to find much in the house. Chyrel's email had included a brief profile from Paul Bender, our forensic psychologist. He'd predicted what the guy would look like and nailed that to a tee. He'd also written that the killer was likely to be a loner and very organized. I'd learned to trust what Paul said.

A figure passed by a window when we got close. All three of us saw it and crouched in the darkness.

"One person inside," I reported.

Staying low, we moved toward the house. "Garcia, take the back."

Menendez stayed with me, both of us leading with our weapons as we approached the front door. Against the porch wall, I removed the Pulsar goggles and stuffed them in my pack.

"I'm in position near the back door," Garcia said over the comm.

Menendez banged loudly on the door. "*Polees!* Open the door!"

Nothing.

She banged and shouted again.

"I can see someone in the kitchen," Garcia said. "Looks like he's washing dishes, but I can hear you through the door."

"Maybe he's wearing earbuds," I whispered, reaching down and trying the knob.

It wasn't locked.

"The front door's open," I said.

"Back's locked," Garcia reported.

"Stay there in case he runs," Menendez said, turning the knob and pushing the door open.

She went in first, crossing in front of me. I followed, going in the opposite direction, gun raised and at the ready.

Nothing moved in the large living room. It was decorated sparsely, similarly to my own house, rough wooden furniture with plush leather upholstery.

Light spilled from the back part of the house, where I heard the sound of running water.

"Help me!" A voice called, sounding far away.

"It came from that door," Menendez whispered.

I nodded.

We moved deeper into the house toward the light. The sound of chains rattling could be heard from the door to my right.

When we could see into the kitchen, we found a man with his back to us. Just as Garcia had said, he was washing dishes.

"*Polees!*" Menendez shouted at his back. "Don't move!"

The man at the sink ignored us and continued what he was doing.

Suddenly, the back door crashed in, causing the man to jump to the side as Garcia came in, training his weapon on him. He was Mestizo and old, maybe sixty or so. He immediately raised both hands as high as he could.

"Where did Casey Jasso go?" Garcia barked at him.

"He did not say," the man replied, his words slurred like he'd just come from a root canal and the Novocain hadn't worn off yet.

He suddenly seemed to realize that Menendez and I were also in the room. "Don't hurt me. I only work here."

Again, his words were slurred and I understood then why he hadn't responded to the banging and yelling.

"He's deaf," I said.

"Please to help me," a woman's voice cried from somewhere below the floor.

"Take care of him," I said. "He can read lips."

I retraced my steps, gun still at the ready. In the living room, I again heard the rattle of chains as I approached the closed door. Opening it, I saw the first couple of steps of a staircase that disappeared into darkness.

The rattling was louder now. I flicked a switch on the wall and the stairwell lit up, as did a basement at the foot of the stairs.

Menendez joined me and we started down.

I heard a moan, which drew my attention to another door on the far side of the basement.

Seeing nothing in the room but shelves stacked with dry goods, I hurried across the floor to the other side. The second door was locked.

A woman's sob could be heard from inside.

"Step back," I said, aiming my Sig at the spot where the deadbolt entered the door jamb. I fired once, shattering the wood frame. The door slowly swung open a few inches, the metal strike plate hanging off the deadbolt, the mounting screws still partially intact.

A woman screamed.

Beyond the door was utter darkness. I felt along the wall and found a light switch. When I turned it on, I saw a woman's legs down below. She was standing on her toes, and as I descended a few steps, I saw that she had no clothes on.

Menendez followed me down and Garcia quickly joined us.

"I cuffed the guy to the refrigerator," he said. "What's down—"

It was easy to see there was nobody else in the small room. I rushed to the woman, looking at the contraption she was hanging from.

Her head was covered, and her wrists were strapped to a beam held up by a chain hoist. I found the control and lowered it slightly as Menendez helped the woman stay on her feet.

"It is okay," Menendez said in a soothing voice. "We are the *polees*."

I quickly unbuckled the straps while looking around at the rest of the room, or more accurately, the dungeon. Everything in there was equipped with leather shackles and restraints. There were whips, chains, and paddles hanging from the walls, and on a shelf, something that resembled a cattle prod was plugged into a charger.

I retched a little at the thought of what all this stuff was for. The depravity a human was capable of knew no bounds once sanity was removed from the equation.

When I'd released her wrists, I quickly ran up the steps to the living room and grabbed a large blanket that was draped over a heavy leather recliner.

I raced back down to the dungeon.

"Here," I said, extending the blanket to Menendez as she started to lower the woman into a chair.

Her hood was off, and I could see her battered face. What I didn't see were any incisions. She had long blond hair, and aside from the black eye, she was very beautiful, which was probably why she was still alive and had all her parts. She'd been beaten severely.

Menendez wrapped the blanket around the woman and eased her into the chair. "You are safe," she said. "We are the *polees*."

"Do you know who the man is who held you here?" Garcia asked.

"His name is Casey," she said in heavily accented English; Russian, or from one of the Eastern European states.

"Do you know who his boss is?" I asked.

"*Da!*" she said, looking up at me. "He is Basil Zotov."

"Basil Zotov," I repeated. "Run that name, Scott."

"You're garbled," Scott said. "Suggest you come up out—"

The rest of what he was trying to say turned to static.

"I need to go upstairs to get that information to Scott," I said, as I turned and ran up the stairs again.

"Do you read me now, Scott?" I asked, reaching the living room.

"Loud and clear. What name did you want me to check out?"

"Basil Zotov," I replied. "He's who Jasso sells the organs to. Get back to me as soon as you know something."

"No need," he said. "Zotov was a well-known weapons dealer and former member of the Russian mafia before the wall came down. *Bratva* kicked him out of the country a couple of years ago. That's the Russian mob. He's been sighted in the Caribbean and South America a few times in the last year, but he's not believed to be smuggling weapons anymore. Jesse, this guy's bad news—ruthless and cunning."

"Roger that," I said, heading back down to the basement. "Get working on Zotov, Scott. Priority one. I want to know his current location.

"Zotov is your money-man," I told Garcia, when I reached the basement where the two cops and the woman were. "That's what I came for. It's just a matter of me finding him now. When Zotov is out of the picture, things can return to normal here; the money *will* be shut off. So, you can find and arrest Casey Jasso on your own."

I turned and started for the door.

"I know where he is going," the Russian woman said.

"Who?" Garcia asked.

"Casey," she replied, as I reached for the stair rail. "He is going after girl on ketch."

CHAPTER TWENTY-NINE

I'd seen a lot of dive boats since we'd arrived in Belize, a few fishing boats and smaller private vessels. I'd even seen a few other sailboats—all sloops. I hadn't seen another ketch since leaving Cozumel.

A cold chill ran down my spine, paralyzing my legs with fear. My left foot suddenly froze in place on the first step. "What did you say?" I asked, as I slowly turned around.

The blue eyes of the Russian woman found mine across the small room. "He say it is poetic justice to kill girl on ketch of old boat bum."

"Change in plans," I said to Garcia. "Jasso's all mine."

I hurried up the steps. "Scott, go dark."

After a moment, he replied, "If you mean take your family and the two cops offline, they are. What did the woman say? We couldn't hear."

"Jasso is headed for *Salty Dog*," I replied, running across the dark pasture while trying to speak coherently. "He can't get to it by chopper...so he'll need a boat. Any luck tracking him...through the airport's radar?"

"Negative," Scott replied. "No problem getting the feed, but he must be flying low. Jesse, there's nothing in his bio that says he's a pilot."

"He might not be licensed," I huffed. "But he can definitely fly. Do I have any backup?"

"Also, negative," he replied. "Not fast anyway. The boat you arrived on is it, and the guy who brought you there is just a hired hand. Charity's offline somewhere in the Caymans and we have one of our research vessels working a site a hundred miles off the coast of Honduras."

A hundred miles off Honduras would be closer to Belize than Honduras. If it was like other research vessels in Jack's fleet, it might only be a few hours away.

"Can you divert the research vessel?"

Jack Armstrong's voice came over the comm, steady and calm as always. "Tell me what's going on, Jesse."

"He's going after my daughter, Jack," I said, already breathing hard from the run with my pack on. "Do we have anyone...who can get to San Pedro...before me? I'm close to an hour away."

There were hushed whispers, but I couldn't make anything out. A thousand thoughts ran through my head as I pulled the goggles on to locate Maui Jim and his go-fast boat.

Jasso had a good head start and the chopper was probably faster than Maui's Donzi, but he'd have to land and get a boat somewhere. That took time. The logical places would be the airport in Belize City or the little strip out on Ambergris Caye. Hell, for all I knew, he might land at any one of a hundred farms near the coast. But once he was on the water, I doubted there were many boats in the country that could match Maui Jim's.

"Jesse," Jack said, as I spotted the glow from a cigarette, "Garcia has local police going to the airport on the island and an officer can be sent out to your boat. I've diverted *Papillon* to rendezvous there, as well. But she can't get inside the reef."

"Let Savannah know," I said as I scrambled down the bank to the sandbar.

"Let's go!" I shouted to Maui as my feet hit the sand.

He was sitting at the helm, smoking a cigarette, his feet up on the other seat. He spun around, flicked the butt into the water, and started the engines.

"Where're the others?" he asked.

I untied the line and vaulted up onto the bow.

"They're not coming," I said, breathlessly. "Get me back to my boat...as fast as this thing can go."

CHAPTER THIRTY

F ast is a relative term. To a sailor, twenty knots is fast. To a man whose family is in danger, the speed of light isn't fast enough. This time Maui Jim did mash the throttles down, and I still thought it too slow.

It was full dark, but a waning quarter moon was up, and the sky was clear. It was a week past the first full moon of the year, known as the Wolf Moon, and Luna provided enough light to see for miles.

I'd given Maui my Pulsar goggles. The Donzi rocketed north-northeast across the smooth water, less than a mile from the reef line.

Off to port, toward the northwest, a flash of light caught my eye, way out over the mainland. I looked that way and saw it again. Lightning.

"Storm's coming!" Maui shouted.

In more ways than one, I thought.

"Don't look directly at it," I yelled. "The flash will overpower the optics."

Maui leaned closer but kept his eyes on the water ahead. "Is there something you're not telling me?" he yelled over the engines and buffeting wind.

We were headed toward a rendezvous with a psycho killer who stole human organs from his victims. Maui had a right to know that. I raised the armrest and got closer to him. "A murderer is going after my daughter," I yelled. "We have to get back to my boat fast."

"We're wide open now," he shouted, the wind snatching his words away. "Is there anything I can do when we get there?"

He seemed like an able enough man, but I had no idea about his background.

"You good with a gun?" I asked, pulling my backpack open.

"Yeah," he replied, waving a hand over my pack. "I got my own."

"I don't know your name," I said. "I'm Jesse."

"Name's Jim," he replied.

I couldn't help but laugh.

Scott kept me abreast of what was going on. David and Savannah both knew what was happening and she was taking precautions. After thirty minutes, Scott advised me that a police boat was near *Salty Dog* but wouldn't approach unless someone else did.

I checked my watch: it was 1950. The chopper had taken off more than thirty minutes earlier. If Jasso flew to San Pedro, he was probably on the ground by now. And hopefully in custody. If not, he was on a boat headed for the cut at San Pedro.

Passing Caye Caulker, I could see the lights of San Pedro ahead. Just beyond Ambergris Caye, lightning flashing across the sky illuminated some very ominous-looking thunderheads.

I could see *Salty Dog's* masthead light as we approached the cut and Jim started slowing the boat. That's when the clouds decided to open up.

Rain pelted us at nearly sixty knots as Jim struggled to get the speed down as fast as possible. You couldn't just yank back on the throttle at high speed in a small boat. The bow would dip and could potentially bury, pitch-poling the boat end over end.

As we turned through the cut, I saw a police boat to the right. The guy on board was struggling to get his anchor up.

To the left, I saw a strange boat tied up to the *Dog*.

My pulse rate quickened as I strove to see through the rain.

I could just make out someone on the aft deck, and someone else was coming out of the cabin. When we got closer, I realized it was Savannah and Jasso.

"Hurry!" I shouted, rising from my seat and drawing my Sig. "Get me closer."

Savannah leapt from the cockpit, then assumed a fighting stance on the aft deck, crouched low. Jasso feinted a lunge for her, but she somehow read it and spun backward, catching him in the backs of both knees with a sweeping kick, following through as if she were a highly trained martial artist. He went down hard and for a second, I thought it was over.

The police boat began to come up behind us, the operator having finally freed his anchor. He had all his lights on, flashing a weird combination of red and blue in the downpour.

Through the rain, I saw Savannah step back, wiping her hair back from her face. She was yelling at Jasso, taunting him as he lay on the side deck near the rail. I had no idea she could be so fierce.

Suddenly, the man was on his feet. He had a pistol in his hand, leveled at Savannah.

Seemingly from nowhere, Finn charged up out of the hatch at full speed. Just as he turned and leapt, Jasso pivoted and ducked. Finn sailed past him, caught a hind leg on the railing, then cartwheeled into the water.

Jasso turned back to Savannah, ready to finish her off. We were approaching from the port side and he was beyond Savannah on the starboard side. He was still out of accurate shooting range and I'd be just as likely to hit her as him.

Time seemed to slow. We were a good hundred feet away, and I was doing my best to put my sights on Jasso's midsection. The boat was moving in the chop and the wind was buffeting me.

Over the rising thunder came a loud boom.

Jasso toppled sideways into the water.

David stood in the companionway, my Mariner shotgun at his shoulder.

Savannah's head jerked around toward the lights from the police boat, then she saw me standing on the bow of the Donzi, my Sig trained on the man in the water.

Jasso wasn't moving and I doubted he ever would. Finn was swimming in circles around the body, barking at it.

"Finn!" I shouted. "Go to the ladder."

Jim maneuvered close as the police boat came up beside us. I holstered my Sig and moved to the back of the Donzi, where the gunwale was lowest. Finn could climb the ladder, but I was worried he might have hurt his leg on the rail, so I helped him up, following right behind him.

In an instant I held Savannah in my arms. "Thank God you got here when you did," she said. "When he arrived, I thought it was you. He was about to shoot me."

"It was David," I said.

She turned and saw the young man standing in the companionway, rain dripping from his hair. He'd laid the Mariner on the deck.

"Get below," I said. "I'll be down in a minute."

The cop on the boat was the same one who'd brought Garcia out to our dive site when we'd found the woman's foot.

"Permission to come aboard, Cap'n?" he shouted.

"Toss me a line," I yelled back. "You too, Jim."

"I'm just a taxi driver," Maui Jim called back. "All the same to you and the officer, I'll just head on home."

The cop looked up at me and I just shrugged. I had more important things to take care of.

To my surprise, the cop told Jim he could leave. The powerful Donzi was roaring away by the time I got the police boat alongside and tied off.

I picked up the Mariner and stowed it under the starboard bench seat as the police officer climbed up.

A moment later, he and I joined the others in the upper salon. Florence handed us towels, for which I was grateful. Savannah was sitting with David, both of them with towels over their shoulders. She was holding David's hand, talking quietly to him, as he stared down at the deck.

The cop turned toward me. "Sergeant Garcia called me," he said. "I am Constable Leo Ramirez, his cousin."

David looked up, fear in his eyes. "I won't resist," he said. "I did it."

Ramirez and I both looked over at him. "Did what?" the constable asked.

"I shot that man."

"I saw what happened with my own eyes," Ramirez said. "You were defending dis lady. Dat man was going to shoot her. You did nothing wrong."

David stared at him for a moment, then looked at me.

"It's all about the situation," I said. "Thank you for being here. You stopped the Ghoul Killer, David."

Florence sat down beside him and took his other hand. "You saved my mom's life, David. To me, you're a hero."

A phone chirped somewhere. Finn and Woden both locked their eyes like lasers on Ramirez. He took a phone from his belt and answered it. "Constable Ramirez."

He listened for a moment then said, "He is down. Everyone else is aboard di sailboat and safe."

He listened a moment longer, then extended his phone to me. "Another boat is coming to help me find di body. Sergeant Garcia wishes to speak with you."

I held the phone to my ear. "McDermitt."

"We are on the way to hospital with the woman," Garcia said. "She gave us the name of the boat she was taken from; Zotov's yacht. It is called *Toyana Devushka*."

"*Toyana Devushka*," I repeated. "Any idea where it is?"

"I'm already checking on it," I heard Scott say, both from the tiny earwig and from the speaker in the lower salon.

We went down there just as the rain stopped completely. Sara's video link was still open, and on the screen, I could see she had her mic covered with one hand. Her head was turned, talking to someone, probably Scott. At the bottom of the screen I read the words, *Scott, go dark.*

Savannah took my hand and stood up on her toes to whisper in my ear. "Don't you *ever* hang up on me again."

"Got it," Scott said, as Sara turned back to her keyboard, typing furiously.

"Connecting telemetry," Sara said.

The TV screen switched to a chart of the Central American coastline. A red dot appeared where we were anchored just off San Pedro. Then two more dots blinked on. One, I guessed to be a good fifteen miles due east of our location and the other about the same distance to our southeast.

"The other two icons are the *Toyana* and *Papillon*," Sara said. "*Papillon* is to the south.

"What assets are aboard *Papillon*?" I asked.

"The usual security detail with small arms," she replied. "Exploration assets include dive gear, compressor, rebreathers, two full hard-hat suits, and a two-person mini-sub."

I stared at the positions of the three dots. Together they formed a nearly perfect triangle, just like the one on the ARMED logo, pointing to the depths. That gave me an idea about how I could get to the yacht unseen.

I considered what I had on board. In a hiding place down in the workroom was a block of about four pounds of C-4, fuses, timers, and det-cord—all waterproof.

I stared at the blue dot on the screen to our east. If I could just push a button and send a missile on its way to dispatch the yacht to the bottom, I would. People like Casey Jasso and Basil Zotov had no place in society. They were nothing more than a blight on humanity.

Savannah looked up at me. "If violence wears a *look*, Jesse, you're wearing it now."

The mask.

The warrior's mask I'd often tried to hide from those closest to me. It had slipped on so easily over the years but was becoming increasingly difficult to remove.

Thousands of words rattled around in my brain, words meant to explain or at least justify the things I'd done and would probably do again. Those words collided with other messages: tiny dispatches from all my senses were feeding information to my brain about wind, current, distance to target, and submersion time. Those flashes of information always had priority in my mind. So, the words I wanted to say kept getting knocked to the side.

"I have to stop this guy from—" I started to say.

Savannah put a finger to my lips. "Hush now, Jesse," she whispered. "This isn't the time for words. You go to work, and just make sure you're back here by morning." She waved a hand at the console. "And you can turn all this off. I know you'll return safe and if I have any questions, I have Sara's number."

I glanced over at the screen, confused. It switched back to the camera at Sara's console aboard *Ambrosia* and her face once more appeared before me.

Sara smiled. "What do you need?"

I turned back to Savannah. "Do you feel comfortable taking the *Dog* out at night?"

CHAPTER THIRTY-ONE

Someone handed my rebreather, fins, and mask down and then the hatch above my head was closed. I settled myself into the seat and put on a pair of headphones that were hanging by my knee.

The sub wasn't small—nearly thirty feet long—but the compartment for the two-man crew seemed as if it had been built in Lilliput. Of course, it didn't help that I was six-three in bare feet and weighed 225 pounds.

I put my gear on the deck between my knees as a crackle came over the headset. Then a voice said, "*Sea Leopard, Sea Leopard,* this is *Papillon* control."

"*Sea Leopard,*" Marc Fisher replied from the front seat.

I'd only met Marc once, but it was a long meeting. Sara and her father, John Wilson, had trained me in tethered submersibles, but it was Marc who'd taught me to fly through the water untethered in a mini-sub. Jack Armstrong had three others just like *Sea Leopard.*

An hour earlier, after being assured by Garcia that David would never even be mentioned in his constable's report, I'd taken Jasso's boat and met *Papillon* ten miles out at sea. She wasn't as big as *Ambrosia*—only 122 feet in length—but while *Ambrosia* had been converted into a research vessel, *Papillon* had been built from the keel up just for research purposes. Like *Ambrosia*, she was also a wolf in sheep's clothing when it came to speed.

"Ready on your order," the voice in the control room said.

Marc gave a thumbs up to the crane operator. "Let's get wet."

One of the crew climbed onto the side of the sub and disconnected the electrical umbilical and a moment later, I felt a lurch as the crane lifted the sub off the deck. We were slowly swung out over the water, then lowered to the surface.

The conning tower of the mini-sub was our compartment. There were three panes of curved acrylic at the front and three more flat windows down the sides, giving us a sweeping 270° of visibility. The rest of the thirty-foot sub resembled a torpedo with wings. The hull itself was stuffed with batteries and electronics and our little pocket of air kept *Sea Leopard* upright and ballast tanks kept her at the desired depth.

The swaying movement stopped, and I could hear water lapping at the composite hull. The sub wasn't designed for deep dives like the submersibles. In *Sea Leopard* we could only go to 200 feet. The submersibles could go a hundred times deeper. But what she lacked in extreme depth capability, *Sea Leopard* and her sister subs more than made up for in speed and maneuverability. A good pilot could fly her through the water just like an airplane, banking and diving quickly if needed.

Marc was far more than a good pilot.

Divers went fore and aft, and I could hear the clanking as the two lift chains were disconnected.

"All clear," control said.

"Roger that," Marc replied. "Diving to twenty feet."

Air bubbled from the ballast tanks as we started our dive. Once the glass was below the surface, the underwater world all around us lit up as the bright work lights refracted off the surface, dispersing the light in all directions.

Visibility was probably over a hundred feet, but the light didn't penetrate that far.

"Are you sure this is the way to do this, Jesse?" Jack's voice asked over my headphones.

"We'll get the crew off," I said. "But Zotov is staying aboard. We know what he is, and with his wealth, he wouldn't be behind bars more than a few minutes. Then he'd rabbit and disappear."

The whir of the electric motors started, and we began to move out of the light.

"Bearing three-zero-zero magnetic," Marc said. "Speed ten knots, depth at twenty feet, bottom... well over a hundred fathoms, and totally unachievable. All systems are working fine."

"You have four hours of air," control said, "and three hours of battery at full output."

"Godspeed," Jack said.

WAYNE STINNETT

"Diving to two-five meters," Marc said. "Increasing speed to twenty knots. See you on the other side."

The *Toyana Devushka*, which meant Toyana girl, was ten nautical miles away—just thirty minutes. They wouldn't know we were coming and wouldn't see us when we arrived. Marc would keep us outside their lights when we surfaced, and I'd go the rest of the way with the rebreather.

Swift. Silent. Deadly.

Ooh-rah, a voice in my head grunted.

The minutes ticked by slowly. At this depth the sub's antenna was below the surface, so we were completely on our own. But well below the surface, with increased pressure on the hull, parasitic drag was minimized, and the little sub was like a bird, capable of flying at thirty knots, banking, and turning on a dime, much like a fighter jet.

But silent.

"We didn't get much chance to catch up back there," Marc said.

"Sorry for keeping you up so late," I offered.

"You didn't," he replied. "You know I work the night watch whenever I can."

"You okay with what we're doing?"

There was a moment of silence before he spoke.

"At first, no. Most of the time, I think there's a way to negotiate, or a line where local law enforcement should take over. But then I read the reports of what was going on. Stealing human organs, man? That's the kinda shit from nightmares."

"These two have killed at least eight people the authorities know of," I said. "The victims' organs were removed while they were alive and the victims, mostly women, were left to bleed out. They had a woman captive in what I can only describe as a sex dungeon. Chyrel hacked Zotov's email. He wanted Jasso to bring him four fresh organs today. Jasso went after my daughter."

"Sucks for him," Marc said.

"Yeah," I muttered. "Sucks on ice."

"I've heard you use that expression before. What's it mean?"

"You've been in a situation that totally sucked before, right?"

"Sure," he replied. "We all have."

"Think back to that one situation when things sucked worse than ever. Remember how it felt? Now move everything, lock, stock, and barrel, to a frozen wasteland."

He chuckled. "Sucks on ice. You've got a point there. I assume that since we're moving up the food chain, Jasso is no longer among the living."

"That would be a correct assumption," I replied without elaboration.

We flew through the water in silence, the only sound a slight whir coming from the electric motors.

"We're nearing their ship," Marc finally said.

My senses tingled.

The jazz, Russ Livingston had called it. When the adrenaline slowly started ramping up whenever we neared the line of departure and were about to lock and load.

"Saturday night," I said softly. "Rock and roll."

"Huh?"

"Long story," I replied.

The whine of the electric motors slowed, then stopped.

"Tell me about it over a beer sometime," Marc said. "Dead stop."

I really couldn't feel any change in the sub's speed as it slowly drifted to a stop in total silence.

"Four hundred meters to target, bearing three-zero-zero," Marc said. "Blowing ballast."

The sound of pressurized air pushing the water ballast out of the tanks hissed inside the little conning tower. A few moments later, we breached the surface and water streamed down the glass.

As the sub rocked gently in the small waves, I could see the yacht not far away. I removed my headset and hung it by my knee again. Then I pulled on my tactical full-face mask and turned on the little micro-processors or computer chips or whatever it was that made it work.

"Comm check," I said, as a faint image of a chart appeared before my left eye.

"Welcome back," the guy in the control room on *Papillon* said. "We're in position three miles away and will hold here until the package is delivered."

I dialed the chart image's intensity back until it was nearly invisible, then stood inside the small space and reached up for the dogging handle. I turned it and pushed the hatch up, then grabbed my gear, stood on my seat, and climbed out of the sub.

The moon was bright and directly overhead. Less than a quarter mile away, I could see the luxury yacht just sitting there, ablaze in lights. For a second, I was worried they'd see us. But with all those lights, anyone looking would barely be able to see the water around them.

It was far too deep to anchor, but the boat hadn't moved more than a few feet in several hours. We assumed it had thrusters to maintain position.

"Be careful," Marc said, his voice echoing up from below. "Send his ass to meet the kraken."

While grinning behind the full-face mask, I put my rebreather on and checked everything out. Then I put my fins on and closed and dogged the hatch.

"Stepping off," I said, pushing away from the sub.

I quickly dropped to a depth of fifteen feet, unreeling my tiny antenna tether as I went.

I crossed my left forearm in front of me to grab my right elbow and began kicking. The compass on my left wrist showed the direction and my kick count would tell me how far I'd gone. The high-tech mask would do the same thing, but old habits, born of necessity, were hard to break.

If you dived a lot, counting kicks became second nature at some point, and I didn't have to think much about it. Besides, I'd see the lights long before I got close to the big yacht.

Sound travels faster and farther underwater than in air and I heard the air bubbles escaping from *Sea Leopard's* ballast tanks. A moment later, I heard the tiny sub's electric motors spin up as Marc disappeared in the blackness of the sea.

Within minutes, before I was halfway to *Toyana*, I began to see a faint light ahead. I looked at my depth gauge.

"I'm at fifteen feet," I said. "Target's lights are in sight."

"You're just over 300 feet away," the guy in the control room said.

"I'm diving to sixty feet," I said. "To get out of his lights. When you see my marker again, you'll know everything's good, unless I say otherwise. Thanks for the assist."

"Glad to help," control said. "We'd been on that wreck down there for a month. Things were getting kinda boring."

I started angling downward, reeling in my antenna. When I reached sixty feet, I was in near total darkness. Thanks to *Toyana's* lights, I could still see my gauges, but anyone looking down would be lucky to make out a whale shark just ten or fifteen feet below the surface.

I was wearing all black and would be invisible to anyone looking.

Swimming slowly, I reached a point directly below the yacht and began to surface, kicking slowly upward with my hands above my head.

Every now and then, I'd hear a burst of mechanical sound. I guessed it was the thrusters keeping the boat pointing into the slight current and maintaining its position.

Zotov left himself a perfect target. Lights below the waterline shined outward in all directions, but at the keel, I was completely hidden.

I quickly found a suitable location, just in front of the giant starboard propeller. C-4 was a fantastic product. Very malleable, it could be pressed into any shape, in this case a ring around the prop shaft. If the yacht was ever found, and in over 2400 feet of water it was unlikely, it would look like a shaft vibration had caused catastrophic damage at high RPM and ruptured a fuel tank.

I pushed the timer, already set for one hour, into the C-4 and pushed the start button. The numbers 59:59 flashed and started counting down.

Pushing off the hull, I dove to sixty feet again, then leveled off. Counting kicks again, I swam due west at a rapid pace. I wanted a lot of water between me and the *Toyana* when it blew up. I checked my dive watch. It was 0113. At about 0210, *Toyana Devushka* and Basil Zotov would cease to exist.

When I was safely away from the light, I rose to fifteen feet and unreeled my antenna. I continued to swim westward as I switched to the alternate GPS transmitter built into the mask.

Papillon would have seen my GPS signal when I surfaced and then seen it turn off. They'd know then that I'd been successful and would hail *Toyana*. They'd warn them about an explosive device hidden in one of the hundreds of storage compartments I knew the boat would have. They would also be blocking any outgoing radio or satellite transmissions from the doomed vessel.

After that, it was up to the crew. They could leave Zotov, taking the launch, or go down with him. He'd be ordered to remain aboard and if he tried to leave with the crew, he'd be thrown overboard on reaching *Papillon*.

While all this was going on up on the surface, I continued to fin westward toward my pickup point. Diving alone was hazardous. If you got in trouble you had only yourself to rely on. And diving at night wasn't without its own set of dangers. I was diving alone, at night, in the open ocean, with nothing below me to a depth greater than the height of the new World Trade Center.

It wasn't the first time I'd dived in such an environment. I continued kicking and counting. When my count equaled a distance of about half a mile, I started counting over.

Surrounded by nothing but darkness, with only the moon and my compass to guide my way, I continued west, always west. That was the direction of home. At least for now.

After thirty minutes, I knew I was at least a mile from *Toyana*. I checked my dive watch; 0200.

I could hear a rhythmic sound, a small diesel engine running at low speed. Not an idle, but not much above that.

I angled up to the surface and when I reached it, I took the inflator tube in my mouth and inflated my BC to float effortlessly while I scanned the surface of the water to the west, while I reeled in my float.

In the distance, I saw red and green navigation lights headed my way. Just above them was a white steaming light, which all boats under power are supposed to display when underway at night.

The sound of the diesel engine, chugging slowly, grew louder as the boat got near. When it was still fifty feet away, the boat shifted to neutral and the engine sound ceased.

I began swimming toward it as it drifted without power, slowly turning toward the south.

A ladder went over the side.

"Looking for a ride, sailor?" Savannah called out from the side deck.

"Mo-om," Florence said from the helm, turning the word into two syllables. "Just help him up, okay?"

Finn looked over the coaming and barked.

"Hey, buddy," I said, pulling my mask off and handing it up to Savannah. "How's the leg?"

"He's okay," Florence said. "A bit of a scrape, but he let me take care of it just fine."

I passed my fins to Savannah, then climbed slowly up the ladder. When I reached the top, water dripping from my hair and face, Savannah stepped back and looked at me.

"Is it done?" she asked. "Can we leave?"

Behind me, a bright orange fireball rolled up into the night sky, illuminating *Salty Dog's* hull and mast. My shadow fell across Savannah, and she and Florence both gasped as the sound of the explosion reached our ears.

"It's done," I said, removing the warrior mask once more. "Let's go home."

THE END

Don't miss the next exciting Jesse McDermitt novel, Rising Warrior, available for preorder until its release on August 31. 2020.

If you'd like to receive my newsletter, please sign up on my website:

WWW.WAYNESTINNETT.COM.

Every two weeks, I'll bring you insights into my private life and writing habits, with updates on what I'm working on, special deals I hear about, and new books by other authors that I'm reading.

The Charity Styles Caribbean Thriller Series

Merciless Charity
Ruthless Charity
Reckless Charity
Enduring Charity
Vigilant Charity

The Jesse McDermitt Caribbean Adventure Series

Fallen Out	*Fallen Hero*
Fallen Palm	*Rising Storm*
Fallen Hunter	*Rising Fury*
Fallen Pride	*Rising Force*
Fallen Mangrove	*Rising Charity*
Fallen King	*Rising Water*
Fallen Honor	*Rising Spirit*
Fallen Tide	*Rising Thunder*
Fallen Angel	

THE GASPAR'S REVENGE SHIP'S STORE IS OPEN.

There, you can purchase all kinds of swag related to my books. You can find it at

WWW.GASPARS-REVENGE.COM

AFTERWORD

Sometimes, the research I do for a new book is nearly as much fun and entertaining for me as telling the story. Not in this case. *Rising Thunder* is a tad darker than most of my previous books. I say a tad, because I wound up deleting a good portion of what I'd written before anyone saw it. But deleting those scenes didn't unlearn the things I researched. As Jesse points out herein, there is no limit to the depravity a person can inflict upon another when sanity is removed from the equation.

This novel contained 79,110 words before it went to my editor. I deemed another 15,000 or so words too dark and cut them from the book before sending it to my beta reading team. That said, the primary story line I used is a reality in many parts of the world, I just moved the location to someplace warm. What's paradise without mayhem?

Thankfully, most of us will never encounter scenes like you've read here. That doesn't mean such scenes do not take place in real life. As a result of my research, I will forever look at others and the world around me with different eyes.

A question came up at a local dock about just what the human body was worth. There were a few guesses, so I thought I'd find out. Then I figured I'd see if I could figure out what that price would be on the black market.

None of us in the discussion had even been close. It may please some of you to know that we are all potential multi-millionaires. Well, that's not exactly true. We'd never be able to collect the money.

An average adult in good health is comprised of about $45 million in parts if sold on the black market. Need a new heart? The going price is a million bucks.

Scary, huh?

So, just who were the victims of my over-fertile imagination, coupled with events that really happened? After I finish a book, I give it to a group of people who I not only call friends but are professionals in their fields. Some are or were members of the Spec Ops community. Others are attorneys, physicians, pilots, boaters, air traffic controllers, local residents of the many islands of the Keys and the Caribbean, law enforcement professionals, military, and a handful of friends I've known since childhood. They provide the feedback for real world and fictional elements of my work, to make the fiction more real and the reality more fictional.

I owe a lot of gratitude to Dana Vilhen, Alan Fader, Katy McKnight, Debbie Kocol, David Parsons, Mike Ramsey, Thomas Crisp, Charles Höfbauer, Ron Ramey, Debbie Cross, Torrey Neill, John Trainer, Drew Mutch, Deg Priest, Glen Hibbert, and lastly, for providing welcome relief that the pervasive evil I was depicting wasn't too dark, Dyana Connell, who works at Lady's Island Marina Store and is quite possibly Jesse's biggest fan. Without the help from all y'all, I'd still be selling paperbacks in a truck stop.

I wrote "The End" in this book on February 21, 2020, and today, March 8, I'm writing this foreword in preparation to send the manuscript to my editor, Marsha Zinberg by morning, who will have it for the next two weeks. Marsha brings more than 30 years of publishing expertise to the table and has worked for some of the biggest names in the business. She's responsible for turning my rough words into a readable story. But Marsha isn't the last one to read my books before they go to print.

Donna Rich always has last eyes on my work before Nick Sullivan records it for an audiobook. These two find the last few errors and offer advice as to how the story might read better.

Lastly, through thick and thin, in good times and bad, Greta Stinnett has always had my six. It takes a lot to succeed in this business and I know I can always count on my wife for support, ideas, and the occasional smackdown when my ideas are crap. Love ya, Babe!

Made in the USA
Las Vegas, NV
28 July 2023

75371692R00210